AGE OF THE ASHERS

THE PETROS CHRONICLES

DIANA TYLER

Published by Diana Tyler 2017

Copyright © 2017 Diana Tyler

www.dianaandersontyler.com

Book cover design and formatting services by BookCoverCafe.com

First Edition 2017

ISBN: 978-0-692-84546-2

*To Mr. Kent Travis, my ninth grade history/
English teacher at The Brook Hill School,
whose passion for ancient Greek drama and
mythology will remain with me all my life.*

CONTENTS

CHAPTER ONE
VOYAGE

The sky was clear, and the sun was so bright and high overhead that their bodies cast no shadows. Iris and Tycho stood hand in hand at the stern of the ship and looked out over the sapphire sea, the sweet smell of the cedar mast and the saltiness of the breeze welcoming them onboard. There had been a time when a sense of adventure would have overtaken Iris as she took in the beauty of the water, the vastness of the horizon, but today she was too weary to feel it...if it was there at all.

"Just one more time," Tycho said to her, as if reading her thoughts.

The words were poetry in her ears. It had been nearly three years since she'd slept in her own bed, hundreds of miles away in Eirene. Their young daughter, now drooling as she slept on a blanket at their feet, had seen more of the ocean than dry land, heard more sailors' shouts and seagulls' squawks than nursery rhymes and lullabies.

Just one more voyage on the small merchant ship and they could go home: home to picnics on the cliffs, festivals at the temple, and suppers at the table of the old couple that had become grandparents to them.

Iris yawned as she heard the oars drop into the water and the crew become quiet as the captain prayed to Poseidon for fair weather.

"Miss?" a voice whispered.

Iris turned to see a young man, more boy than man, looking up at her with round, frightened eyes. "You're Iris the Asher, aren't you, miss?"

Iris nodded as she scanned the deck for eavesdroppers. On a ship full of rough mariners who liked their women weak and docile, a woman with a notorious power had not made her a welcome passenger. But in recent years, people had begun approaching her not with rage and hatred in their eyes, as they would a beast they wished to tame or kill, but with hope and desperation, as they would an angel that might deliver them.

Since the Feast of Therismos almost a decade ago, the name Iris the Asher had become more respected, and indeed more revered, than Iris the Goddess. In fact, many of the mystics were teaching their pupils that she was an Olympian incarnate, perhaps Hera or Athena, a notion that made Iris shudder.

Why couldn't they believe her when she explained that her power was from the All-Powerful, that her gift was from the One who gave life and took life away? All she was, all she had, and all she had overcome, was by the grace of Duna. Every day she prayed that not one pagan sacrifice would be made to a blasphemous statue of her image.

But apart from the mystics, with their oleander-induced delusions, countless Eusebians and Alphas were listening to Iris and Tycho's story and accepting their faith as their own. They gathered into the temple courts by the hundreds to hear them, and, yes, to see if they might catch a glimpse of the mysterious fire that dwelled in the palms of Iris's hands.

She'd mastered the power of her *doma* so well that she could conjure a flame as easily as she could blink. If providing an exhibition led to further discussion of the might of Duna and the love of Phos, she would happily acquiesce to the crowd's wishes. But if she sensed that the crowd just wanted to see a show of sorcery, she'd ask Tycho to talk of his own miracle stories while she stayed hidden in the shadows.

3

Iris had seen what unbridled power could do to people. Each day, she prayed for Duna to use her only as a Vessel of the *doma*, and to forbid her from ever becoming its overlord, or worse, its slave.

Iris nodded again at the boy, this time remembering to smile. "Can I help you?" she asked.

Tycho squeezed her hand, a habit of his when he could detect her nerves. He often teased her, saying that for one who could destroy a man with a single flick of her wrist she was awfully skittish around strangers.

"I am an Alpha, miss," the boy said, "but I don't trust Poseidon for safe passage like my father does."

"Your father is the captain?" Iris asked.

"Yes. And he knows who you are, but don't be afraid. Though he won't admit it, he fears your power. They all do."

Tycho had been right. The reason it cost them one hundred drachmae each time they boarded a ship was not because they despised her, but because they feared her. If the sailors were going to risk their lives spending hours alone at sea in the presence of a presumed goddess, one likely to prove as testy and capricious as the rest of the pantheon, they insisted they be handsomely compensated. Iris couldn't blame them. If she believed herself to be at the mercy of a fierce deity that could swim beside their boat as a sprightly dolphin one minute, then spring into the clouds and plague them with lightning bolts the next, she would also expect a wage to match any potential peril.

"Thank you, that is reassuring," Iris said, expecting that to be all he wished to tell her.

But he took a breath to say something further, then stopped himself and started again. "Could you..." He almost squeaked the words. "Could you pray for ... my father?" He sighed with relief when the question finally escaped his lips. "I heard your letter read in Ourania last year and my life has been changed ever since. I would give anything for him to know the truth as well, but when I told him of the letter, he said that if you had any power, it came from Python, for he is the only god."

The boy's sad gaze dropped to the sea. "My father has a stubborn heart. I doubt he's capable of changing at his age."

"Trust your father in Duna's hands," said Tycho, his voice stern, but his expression gentle. "He delights in doing the impossible, like when he helped a teenaged slave girl named Iris overthrow a tyrant," he said, raising an eyebrow before kissing his wife on the forehead.

The boy smiled and stared at Iris a moment. She knew he was likely imagining her as that famed warrior-goddess who'd saved the temple from decimation, and mercifully proselytized the heartless maniac who slew his own people for power. But, as everyone knew, Diokles denied Duna to the last, wheezing threats and spewing contempt until his heart had finally stopped beating.

Surely it had crossed the boy's mind that his father could very well reject Duna, and die proud and blind like Diokles. While the captain didn't have innocent blood on his hands, how well Iris knew that sometimes the hardest people to reach were the ones who were noble and good in the world's eyes, those who slaughtered bulls and rams to appease the gods and beseeched them for all to see.

Seeing the worry rise as glistening tears in the boy's blue eyes, Iris took his hand and bowed her head before another care could invade his mind. "Duna," she prayed, closing her eyes. "Our king and our protector. Thank you for this boy."

"My name is Pontus," he whispered.

"Thank you for Pontus," Iris continued. "Thank you for the love he has for his father, the captain of this ship. I know, perhaps better than anyone, what it feels like to be utterly far from you, and yet, at the same time, to sense you chasing after me with a relentless fervor no Petrodian will ever fathom.

"Duna, I felt the rebellion in my heart toward you burning hotter than my *doma*, which can incinerate entire forests if I allow it to. So hostile was my soul toward any sort of love, most of all love from the one who allowed my family to die, leaving me an orphan and a slave to a sadistic soldier. But still..." Iris's voice cracked as she felt the boat begin to glide out from the pier. "But still you pursued me. Still you brought people into my life to give me hope and show me what true love looks like. Still you set the Moonbow in the sky, not just so I could solve its mystery, but so that I might share its meaning with the world.

"My king, we ask that you would pursue the shuttered heart of Pontus's father. Use whatever means necessary to melt the ice that covers it. We thank you for hearing our prayer, and we trust you to answer it. Your will be done."

"Your will be done," echoed Tycho and Pontus.

Iris and Tycho opened their eyes just in time to see a long, slimy black tentacle retracting fast as a snake's tongue over the side of the ship, and that Charis, their three-year-old daughter, was missing.

CHAPTER TWO
SCYLLA

It's Scylla!" the sailors cried out.

Iris turned to see them, at least fifty sailors in total, bracing themselves around the mast, holding tightly to the forestays and backstays as all color drained from their faces. They flinched and stumbled as violent movement from the unseen beast rocked the ship, drenching the deck far better than any tempest, and pushing it farther from shore. The pier might as well have been a thousand miles away; no one was brave enough to try swimming back to it.

Tycho lifted his arms, preparing to hurl himself into the ocean after his daughter.

Pontus grasped his hand and yelled, "Don't! You'll die in seconds."

"I know how to swim, Pontus. Let me go!" Tycho shouted back.

"What's 'Scylla'?" Iris asked when her breath finally returned, fire already kindling in her fists.

"The sea monster, miss," said Pontus, as he dropped to his hands and knees and crawled toward a tiny hole in the hull. "A legend, or so we all thought."

"We never should've let her on board," barked the captain from the bow. "No fortune is worth losing my ship and crew."

Iris lifted her hands, a thin haze of flame floating before them. A hush fell over the ship as the men stared, transfixed and terrified, at the fire formed from human flesh.

"It isn't your crew it wants," Iris said.

She turned away from the crew and captain as the splashing stopped and a shadow the size of a thunderhead stretched across the deck. The first thing Iris saw when she looked up was her daughter Charis, stricken silent with fear inside the clutches of one of the dozen or so tentacles that protruded from the monster's bloated gray belly.

Hearing the sound of growling dogs, her eyes traveled up to the mud-colored middle section of the creature and saw that it was surrounded by the heads of wolves, whose sulfurous breath was enough to slay a man. Should that tentacle—now threatening to squeeze the life from Charis's body—move just inches closer to Scylla's side, how easily one of those dogs might puncture the toddler's skull with their sword-sharp teeth.

Iris decided to first send her fire to them.

Twin bubbles, gleaming like gold, broke free from Iris's palms. She softly pushed them toward the six female heads at the top of Scylla's body, each one a horror of tangled braids, hissing tongues, and haunting, hollow eyes glazed over from eons spent in Hades' darkness. Every eye followed the fiery spheres as they traveled slowly over the ship's edge before quickly swelling to triple their size and spewing sparks into the air.

The monster gave an earsplitting shriek, and the wolves turned their bristling necks and barked, distracted from the child just as Iris had hoped. With the beast's attention fixed momentarily on the flickering diversion, Iris clenched her fists so tightly that her fingernails drew out drops of blood that worked to kindle the flames all the more.

She opened her red-hot hands and lunged forward, thrusting out her arms as far as they could reach. A string of fireballs rushed toward the wolves in a blazing blur, silencing each one on impact. Smoke settled over their lifeless heads.

"Give me my daughter or I'll rid you of all your other heads, Scylla!" Iris yelled as she pressed her hands into her thighs, trying to suppress the throbbing pain left behind by the fire.

In perfect synchronization, all six heads spun back toward her. Their forked tongues flashed out and in, smelling the fear of the crew. Their matted braids danced wildly in the wind, and their eyes filled with chilling orbs of light that Iris had seen only once before in the most evil of men.

The tentacles lifted toward the cluster of repugnant faces, the one holding Charis trembling like an ice-laden branch.

"I only wanted to see the magic doma for myssssself. I thought it was nothing but a ssssilly ssssailor's tale," said Scylla, all mouths speaking together. "A ssssilly tale like Sssscylla," she hissed. "We monsters must sssstick together, lest hissssstory forget all about usssss, don't you think, Irissss?" The tentacle flexed, curling in closer to the monster, causing Charis to squeal with pain.

With no time for them to heal, Iris's hands birthed two new scorching flames that soared like asteroids straight into the heads' vile ring. Two of the heads fell limp while the remaining four howled like harpies.

"You're just making her madder, miss," whispered Pontus, but the monster's hearing was keen.

"Lisssssten to the lad," the heads screamed, as the tentacles flailed up and down, plunging Charis's bare feet into the water.

"Why do you want her?" shouted Tycho. "What's a three-year-old child to the likes of you?"

The heads rotated three hundred and sixty degrees as they cackled. "I made a little deal with Apollo. I bring him one of the Hodossss, and he givesssss me back my former form. I onccccce rivaled Aphrodite, I did. Thissss runt wassss a mossssst eassssy catch. I'd better be going back to the pit. The Dark Lord hatessss to wait..."

And with that, the squid-like creature lowered herself into the sea as flame after flame escaped Iris's hands. Each one fizzled in the waves.

"That's it," said Tycho, removing his cloak and throwing off his sandals.

"Tycho, don't!" Iris pleaded. "I can't lose both of you."

"Iris, have faith."

Two tears slipped down Iris's cheeks as fear and faith waged war within her. Neither she nor Tycho noticed that Pontus was no longer standing at the rail.

"Where's my son!" shouted the captain, stepping out from his hiding place behind the mast.

For a minute or more, not a sound was heard, only the mournful cry of gulls that flew above the encroaching wall of clouds. The clouds were so thick and tight around the ship that Iris felt as if they were being entombed, slowly suffocating inside Apollo's well-set snare. She grasped the side of the ship, searing the wood with fresh fire still hungry for a target.

"Duna, help us," she prayed. "Help Pontus now. Greater are you than any weapon or warrior of Apollo."

Crimson water appeared and expanded on the surface of the sea. Iris took a deep breath, resolved not to let it go until she saw her daughter alive. A severed black tentacle emerged and bobbed up and down, a dead snake still fearsome to see. Blood flowed from the tendons that had attached it to Scylla's gut, and it twitched like a fish on the sand.

Iris gasped at the sight of Charis's head popping out of the water, spitting and coughing, but very much alive. Pontus had the child by her tiny torso. He began kicking frantically toward the ship.

"Turn and hold onto me," Pontus said to Charis. She obeyed and clung to him like a startled monkey as Tycho threw down a rope and began hoisting them up. The crew, dumbfounded by Pontus's bravery, simply stared.

Iris hung over the side of the ship and pulled her child into her arms. She snatched Tycho's cloak from the deck and wrapped it around Charis, making her look like a caterpillar nestled inside its cocoon. Iris kissed her face over and over, and vowed never to board a ship again. If letters needed delivering, she'd gladly let Tycho be the messenger. She doubted she'd ever let Charis out of her arms again.

13

"Pontus!" Tycho shouted, then jumped back as the ship quaked, the rope falling from his hands.

The captain ran full speed to the stern, and peered over it as a blinding ray of sunlight pierced through the clouds. The waves settled, the whole sea returning to immaculate glass containing nothing but a silver school of mackerel.

"Where is my son!" the captain's voice boomed.

"He saved our daughter," said Iris, her voice shaking from the panic and pain still seizing her.

"That isn't an answer!" When he realized that he indeed knew the answer, the captain turned and slid down onto the deck. He stared up hopelessly at Iris, as if waiting for someone to make sense of what had happened, or to undo it altogether.

He began pounding the sides of his head and cursing under his breath. "What did she want with him?" he bellowed. He staggered to his feet like a drunkard and yelled into the sea, "Take me instead, you reeking wench! I'll give you all I have."

Charis stirred and turned toward her father. "That's what he said, Papa."

The captain neared the child with a half-curious, half-furious sneer on his lips. "What who said, child?"

"The boy who saved me," she answered. "He told the monster to take him." Charis then laid her head on Iris's shoulder and began sucking her thumb.

"You raised your son well, sir," said Tycho. "He sacrificed himself for our daughter, just as you were willing to do for him."

"It was too late for me to do anything," the captain said. "I was a spineless coward hiding like a rat with all the rest of them." He motioned toward the crew, who were working at a feverish pace, readying the ship to sail away from Scylla as fast as possible.

"Scylla wouldn't have accepted your offer anyway, sir," said Iris. "From what I understand, you're not a part of the Hodos."

"And what in Zeus's name is that?" he demanded, nearly spitting in Iris's face.

She took a breath, praying silently for patience. "Hodos means 'the Way.' You don't follow the Way of Duna. Apollo— or Python, as you call him—doesn't trouble himself to capture those who are already on his side."

"I'm on no one's side," the captain snapped.

"We're all on someone's side, Captain," said Tycho, stepping forward. "Whether we know it or not."

"Do you know what your son was doing before we were attacked?" asked Iris. The captain shook his head, his eyes squeezed closed as if bracing himself to hear what was coming next. "He was praying," she said. "For you."

The captain's eyes opened, pure crystal tears welling in each one.

"He wanted you to believe, as he believed, that Duna is the true god. Pontus was following that example of selflessness.

You can trust that he has an eternal reward, sir. He did a great thing. A rare thing."

The captain's tears fell uncontrollably.

Iris and Tycho turned aside, letting him have his privacy as the weight of grief fell down on him like an avalanche. Iris knew the feeling too well. And she knew that no amount of pretty words or consoling embraces could lift it.

A few minutes later, the Captain heaved a final sob, and uttered his son's name as tenderly as a father can.

"I was always hard on him," the captain said, to no one in particular. His eyes were swollen and bloodshot, his hoary beard wet with tears. His clasped hands shook as the lines in his brow deepened. "He never wanted to be a sailor. Didn't like the water. But I pushed him...I kept pushing him. He'd only just learned how to swim." He kicked the ship and buried his head in his hands as rage and regret churned inside him.

Iris's heart sank at the sight of him. Overcome with empathy so strong that it mimicked nausea, she placed her daughter in Tycho's arms. She remembered one of the oracles her ancestor, the first Asher, had written centuries ago: *Duna comforts us in all our afflictions, so that we may be able to comfort those who are afflicted.*

"I know words are useless, Captain," she said, placing a hand on his back. "Nothing I can say or do can make this easier. Your son is a hero, and I pray that one day you'll be able to celebrate his life as much as you mourn it now."

The captain wiped his face and nose, and then smiled when he saw a dolphin laughing up at them from the ocean. "My boy's favorite animal," he said. "The first time he sailed with me it was because I'd promised he'd get his fill of them. He never did see a single one, though. Only heard about them in the myths."

"He never saw them, but he knew they existed. Like Duna," Iris mused, watching the dolphin jump and greet two of its pod mates, all chattering together in their high-pitched language.

"Do you..." the captain began, his apprehension reminding Iris of Pontus when he'd asked her to pray for his father. "Do you think I could come with you into to Limén? If you read the letter there, I mean. I think I would like to hear it." Instantly, his countenance brightened with a mixture of surprise and relief at his own words.

Iris watched the dolphins swim away as quickly as they'd appeared, as though their mission had been completed.

"I would love nothing more, Captain," replied Iris.

She was tempted to fetch the scroll now and read it from start to finish before the captain changed his mind, but something told her to wait. Faith, she reminded herself, is not knowledge to be acquired, or even a life-shaking event to be experienced. Not at first. At first it is a seed that can't be forced to germinate and grow.

Iris thought of her beloved brother, Jasper, named after the blood-red rock that always hung around her neck and was now pressed to her lips. He had died a criminal's death, burned alive on a pyre at sea, yet he had committed no crime.

That night at Enochos was indelibly etched into Iris's memory. She could recall the sadness, anger, and fear she felt then as readily as she could summon the flames from her hands. Of course she'd been furious at Acheron, the sadistic guardian who'd ordered her brother's execution. But she'd also developed an intense hatred toward the god Jasper had worshipped so zealously. How could Duna let one of his most devoted followers perish at the hands of an egomaniacal brute? How could he do nothing as he watched an orphan child lose her brother and then become slave to his murderer before the night was over?

Now, every time she thought back to the night when Python intended to destroy her life, she could see Duna's invisible hands weaving each and every thread—the good and the bad—into a dazzling tapestry. She thought of the beautiful smooth pebbles she and Jasper used to collect from the shores near their home. Their father had said that the reason the stones were so perfect was because they'd been trapped in merciless waves. The constant tossing, rolling, and rubbing together had polished them with more skill than the pagans' revered Hephaestus.

Iris believed that she was such a pebble. Had she lived a carefree life sheltered in some quiet cove, she would be rough, unpolished, and devoid of compassion.

She left the scroll alone with Tycho, but couldn't help but recite her favorite oracle of all to the captain before leaving him in peace and scooping up Charis again.

"Captain," she began, her voice confident and clear, "the oracles wrote this on their tablets thousands of years ago, inspired by Duna to do so. It has proven true time and again in my own life, and in Tycho's. I believe Duna wants you to hear it now: '*Python intended to harm me, but Duna intended it for good to accomplish what is now being done.*'"

CHAPTER THREE
CHLOE

Chloe Zacharias forced herself to try to see the good in everything. It was a habit instilled in her as a little girl when, at no older than four or five, her mother showed her a rainbow for the very first time. A summer thunderstorm had been busy shaking the windows and picture frames on the wall all afternoon, and while her brother and father were content playing games on the floor, Chloe couldn't stop crying.

"Shhhhh, sweet girl, don't hide or you'll miss the good part," her mother had whispered to her as Chloe retreated beneath a threadbare baby blanket.

"It's all scary," Chloe said, curling herself up into a ball on her mother's lap.

"I bet there'll be sunshine soon. And maybe even a rainbow. You wouldn't want to miss that."

"What's a rainbow?"

"You'll just have to wait and see," her mother said, and winked at her.

Chloe fell asleep a few minutes later, and when she woke up she was in her mother's arms on the back porch.

"Look, Chloe," her mother had said, pulling the blanket off her daughter's warm head.

Feeling a drop of rain from the drip-edge above strike her on the nose, Chloe winced and strained to reach the blanket as her mother set it on the porch swing. "No!" Chloe protested, her body going stiff with antagonism toward the outdoors.

"Just open your eyes and look at the sky."

It was then that Chloe first beheld the majesty of a rainbow, its vibrant bands of color a most soothing valediction after the clamor of thunder and rain. From that day on, she always looked forward to storms for the chance to see rare beauty unveiled. Even if she didn't see a rainbow, the end of a storm always reminded her of her mother. And she was happy.

Now it was a crisp fall day, with a few white wisps of clouds in the sky but no threat of a storm. But had Chloe, eighteen years old as of eight o'clock that morning, still had her baby blanket, she'd be hiding under it by now.

Her aunt Maggie and uncle Travis had been trying to keep the birthday party under wraps all week, but like all other parenting-related activities, surprise-birthday planning was not their forte. On Monday Chloe's brother, Damian, had noticed the yellow phone book open at the catering section, and answered calls from three different cake companies while Maggie and Travis were "grocery shopping." Except for a large plastic bag, they returned that evening empty-handed.

Little clues such as those popped up every day, and Damian and Chloe decided it was best to play dumb. "It's what Mom and Dad would have wanted," Damian had said.

For the life of her, Chloe couldn't figure out why her aunt and uncle were going out of their way to do something nice for their niece and nephew. Since they'd become the twins' legal guardians, they'd behaved more like bored babysitters than parents. Damian thought their parents must have written something into their wills about mandatory eighteenth birthday parties for their children.

Eighteen was a monumental year for Petrodians, one that distinguished them as official adults. In just a few months, Chloe and Damian would be graduating high school and leaving home to make something of themselves, either at the university or in Limén, where they could learn a trade and start earning money in under a year.

Chloe said to Damian, only half jokingly, that Maggie and Travis were probably in a celebratory mood because they would soon have their house to themselves again. They wouldn't have to help her with homework, or drive her to doctor appointments when her brother was occupied. Ignoring his own previously stated cynicism, Damian told her to lighten up and enjoy their generosity, whatever the reason for it.

But enjoying a large group of people she hardly knew, who were presumably at her house to celebrate the day she was born, was a Herculean task for Chloe. That afternoon she watched from her treehouse as thirty or forty of her high-school peers stood around in their various cliques, stuffing their faces with the bright blue, fondant-covered kiddie cake and acting a little too chipper after sipping the pomegranate punch—although she couldn't blame whoever had spiked it with what she guessed was an exorbitant dose of Nirvána, a psychoactive powder meant only for adults whose social anxiety impeded their ability to work.

The party's only chaperones, her aunt and uncle, had been M.I.A. since the party had started over an hour ago, their absence practically asking for their guests to break the law by braying and prancing about like inebriated donkeys.

Chloe sent a text to Maggie, warning her that the police could have them put in the stocks overnight on grounds of parental negligence, but by the time her aunt had made it to the punch bowl, it had already been drained. At least the evidence was gone.

Chloe watched as Damian waved a group of guys over toward the dinosaur piñata. After they'd demolished it, they stumbled into the castle-shaped bounce house and let the drugs transform them into juvenile chimpanzees. Chloe rolled her eyes. She might've actually had fun at this party were she turning eight and not eighteen—and if the punch wasn't contaminated. She embarrassed her brother enough without the "relaxing" effects of Nirvána.

Chloe leaned against the wall on which at least a hundred homemade cartoons were nailed, most of them posted there during her first summer as an orphaned ten-year-old. Starving to escape the ordinary, she'd created extraordinary best friends for herself: a young yellow-haired girl named Rhoda, and Farley, her imaginary dragon. Like Chloe, Rhoda was always alone because, like Chloe, her parents were dead, too.

Whenever Rhoda was feeling bored or sick or sad, Farley would appear in a puff of smoke, and together the girl and dragon would travel to different places around Petros, stir up mischief, snag a few souvenirs, and then return home in time for dinner.

Chloe thought she was now too old to have imaginary friends, but she still lived vicariously through the old adventures of Rhoda and Farley, preferring their company to real children her own age. She told herself that Damian had enough social interaction for the two of them. He was the quintessential high-school jock whom every girl wanted to date and every boy wanted to be.

Chloe, on the other hand, was the invisible nerd that people talked to only when they needed help with an algebra problem. But she knew she had no one to blame for her lack of a life but herself.

No, that wasn't true. She could—and often did—blame the car accident that claimed her parents' lives, and the hit-and-run driver who got away. The first ten years of her life had been an endless daydream, filled with the assurance of safety and sunshine that every child deserves. The day her parents died, a part of her soul crept into an early grave, and every birthday buried it farther down.

Chloe scooted into a soft sunray and closed her eyes, basking like a lizard in the mild warmth it offered. She watched the colorful squiggly lines behind her eyelids dance and squirm, an activity that helped her fall asleep when her mind was fixed on problems she couldn't solve. Soon, the cacophony from the party below faded away, muted by the sweetness of an impromptu nap.

☾

"I know how to swim, Pontus, let me go!"

Those idiots are trying to go swimming in a sixty-degree pool, Chloe thought, her eyes still sealed shut, ready to plunge back into sleep. Then came her second thought: *Who in the world names their son Pontus?*

"It's Scylla!" shouted a group of voices, not a single one familiar to Chloe.

Scylla? Chloe groaned and peeled open her eyes. What she saw took her breath away.

There was water all around her, and it definitely was not a swimming pool. She'd never seen the Great Sea in person, but judging by the deep-blue ocean waves, this was it.

She suddenly lost her balance and fell back onto a thick rope. She grabbed hold of it with both hands, only then realizing that she was on a ship that was being tossed like an unruly child's bath toy.

"Everyone, get down!" yelled a man beside her, whose white knuckles were holding onto the only oar that hadn't been abandoned. But a few seconds later, he too was on his belly beside a heap of trembling men as whatever was aggravating the ship continued to splash and spin around them.

And then Chloe saw it, the thing the unknown sailors had called "Scylla."

26

Chloe squeezed her eyes closed and blinked them rapidly when she opened them again. Her eyes had to be playing tricks on her. She pinched herself. She had to be dreaming. But no matter how many times she squinted or blinked or tapped and slapped her forehead, the terrifying scene stayed put.

Scylla was like no marine animal she'd ever seen, not even in the discovery shows on TV. It was impossible to say how tall it was because its lower half was submerged in the sea. The upper half was a repulsive blend of dog, squid, and woman. The only normal thing about it was a human child with fair skin and red hair. What wasn't so normal was that this child was wrapped inside one of the animal's black tentacles.

Wake up, Chloe! Wake up wake up wake up! But it was no use; Chloe felt as awake as she did after three cups of coffee. This was no dream.

Chloe tried to compose herself. She took three deep breaths and crouched down, forcing herself to think optimistically. *Just wait it out, she told herself. Once this thing passed by they would get back to land.*

Peering around a broad man hiding behind the mast, she could see three people: two men and a woman. They were standing at the stern, holding their ground. The shorter and slighter of the two men began to crawl closer to the edge of the deck as more commotion rang out among the crew, but it was all a muddled noise to Chloe. *Why weren't they afraid?*

Chloe watched as the woman slowly raised both of her hands, as if to surrender to Scylla. But when the ship became deathly quiet, Chloe knew surrender was on no one's mind. She watched carefully as the woman's palms began to glow with yellow-orange light. Chloe's mouth fell agape as the pair of lights, now pulsing like flames, proceeded to float languidly out of the woman's hands like miniature spirits.

"Chloe! Chloe!"

Chloe's eyes darted around the ship. Who knew her here?

"Chloe!"

She continued to look, but no one was facing her; all eyes were on the woman. More than that, the voice calling her sounded just like her brother's.

"Gross, Chloe, you're drooling," Damian said.

☾

Chloe jumped back to consciousness and wiped her mouth.

Her brother grimaced. "And why are you wet?"

Chloe looked down at herself. She was back in the treehouse, and indeed she was drenched with water, water that smelled to her like salt. She knew why she was wet, but she couldn't very well tell Damian. He'd have her committed to a mental hospital before the party was over.

"It rained while you were in the bounce house," she lied.

"Right..." Damian said. "Well, come down now. We're opening presents."

"Be right there. Can you grab me a towel?"

Damian rolled his eyes and nodded, then started down the ladder.

Chloe quickly rocked up onto her feet and looked down out of the treehouse. No ocean. No Scylla. She opened her hands; they were rough and red from where she'd been gripping the rope for dear life just moments before.

Chloe turned to the wall of comic strips behind her, to the big-eyed, yellowed-haired girl and her polka-dotted dragon. "Well, guys, I think it's time I socialized with real people a little more often. Eighteen years old and I've already lost my sanity."

CHAPTER FOUR
FANTÁSMATA

One of the many downsides to being a twin was that people often viewed you as one individual instead of two. For instance, Chloe's mother had loved dressing her and Damian in matching outfits. Their scrapbooks were full of photographs of the twins in identical onesies, themed birthday get-ups, and wolf costumes that they wore to the Lycaea festival, an age-old holiday that honored the Unknown God. It didn't matter that Chloe was terrified of wolves or that Damian enjoyed paint on his face as much as he enjoyed fire ants attacking it. They were twins, and twins did things together.

It was the same when it came to presents. Every year, without fail, two-thirds of their gifts were identical—and they weren't even identical twins. Far from it.

Chloe's eyes were an ordinary shade of blue, but Damian's were an enviable gray-green that became lighter or darker depending on his mood, at least that was according to Chloe's unspoken observations. Chloe's skin was what her mother called "porcelain"; her mother hadn't lived long enough to watch it morph from porcelain to pimply when Chloe reached puberty. Damian's complexion, on the other hand, was sun-kissed and nauseatingly flawless, as was his physique. He also had the better hair—thick and dirty blond—whereas hers was stringy and the unfortunate color of turbid dishwater. And it was much too long.

There wasn't a sport Damian wasn't good at, and his lithe, muscular body had prospered because of it. Chloe had tried sports with her brother when she was young, but only because of the common misconception that they were joined at the hip. It was only after throwing an exorbitant amount of tantrums that her parents finally relented and left her to her books and dolls. She wasn't fat, but she wasn't exactly the Aphrodite to her brother's Adonis either.

After the birthday revelers had said their goodbyes, Chloe retreated to the downstairs office and curled up in her father's "thinking chair," a cup of untainted punch from the fridge in one hand and one of her many ho-hum birthday gifts in the other. She started sorting through them and making piles: one for those she'd donate to charity or give to the few friends she had at school; one for those she'd re-gift for her aunt and uncle who'd have no idea they were originally intended for her; and finally, one for those she thought she might enjoy should she ever get struck by lightning and forget who she was.

"Chloe, you missed one." It was Damian, sneaking up on her as usual and speaking at an excessive decibel level.

"Geez, don't scare me like that!" Chloe said, pressing her hand to her chest.

Damian tossed her a tiny gift bag stuffed haphazardly with neon-pink tissue paper. "It was on the front porch," he said.

"Thanks," Chloe replied, suspiciously eyeing the bag as though it were booby-trapped.

"You got a boyfriend now or something?" Damian asked, his whole face crinkling the way it did when he bit into something sour.

"None of your business," Chloe replied, sending Damian on his way. One good thing about having a brother for a twin was that he didn't needle her for info as a sister probably would.

When she could hear Damian's footsteps heading upstairs, Chloe ripped the tissue paper out of the bag and flicked open the envelope, inflicting a minor papercut on her thumb. The card read: *Dear Chloe, I can only give one of these away. I hope your brother doesn't mind. I just thought you'd enjoy it more since I know you're pretty good at O&M. See you in class, Ethan Ross.*

O&M was an abbreviation for "ontology and mythology," a class everyone at school hated. Everyone but Chloe and, she presumed, this Ethan chap, who she knew next to nothing about. All she knew was that he ran track, was on the wrestling team with Damian, and sketched and wrote what appeared to be poetry during study hall when all the other students were rushing to get their homework done. To Chloe, "athletic poet" was quite the oxymoron.

Damian and those of his ilk thought O&M was the biggest waste of time. They were probably right. After all, the purpose of the class was to study and discuss the theories about how Petros came into existence, as well as the history of the so-called gods and ancient creatures that once inhabited it.

There was some compelling evidence to support these theories, but the most prominent and promising archaeological sites situated near Ourania, the Colony of Commerce, had been completely destroyed, literally wiped off the face of Petros and into the ocean by some unknown catastrophe millennia ago. But the mystery of it all is what captivated Chloe the most. It appealed to the ever-expanding side of her that preferred unseen, even speculative, worlds to the real one.

Chloe put the card aside and pulled a small white rectangle out of the bag. It was laminated with Eirene's territorial seal of an embossed serpent coiling around a crescent moon, and underneath, in bold black text, were the words: *Eirene Museum: FREE One-Day Pass.*

"Huh," was all Chloe could say. She couldn't believe she'd finally opened a gift she wanted to keep.

The week before, a nondescript newspaper ad had announced the museum's opening. It stated they would be using the museum to unveil artifacts and documents that had hitherto been withheld from the public for certain unnamed and "immaterial" reasons.

This news, of course, piqued Chloe's interest, but her hopes of visiting were promptly dashed when she learned that the admittance fee was two hundred drachmae, enough money to buy a nice used car. Why in the world it cost that much to see a bunch of dusty old shards and deteriorating scrolls was beyond Chloe's realm of understanding.

She dialed the number at the bottom of the card and found out they were open until six p.m. *I wonder if they know anything about ol' Scylla, she thought.*

Chloe slipped her ankle boots back on, the red patent leather ones she wore on special occasions, and stood at the bottom of the stairs.

"I'm going to the museum! Going to use the car!" she yelled up at Damian, and was out the door with keys in hand before he could object.

Her aunt and uncle waved from the living room couch, eyes glued to the TV.

((

Chloe couldn't wait to get out of the car. She'd been driving for half an hour up Archaíos Peak and already the winding narrow roads were making her feel carsick.

Continue straight, her cellphone told her in its chipper, albeit untrustworthy, tone.

"You're gonna lead me right over a cliff, aren't you," Chloe said as large drops of rain began to pelt her windshield. This was starting to feel like a scene from a teen slasher movie. Girl receives gift from psycho peer. Girl stupidly goes alone to remote location. Psycho intercepts girl and—

A yellow sign interrupted Chloe's thoughts; it instructed her to turn left onto an unpaved driveway that was barely wide enough for the compact sedan. A few seconds later she found herself gazing up at two white, egg-shaped buildings standing opposite one another with a few pretty cacti and succulents planted around them. Between the buildings was a freshly paved parking lot, the visitors' section of which was completely empty.

Chloe gave a resigned sigh as she pulled into it. *Psycho lures girl into museum exhibit...*

She turned off the ignition and silenced her phone. She sent a text to Damian: *If I'm not home in two hours please send a search party to 3309 Archaíos Road. By the way, what do you know about Ethan Ross? Good or psycho?* As she trotted toward the porte-cochère, her phone vibrated with his response: *You're the psycho.*

Unfazed and unsurprised, Chloe dropped her phone into the dark depths of her oversized messenger bag and approached the building. She tried pushing open the door. Locked. Able to make out a woman standing at a desk in the center of the foyer, Chloe knocked until she got her attention. The woman strode toward her, wearing a ruched burgundy wrap dress and a pair of intimidating black pumps Chloe could hear echoing through the glass.

"Do you have an appointment?" the woman asked behind the closed door.

"No, ma'am, but I have this." Chloe pulled the wrinkled one-day pass out of her pocket and held it up.

"Who gave that to you?"

"Ethan Ross?" Chloe said, unsure whether his name would gain her entry or banishment.

The woman pressed a button on the wall and the door slid open. "Welcome," she said. "You can follow me."

"I'm assuming you know Ethan," Chloe said as her boots clip-clopped across the gray cement floor.

"He's my son," said the woman. "He's always been interested in ontology and mythology, so I thought this would be a good weekend job for him."

Chloe looked around the foyer. It was so sparse and uninviting that it seemed more like a sanitarium than a place of conservation and study. Three of the sloped walls were white concrete and completely bare. The fourth and furthermost wall was entirely glass and stretched from floor to ceiling. Through it, Chloe could see a cluster of wooden benches overlooking the valley below.

"What does he do here?" Chloe asked.

"Docent," the woman said with a laugh. "But mostly he just studies everything. As you can see, there isn't much of a need for tour guiding." She pointed to a clipboard on the desk and handed Chloe a pen. "If you could just fill this out. The Fantásmata require it."

"I'm a little surprised there aren't more people here, actually. But I guess it's cost prohibitive," Chloe said as she skimmed carelessly over the fine print and signed her name.

"Exactly. 'Serious interest only,' is what the Fantásmata say. I guess if people want to see what relics we have, they'll find a way to pay for the privilege."

Chloe could tell that Ethan's mother was less than thrilled about the circumstances. "So are you the curator?"

"Precisely. Technically, I'm an archaeologist. I used to work at the ruins mostly, at the coast in Ourania. I was recently reassigned after this was built." She looked up at a dropped screen of metal mesh separating the room from the ceiling. In the soft light that filtered through it, Chloe could see sadness spreading like a net across the woman's face, trapping her.

She probably feels like a caged bird, Chloe thought.

"Why did they build a museum if no one can come to it?" Chloe removed her jacket and set it on the minimalist black sofa that composed the waiting area.

"Oh, people come to it," the woman said. "I just don't know who."

Chloe stared at her blankly. "That doesn't make much sense."

The woman shrugged and handed Chloe a museum sticker, which Chloe stuck onto the side of her purse.

"The Fantásmata don't seem to care whether their rules make sense or not," came a voice from the back corner of the room, echoing in the open space.

Chloe turned to see Ethan standing in a doorway that she was certain hadn't been there before. When he stepped forward, the door sealed itself behind him, returning to ordinary wall.

"Cool," said Chloe, feeling like she'd just been shown a magic trick. She was tempted to ask him to do it again. "How many of those doors are in here?" Her eyes searched the walls for traces of hidden switches or camouflaged dials.

Ethan's mother smiled. "A few. Thieves don't have time to search for invisible entrances. Quite clever, isn't it?"

Chloe nodded and smiled at Ethan as he extended his hand to her.

"Happy birthday," he said.

"Happy birthday," she repeated, shaking his hand. "I mean *thank you*."

She gave herself a good hard mental kick. Why was casual conversation so difficult for her? Ask her to talk about how the Olympians overthrew the Titans, or how Apollo slew the Python that guarded Petros's most powerful oracle and took it over himself, and she was articulate and suave. But ask her to talk pleasantries and make introductions, and her mouth refused to receive signals from her brain.

"Like your gift?" Ethan asked. "I mean, I guess you do if you're here, right?"

Chloe detected a smidgen of nervousness as he ran a hand through his dark hair. Maybe she wasn't the only awkward one.

"Sorry I couldn't come to the party," he added before she had a chance to answer.

"It's okay. Your mom told me you work weekends," Chloe said. "Fun job?"

Ethan shrugged and looked to his mother. "Did Mom tell you you're the first patron?"

"I'm the *first*?" Chloe said, pointing at herself incredulously.

"The first *civilian* we have on record," his mother clarified. "The Fantásmata come occasionally—and unexpectedly. I come into work some days and the place is a fortress. I can't get in. Someone has the master key, and it isn't me."

"So," said Ethan, "wanna see what the crazies are hiding?"

Chloe had half a mind to turn and run. The last place on Petros she wanted to be was on the Fantásmata's bad side. It was obvious they didn't want just anyone visiting this place. How would they react when they found out a measly civilian had laid her measly civilian eyes on their priceless artifacts? But then again, they had assented to the dispensation of one-day passes, a notion that baffled her even more.

If she were accused of committing a crime by coming here, surely the court at Enochos would rule in her favor. And if not, she could only hope she wouldn't be sentenced to anything as traumatizing as the encounter with that Scylla monstrosity.

CHAPTER FIVE
STRANGER

Chloe followed Ethan to the part of the wall from which he'd entered. He slowed down to inspect a section, and when he found whatever it was he was looking for he stepped closer until he was mere inches from the wall. Then he opened his eyes wide, and stared. After a few seconds, a door appeared in the wall and slid back, revealing a steel staircase leading down into blackness.

"I'd spend my time just opening doors if I worked here," Chloe joked, refusing to succumb to the urge to relinquish her one-day pass and flee. *He's not a psycho, he's not a psycho*, she told herself.

"That's mostly what I did on my first day," Ethan said. "Sort of dried my eyes out after a while, though."

Unsure if he was serious or just had a dry sense of humor, Chloe laughed anyway and felt her nerves ease up a bit.

When they reached the bottom of the stairs, Ethan flipped a switch, flooding the narrow gallery with light. Chloe's attention was immediately drawn to a humongous fossil in the center of the room. Stepping closer, she saw that it was a footprint, or, more accurately, a talon print.

"That's half the size of me!" she exclaimed. "What in Hades is that?"

Ethan smiled, evidently amused by her enthusiasm—or her ignorance. "Remember the stories about the Gryphons?"

"You're kidding me. This belongs to one of the things that pulled Apollo's chariot and slaughtered Cyclopes? Do you have Cyclopes fossils, too?" Chloe's heartbeat accelerated. She wasn't afraid anymore; she was riveted.

"It's speculation, of course. But it matches the written record we have. And no. No Cyclops remains yet. I'm not sure that's something I'd want to see."

Chloe kneeled in front of the fossil. She reached out to touch it, but stopped herself.

"You know what's even more awesome?" Ethan pointed to another fossil at the opposite end of the room.

Chloe sprang up and approached the rock, stopping when she made it halfway and could clearly see what it was. "No way," she said, goosebumps rising on her arms.

"One of the gryphon's back feet," Ethan said. "It has the exact same dimensions as the forward talon. And again, it fits the mythology perfectly."

"Wait," said Chloe, her logic short-circuiting her excitement as she stared at the gargantuan lion paw impressed in the stone. "How do you know it's not a fake?"

"Well, first of all, my mom ran every test known to man, including thermoluminescence and radio-carbon dating. And second, the last time someone fabricated an artifact—I think it was an amber scroll—the court sentenced him to death. They made him drink hemlock."

Chloe shivered, not only because of the grisly punishment, but because it stood to reason that if the gryphon had existed, then Scylla had, too.

"So your mom dug all these up?" Chloe asked. She didn't want to consider a real-life Scylla a second longer.

"She and her team. They'd been laughed at for years because they hadn't found anything more than pottery. When they found the fossils and the scroll, the Fantásmata pulled their funding and made them clear the site."

"Why? Why would they shut them down as soon as they started making progress?" Chloe asked. But then she remembered Ethan's remark about the Fantásmata not

43

caring whether their decisions make sense. She couldn't help but wonder what other fossils and relics were buried. "Have there been any...um...giant squid fossils found?"

Ethan raised his eyebrows in surprise. Then he laughed. "No, why do you ask?"

"I'd just like to know if Scylla, the mythological sea monster, ever really existed."

"I guess we'll never know," Ethan said.

"I *hope* we'll never know," Chloe muttered under her breath.

"What did you say?"

"I said I'd like to see the scroll. You said there's a written record."

Ethan nodded. "Iris's Scroll, we call it. It isn't much, but it's intriguing nonetheless. There's more to it, my mom said, but the Fantásmata are still studying it on their own."

"How do you know they didn't just dump it all back in the Great Sea?" Chloe could feel herself resenting her planet's secretive government a little more each minute.

"That wouldn't make any sense." Ethan shrugged. "But I wouldn't put it past them." He walked past a display of water pots and weapon remains—which, given the evidence of a gryphon that surrounded it, didn't interest Chloe in the least—and stopped in front of the back wall.

Instead of waiting for the high-tech wall to scan his retina, Ethan tapped out a pattern on the surface. The wall stayed put this time, but Chloe's eyes lifted up as Ethan's did, and she saw a square of four ceiling tiles fold up. Out of the hole descended a cylindrical glass case with a few torn, discolored pages positioned in a circle around it on plastic display stands. Ethan was right; it wasn't much.

Chloe squinted at the unfamiliar alphabet etched into the scroll fragments. "Can you read Próta?" she asked Ethan.

"I'm working on it. My mom has some of the only Próta textbooks still in print. Studying is another way I spend my time here when I'm not opening secret doorways."

"Do you know enough to know what these say?"

"I can work it out." Ethan shrugged.

"Good enough for me."

Ethan joined her by the case and pointed to the stand on the far left. "This one talks about something called a 'Guardian.' His name is Acheron, and he's a pretty mean dude. He had five Eusebians executed because they asked him to stop the Alphas from sacrificing in their temple."

"What are Alphas and Eusebians?"

"My mom says that it seems like there were two classes— more like religious groups—back then, at least according to one scroll that got confiscated a long time ago. One class worshipped the gods and goddesses, like Poseidon, Apollo, and Athena, and the other worshipped one god, named Duna."

"I wonder when all that changed. Do these say?" Chloe asked, touching the glass with her knuckle.

Ethan shook his head. "I have a feeling only the Fantásmata know."

"What's this one say?" Chloe gestured to the second stand in line.

"That one mentions a messenger named Carya. She's sort of weird, and supernatural, I think. She only talks in rhymes. She heals a slave girl who's been whipped by Acheron."

"Who's the girl?"

"Her name's Iris. She's the sister of one of the people Acheron had killed. I guess he made her one of his slaves after that. I'd like to know what happened to him. I hope Iris sicked her doma on him."

"Her what?" asked Chloe.

Before Ethan could answer, a loud beep blared from two speakers above their heads, causing Chloe to jump.

"It's okay. It's just the intercom," Ethan assured her.

"Ethan, it's time to come back upstairs." The voice belonged to Ethan's mother. "We have to close up for the day."

"I'm sorry," Ethan said to Chloe. "You haven't heard about Diokles yet. He's the last person mentioned in these sections. Maybe you can come back since your time was cut short today."

Chloe found it refreshing that Ethan referred to these ancient people in the present tense, as if they were living now and he'd just talked with them over coffee. Perhaps they were to him what Rhoda and Farley were to her: imaginary characters whose faraway stories offered solace and escape. It felt good to consider that she might not be the only one who felt the need to escape every now and then.

"I'd like to see you—*it*—again," Chloe stammered. She told herself that Ethan hadn't noticed her slip.

He smiled. "I'd like to see you, too."

Chloe remained silent, letting his words settle in the air long enough for her to make a memory of them. She'd never been told that before, and the feeling was incomparable, especially because she knew, instinctively, that he meant it.

"We'd better go," Ethan said, then he spun on his heel and rushed to the foot of the stairs like he couldn't wait to be rid of her.

Men, Chloe thought. They were either liars who didn't mean what they said, or they were cowards who meant what they said but didn't have the guts to stand by it.

Ethan offered to walk Chloe out to her car, but she told him no thank you. He said he would see about getting her another one-day pass, or at least a half-day pass, but she wasn't going to hold her breath.

She got into her car, happy to see that the rain had let up and there was still enough daylight to keep her drive down the mountain safe from her made-up, horror-movie scenarios. She put the car in reverse, looked in the rearview mirror, and then screamed as her heart leapt into her throat. Sitting in the backseat, looking back at her in the mirror, was a girl.

"Who in Zeus' name are you?" Chloe shouted as she turned to face the interloper. She pulled a bottle of pepper spray out of the console.

The girl smiled softly and folded her hands, clearly unalarmed by Chloe's threat.

"Do you know what this is?" said Chloe. "It's pepper spray. It burns really, really bad. Get out of my car or I'm going to blind you with it." This made the girl giggle a bit and twirl the ends of her wavy, auburn hair. "You think that's funny?" That made the girl giggle even louder, and Chloe began to wonder if she was a bit slow. "Are you deaf?" Chloe said, raising her voice and enunciating each word so much that her jaw popped.

The girl stopped laughing and shook her head, then she opened her mouth and said,

"I can only speak what I've been sent to say,
So listen well before I fly aw—"

"Why are you talking in rhymes?" Chloe interrupted. "Wait. Are you...are you..." She could feel her chin quivering as the answer to her own question was becoming all too clear.

Carya.

Was she hallucinating as she had in the treehouse? She pinched herself up and down her arms. She tugged on her ears.

48

She was tempted to spray herself in the face with the pepper spray just to ensure she wasn't dreaming.

Then the girl spoke again.

"Do not harm yourself; you're wide awake,
But you must know what steps to take.
If more of the past you wish to see,
Take and eat from the walnut tree."

The girl held out both fists and opened them. In the center of each ivory palm sat a walnut still in its shell.

As Chloe stared at the walnuts, she noticed that her car had never smelled so good, not even when Damian had put a wintergreen-scented air freshener in it after Chloe spilled a milkshake in the backseat and waited five days to clean it up. Now it smelled like lemon and lavender, rosemary and thyme all mingled together.

Before Chloe could ask another question, the girl began to speak again, only this time her voice was louder as she pronounced every syllable with urgency.

"There's just one warning you should heed:
Do not eat of the enchanted seed.
Take a lesson from Hades' wife,
Who descended to hell, though she kept her life."

"You're a funny little thing, you know that?" Chloe turned back toward the steering wheel, where the car didn't smell so fresh. "Now get out of here before 1—"

Before she could finish her sentence, the image of the stranger vanished from the rearview mirror. The only sign she had ever been there were the two walnuts hovering in the air where her hands had held them up.

"This birthday just gets better and better the crazier 1 get," Chloe muttered. Then she took the walnuts and stuffed them in her purse, wondering why in the world she wasn't hurling them out the window instead.

CHAPTER SIX
ORPHEUS

The Underworld was divided into several sections, into which mortals' souls drifted the moment after their final breath. There were the Fields of Asphodel for those who, in life, committed neither heinous acts of evil nor honorable deeds of greatness. Beyond them was the Plain of Judgment, where Hades took pleasure in devising modes of torment that fit its inhabitants' crimes. And between these two realms lay what was perhaps the most miserable of all the lightless lairs hidden deep beneath Petros, the Vale of Mourning, reserved for spirits consumed by tragic love, even in death.

The Vale of Mourning was no Elysium—where the occupants enjoyed sparkling white shores and soothing hot springs with fruit trees blossoming all around them—but it possessed a beauty that most mortals never had the opportunity to see. Wrapped around the Vale was a dormant range of volcanic mountains that stretched for miles toward Petros's crust. From them flowed four rivers that Achelous, one of Apollo's dark rebels, created so his beloved Deianeira could bathe in them and be reminded of their short-lived love before Heracles subdued him and whisked her away. These supernatural rivers converged within a vast crystalline lake filled with exotic fish that swam together in colorful schools, the only creatures in hell awarded freedom.

While there was no sun in the Underworld, Apollo possessed the ability to fabricate light with a snap of his fingers. He suffused the Vale with summer sunshine and filled its trees with music, though there were no birds. There was just one musical instrument, which belonged to a man named Orpheus; he played it seldom and softly.

This land of woe and regret was made beautiful by cruel design; its beauty meant to taunt the brokenhearted with scenes of rapture and songs of enchantment they would never be able to share with the ones they loved. Many of them stayed curled up in the shadows of the cypress trees with their ears covered, trying in vain to ignore the false heaven around them. Others made the best of their fate and befriended each other, spending their time reminiscing about their romances and how they went awry.

Orpheus was unlike any of his peers, for he neither hid from the majestic, lonely world nor babbled about his dear Eurydice to downcast wraiths who didn't care. Apollo had allowed Orpheus, one of his many sons, to keep his golden lyre, the one that could charm or sedate any living thing depending on the song he played.

To be sure, the Dark Lord was not showing mercy. The lyre was to be a thorn that drew blood whenever it was strummed, causing stabbing memories of Eurydice to play through the melody.

But Orpheus cherished the instrument because it made him feel close to his departed wife, Eurydice, who was taken from him by a viper's bite. She had touched it, played it, loved it, sung along with it, just as he did on days when the pain of missing her made him cry aloud for death to take him again and send him this time to the Plain of Judgment, where the physical anguish might mask the torture wrought by his own emotions.

On this day, just after the peach light of dawn had spread over the ash-colored mountains, Orpheus took his lyre and began to play the song he had composed the morning he first laid eyes on Eurydice. The words rolled off

his lips like water burbling in a brook as he closed his eyes
and recreated the moment within the dreamlike haze of his
most darling memory.

> "When I would grow weary of people
> and forget how to form a smile,
> I would wander into the woods and
> follow the river a while.
> I would lean against a tree, invite
> the songbirds to be my muse,
> Then play as many melodies as the
> morn has different hues.
> But the day the oak nymph crossed my
> path with hyacinth in her hair,
> My fingers refused to touch the lyre;
> all I could do was stare.
> She was the most exquisite creature,
> with ivory arms and cheeks,
> One look at her and my heart went soaring
> past Zeus' snow-capped peaks.
> She was enchanted by the music,
> overcome with rapt desire,
> By the quivering of the lyre's strings,
> their notes of mirth and fire.
> She had a voice like honey, and that
> day it soothed my soul,

It sweetened my heart with gladness
    and made my being whole.
Though a son of gods I was, I would
    have cursed them all to be,
A worthless worm in the wondrous
    presence of my sweet Eurydice."

"Mercy, mercy, Orpheus. Have mercy on our pitying ears."

Orpheus turned to see Clytemnestra, the murdered queen, pulling at her hair with one hand and her ragged robe in the other, imploring him to stop.

"Give me that loathsome instrument this second," hissed the queen as she pointed to a plume of smoke rising out of the tallest mountain. "I will rejoice with every step as I hike up there to drop it into the Tartarus cauldron. I know the Titans will have no greater pleasure than to take their turns tearing it to pieces. No doubt the music curses them all as well."

Orpheus dropped the plectrum onto the grass and leaned the lyre against the dewy slope he sat upon. "Fair queen, why do you seek to bless the Titans while begrudging me the only speck of bliss I have to enjoy here in this cesspool of suffering? I took my own life to be with my Eurydice, but even death could not end my agony. Why must you plead like a beggar that I spare you from a moment's worth of relief within an eternity of gloom?"

"Let him play," called another voice from the branches of a frankincense tree.

"Mind your own business, Leucothoe!" shrieked Clytemnestra, as she charged toward the tree and stared into it like a bloodthirsty hound chasing after a squirrel.

After a few seconds of silence had passed and it seemed Clytemnestra would get her way, the princess's olive arm darted down from the leaves and seized the queen by the shoulder.

"I do not take orders well from *murderers*," said Leucothoe as she slid out of the tree and planted her feet on the rocky earth. "I side with those who, unlike you, are undeserving of their lot in Hades. Husband killers deserve the Plain of Judgment, where the condemned would pluck out their own eyeballs just to hear an hour's worth of song from Orpheus's lyre."

"Do not speak of what you do not understand, you vile strumpet," Clytemnestra barked as she righted the robe at her shoulder. "Oh, why didn't Apollo leave you in the form of that hideous tree as your lover intended? Or better yet, why didn't Helios, your weak-willed lover, leave you buried dead in the sand in the first place, rotting away where your father rightly put you when he learned of your fool-headed trysts? When will mortals learn that nothing good ever comes from dalliances with the gods?"

"I have this frankincense tree to console my spirit as I weep for Helios, my radiant, sun-born love." Leucothoe stepped forward and stroked the crossbar of Orpheus's lyre. "The famed poet has his instrument to fill his thoughts with his wife, the ravishing oak nymph. But what do you have to assuage the festering hole of your guilt-blackened heart?" Clytemnestra's eyes narrowed with anger. "That's right," said the princess. "*Nothing*. And so you despise those of us with remnants of love still to cling to. You may hate me, great queen, but I pity you."

And with that, bold Leucothoe climbed back up the tree, into her abode of salty tears and piney resin.

Orpheus stood and took the lyre into his arms, sure the queen would snatch it away and make good on her word to carry it to the tallest peak and fling it into its flames. But Clytemnestra didn't approach him. Instead, she threw on her cowl and scurried off across the valley, leaping across a brook, squealing like a doe with an arrow in her flank.

As he watched her flee, Orpheus pondered the double-edged power of words, at their ability to both heal like medicine and cut like swords. He picked his plectrum up off the grass and tried to play something light that might cheer his spirits, but his fingers felt paralyzed; they were unable to move in the wake of the women's feud. The bitter queen had gotten her way after all. .

"Oh, Eurydice," Orpheus half sung, half said as he walked toward the lake. "Wherever you are—basking in Elysium, I'm sure—do you have any idea what I wouldn't do to sing with you for one quarter of a note? Or to see you for one fragment of a second?"

Orpheus stood at the edge of the lake and dipped his big toe into the water. He tried to remember what it felt like to do so on a hot, sultry day after walking miles in the woods, or threshing wheat in the fields. He wanted to feel the desperate urge to dive in, and then to have relief wash over him as his body went weightless in the water. He wanted to feel the reward of ecstasy after a hard day's labor, or an afternoon spent composing or performing for throngs of merchants in the agora.

Most of all, he wanted to feel Eurydice's hand around his wrist, pulling him from the tepid shallows into the colder deep, splashing him as she sung and spun, cleansing him more completely than the purest spring could ever do.

The poet looked down at the lyre, his closest companion; his only companion. He thought of the thousands of songs it had birthed and the millions of tears it had evoked, tears of both sorrow and unspeakable joy. He'd stopped counting the number of years the lyre had been with him there in the Vale, how long it had served as the angelic voice of his hellish grief. But he knew one thing: the day had come to part with it.

Orpheus raised the lyre to his shoulder and admired its turtle-shell sound-chest, its six strings made of the gut of a goat Apollo had killed in the foothills of Olympus. More lyrics flew from his lips.

"Like I've been pierced through with Achilles'
spear, or flung from Troy's great wall,
Still, a greater pain would it surely be
to never have loved you at all."

His eye released a single tear as he rotated his torso, preparing to fling the hallowed instrument into the lake where it would rot and fade to legend.

"Don't be rash, Orpheus," came an impish, high-pitched voice behind him.

Orpheus lowered his lyre and said, without turning around, "What foul mischief brings you to our charming sector, Hermes?"

"The only charming thing here is that divine instrument, of which you are about to dispose," replied Hermes, adjusting the dog-skin cap that made him invisible to the living and dead alike.

"What charm does it bring to you, Uncle?" asked Orpheus, shifting his focus back to the lake. "You never subject your ears to the wailing ghosts of the Vale unless my father has sent you on some spiteful errand. Take your business elsewhere."

The poet raised the lyre again and took a firm step forward, then, like an Olympic athlete with a discus, he swung the lyre five times back and forth, releasing it on the sixth. The instrument went sailing through the humid air, bound for the murky center of the lake where it would sink into oblivion.

But then, in its apogee, the lyre stopped and hung still, suspended by Hermes' magic.

"Stop your sorcery, Hermes!" shouted Orpheus as he pivoted back to his puckish visitor.

Hermes just gave his boyish smile, a smile that one could describe as endearing had it not belonged to Apollo's slyest emissary. The spirit twirled his golden rod, then, mimicking a sailor heaving an anchor out of the sea, he leaned back and tugged on the wand, grinning as he pulled the lyre to shore.

"You didn't create this treasure," said Hermes, cradling the lyre like an infant. "What makes you think you can destroy it?"

Orpheus could feel his normal, equanimous deportment being undermined, replaced by the basest of territorial instincts. "What makes you think you can stop me?" He lowered his head like a bull and charged the saboteur.

Just before a collision could occur, Hermes lifted the wand and carved a fair-sized frame in the air between them. Orpheus stopped dead in his tracks when he saw the silhouette forming inside the frame's silver edges. At first there was nothing but white wisps of mist, starting at the top and curling back in faint tendrils until they met the outline of a royal diadem. But then, in the middle, sharper features formed: an eyebrow, eyelashes, a nose, and lips Orpheus had dreamt of, waking and sleeping, every day and night.

"Eurydice!" Orpheus gasped.

He watched the image take on color. The diadem shone brightly with amethysts and emeralds. The white hair turned to pale honey. The eye glowed green; the lips became scarlet. As Orpheus reached out his hand to touch the cheek, the face became flesh and turned toward him.

"Orpheus," the image whispered, Eurydice in solid form.

Orpheus stumbled forward, both arms outstretched, but the poet could not steal a single kiss; Eurydice disappeared in an instant.

"Get out of my sight, Hermes," Orpheus growled. "Take the lyre back to your brother, or find someone else to torture with it."

Then he stomped through the air where his wife's face had been and kept on walking, toward woods so dense no light or sound got in. There he would join the others who, by lying down in darkness and denying their senses stimuli, sought an impossible end to their death.

"You think that was the end of my mission here, dear nephew?" Hermes called after him. "To conjure the image of your beautiful wife only to break your heart when you do that very well yourself?" Orpheus said nothing and continued his listless trudge. "Well, you are wrong. What if you really can have Eurydice back, to hold in your arms in Elysium for all eternity?"

Orpheus heard Hermes leap into the air, then saw him flying high over his head.

"Hear me out, Orpheus." The wings of Hermes' sandals fluttered as he hovered five feet above Orpheus's reach. "That's all I ask. No more tricks. There's no worse Apollo can do to you if you refuse the message I have to relay, but trust me when I say there's no worse punishment than to miss this opportunity. It may never come again."

"What opportunity?" Orpheus muttered, eyes still fixed on the woods just yards away.

"Apollo needs your gifts for a task in the mortal realm. In return, he will raise your spirit to Elysium to be joined with Eurydice's forever."

Orpheus stopped walking and looked the imp in his twinkling eye. "What sort of task? And why should I believe you?" He scowled, shaking his head at himself for slipping into Hermes' trap. "What reason do I have to trust you—you, the notorious knave who thrives on deceit like a tick on a dog?"

"What do you have to lose?"

CHAPTER SEVEN
MISSION

Hermes escorted Orpheus through the Vale, and when a swarm of jealous souls began to moan and shout and yank hard at the travelers' cloaks, begging to follow behind, Hermes turned them to stone until he and Orpheus were out of sight. Those less hostile were lulled to sleep with a few notes of Orpheus's lyre before their indifference could morph to madness as their chance at escape strode past them.

"Where are we going?" asked Orpheus.

They'd reached the end of the Vale, which was designated by a dolomite cliff overlooking a churning sea of lava; mourning souls sometimes flung themselves into it, only to be ushered back by Hermes to their sphere, their memories of life feeling more recent, raw, and sharper than on the day they'd died. Perhaps that's how Apollo could punish him should he refuse to do his bidding—send harpies to throw him over the cliff, again...and again...and again, burning his thin, ghostly flesh, searing his heart with a fresh recollection of love when it knew no threat or foe.

"Up," was all Hermes said before adjusting his cap, clicking his heels, and grabbing Orpheus's arm as he leapt out over the cliff, flying them across the lava toward the foggy Fields of Asphodel.

Orpheus had sung about birds, but never had he imagined he might one day fly like one, much less do so in the grim dome of the Underworld. But, as when he'd dipped his toe in the lake and felt no sensation of relief or release, he felt nothing as Hermes sped them through the air between Asphodel's grayness below and Hades' iron mantle above.

There was no breeze to guide them, no zephyr to sweep them higher or soften their descent. There were no birds to fly beside, no creature to call to or to follow, and no aerie on which to perch. There was no landscape worth encircling, no scene to admire, no treetops to dance upon.

All was a wasteland. The Fields of Asphodel consisted of nothing but confused clumps of souls whose memories had been washed away the moment they'd drunk from the River Lethe. Like cows grazing tirelessly in a pasture, they picked and picked at the pallid Asphodel blooms, filling wicker baskets and counting them one by one. They were witless, senseless, and for the very first time, Orpheus felt grateful for his plight in the tear-stained Vale.

"Would you like to go the long way, to the Plain of Judgment?" Hermes shouted into Orpheus's ear. "You can get a good look at Sisyphus rolling his boulder uphill, only to have it crash back on him as he nears the top. And Tantalus, too. He's the wretch who killed his own son and fed him to his dinner guests. Now he stands in a pool of water that recedes the second he bends down for a drink. And the branches of low-hanging fruit above his head recoil at his touch." He laughed. "It's quite pathetic."

"I think not, Uncle. Unlike some, I do not derive joy from observing others' pain." Orpheus half expected Hermes to drop him into the River Lethe below, where his mind would be wiped clean.

"We'll see about that," said Hermes.

Their surroundings blurred as they shot fast through the sky, and Orpheus hummed an old tune.

☽

Hermes slowed as the palace of Hades pierced through the smog of sulfurous ash. He landed them along the wall, near two towers and the roaring Chimera that kept watch between them.

Orpheus gazed in awe at the gigantic creature, marveling at its leonine face and torso, the buckskin goat head bleating from its back, and the hissing snake that comprised its tail. *"I thought it was just a legend,"* he said.

Hermes batted the Chimera on its rump, causing the lion head to whip around and roar so loudly that the walls around them shook. It lunged toward Orpheus and took a swipe at him with its paw, missing him by an inch or two. Then it bucked and turned, allowing the serpent tail to dance and strike as Orpheus sidestepped to avoid it. But it never hit him; he was only being teased.

"That's enough, my dainty doll," Hermes cooed as he stood on his tiptoes and rubbed the lion's chest. "You really should work on being more hospitable to our guests, you know."

The lion purred as the goat head lay down and the snake went slack, stretching itself gracefully toward the granite ground.

"That's the problem with the living, and even some of the *dead*," said Hermes, glaring over his shoulder at Orpheus. "If they can't see something with their own eyes, they write it off as fantasy or futile speculation."

"I didn't write anything off," said Orpheus. "But never mind; there's nothing I'd rather do less in this miserable place than philosophize with *you*. I came to—"

"To see me?"

The voice rumbled like thunder in Orpheus's ears. He turned to see the bright white figure of a man the size of a giant standing near the gated entrance that led down to the palace below. A soft yellow glow seemed to pulse above the man's skin, shrouding even his eyes in a shimmering gossamer layer of light.

Orpheus hadn't seen his father since the second most tragic day of his life, the day he lost Eurydice once again to the shadows of Hades. Her second death was more unbearable, because he'd caused it...

☾

After the funeral, Orpheus had taken his lyre into the woods, intending to travel to the Cave of Charon, named for the ferryman who sailed the newly deceased across the River Styx. The cave was where Orpheus had planned to breathe his fill of poisonous vapors, fall down dead, and try to persuade Hades' judges that he belonged with Eurydice, wherever they'd placed her. He had almost reached the cave's mouth when Apollo had appeared and spoken words the poet could scarcely comprehend; his mind was so muddled with grief.

"Had I known how beautifully you'd play it, I'd never have given you that lyre," Apollo had said. *"It seems it has the power*

to persuade even the Lord of Death to let your Eurydice rejoin you in life."

Orpheus had stopped strumming for the first time in days and waited for the apparition to fade or beckon him into the cave to meet his end. But Apollo had remained and continued with his proposition.

"Hades' ears have been bewitched by your playing, my venerable son. He wishes to grant you back your wife." Apollo paused just long enough to see dead hope quicken and rise into Orpheus's eyes, then he extinguished it with the following condition: "However, the path to your love is not without its perils."

He stopped again, this time to observe Orpheus's reaction, but the poet was stone-faced. He would face a legion of hellish hybrids, empty-handed if he had to, for a single glimpse of his beloved's face, let alone have her company forever.

"You must go to the Underworld," continued Apollo, "enchant three-headed Cerberus until he sleeps, retrieve Eurydice, and then lead her out yourself. Should you turn to regard her as you depart, she will be swallowed back into whichever compartment the judges have assigned her. She'll be gone forever, Orpheus."

Orpheus nodded his understanding, still too shaken to speak. Which god of fortune was he to thank for this mercy?

Apollo waved his hands across his son's face, cloaking him in a mystical nimbus meant to shield him from the cave's fatal fumes.

68

Orpheus had chosen the most mellifluous ballad he knew and played it continually as he followed Apollo down into the smoldering bowels of Petros. When he reached the bronze threshold, he had no trouble charming the guard dog, Cerberus. In fact, nothing had ever so easily swooned under the spell of his music. He dropped the lyre when his eyes spotted Eurydice waiting for him in a dreary courtyard flanked by porticoes that flickered with lamplight and the eyes of on-looking spirits.

And then, with his love liberated and their freedom in sight, Orpheus made his irreparable mistake.

When he saw pink dusk appear before him, he had peeked back over his shoulder to make sure Eurydice was still there. In horror, he watched her scream his name as she dissolved into the twilight, her spirit translated back to Hades' lair.

☾

Orpheus became dizzy as Eurydice's last anguished cry echoed in his brain, causing his head and neck to sweat, and his phantom heart to ache. He fell to one knee and held his hand to his chest, his guilt coursing hot through his veins like venom.

"My son, why do you cower in my presence?" Apollo said, stepping closer.

Orpheus mustered the strength to lift himself off the ground. He drew a breath, wiped his brow and tried to find his father's eyes, well hidden behind the yellow aura.

As if sensing his son's desire, Apollo let out a long exhale, melting the web of light around him and revealing exquisite armor, which was, from embossed breastplate down to shining greaves, entirely made of gold. His cerulean eyes sparkled like jewels set within an amphora of marble. The pupils dilated with a piercing glow that made Orpheus shiver for the first time since he'd been dead.

"I'm sorry, father. It's been ages since we last met." Orpheus lifted his eyes to the black mountain range that cut across the horizon. If Apollo was so powerful, why did he choose to live in the roiling belly of Petros and not aloft somewhere—anywhere—in the starry cosmos?

Orpheus had never seen his father's face. It had always either been masked by hoods or surrounded with that impenetrable mist: it was a thing of beauty, more magnificent than anything his peers had ever carved or painted, spoken of, or sung about. But it contained something terrifying, too. Something Orpheus couldn't put words to. Something he could only feel in the remote reaches of his being. It seized every muscle, chilled every cell, and stiffened the very marrow in his bones.

"I've missed your music, Orpheus. I'm glad Hermes got to you before you fed it to the fishes." A smile played on Apollo's lips, and then, without moving, he pulled the lyre out of Orpheus's hands and held it in his own. "I have a job for you and this lyre. And I think you'll find the offer rather irresistible."

"Forgive me, father, but the last time you presented me with an offer, it separated me eternally from my wife and expedited my suicide."

"And who do you have to blame for *that*?" Hermes shouted, still standing beside the Chimera as all three of its heads slept soundly.

"Come, come, Hermes, don't be cruel," Apollo said, as his fingers plucked a few notes of the lyre. "That was a long, long time ago."

"Hermes is right," said Orpheus. He couldn't deny that losing Eurydice was no one's fault but his own. "I will do whatever you ask under the condition that you ensure my success. Hermes or another of your officials must come to my aid when I need it. And he must escort her to me, or me to her, the moment my task is complete. Lastly, there should be no possibility for this arrangement to be annulled." Orpheus's cheek twitched. Who was he to make demands on the general of Hades' army?

"Oh, Orpheus," Apollo said, his wide eyes glittering. "I'm glad to see that time apart from your muse has put some steel into your poet's heart. That will serve you on your mission."

"So we have an understanding?" Orpheus asked.

"I'm afraid you've overestimated my power, or perhaps my jurisdiction. I can no more control your future than Hades' judges can rule unjustly. Everyone receives what they've earned."

"Fine," grunted Orpheus, embarrassed by his oversight. Though his appearance may have suggested otherwise, Apollo wasn't all-powerful. Mightier than he and his cohort, Hades, was the All-Powerful Creator, whose name it was forbidden even to whisper within the vales of hell. "But I must have your word that if I'm successful, nothing will prevent me from getting her back, and *back for good*."

Apollo set down the lyre and kneeled on the ground. At first, Orpheus thought he was going to lie prostrate as an expression of his sincerity, but he soon saw that his father was enchanting the stone somehow. Apollo blew on the granite, his lips almost touching it, then brushed both hands back and forth across it in opposite directions, forming two large arcs of spotless, translucent glass.

"Come," Apollo said. Orpheus obeyed and kneeled beside his father. "Now look."

Through the glass, Orpheus saw a small, roofless chamber overgrown with dead flowers and withered tamarisks. In the center of the room was a marble bench that seemed to glow amid the gray habitat around it. Scanning a thick trellis of shriveled grapes, Orpheus caught a flash of a vibrant, violet robe, and then a glimpse of flaxen hair.

"Eurydice," he whispered, as if anything above a whisper would make her vanish.

"We're holding her here for you," Apollo said, tapping on the glass with his slender white fingers. "Hades' wife

72

Persephone furnished the cell herself. It's no Elysium, which is of course what your wife is accustomed to, but I'm afraid living things don't fare well in the heart of Hades. Is she just as beautiful as you remember?"

Orpheus pressed his hands against the glass, framing her body with his fingers. He spoke her name louder, trying—foolishly, he knew—to get her attention. She was still too far away, always too far away...

"No song of mine ever came close to describing her decently. 'Rainbows, sunsets, starlight, the sea, none of it compares with my Eurydice,'" he sang softly.

Apollo stood and pulled Orpheus up by the arm. "She'll be waiting. When you're with her in Elysium, you'll have all of eternity to try and write the perfect serenade for her."

Orpheus willed himself to turn away as the glass slowly turned opaque; he couldn't stand to see Eurydice disappear yet again. He picked up his lyre and looked Apollo dead in his bone-chilling eyes. "What do you want me to do?"

CHAPTER EIGHT
EDUCATION

From day one after her parents died, Chloe and her family ate dinner separately. Usually, her aunt Maggie and uncle Travis went to the neighborhood mess hall around the corner, returning in plenty of time to watch an Enochos court case on TV. Chloe and Damian were fortunate enough to have had a chef for a mother, so they knew a thing or two when it came to cooking. However, because it was nearly impossible to find anything other than ice cream and canned soup in the kitchen, they too often resorted to the mess hall's delivery service and ate alone in their rooms.

Only twice a year was the dining room ever used by all four of them at once: Lycaea Eve before the yearly festival, and on the twins' birthday. It was always an awkward occasion. They sat together in the formal, dusty dining room, the only sound coming from the icemaker and the air conditioner.

Chloe knew that sacrificing their nightly veg-out routine and purchasing gaudy cakes was her aunt and uncle's idea of a kind gesture, but Chloe couldn't help but feel patronized. Sitting there in the hard, ladderback chair, staring at a lukewarm bowl of macaroni and cheese, Chloe always felt simultaneously depressed and overjoyed.

She and Damian were now adults, and graduating in the spring would mean freedom. Freedom from the apathy and selfishness of her aunt and uncle was what she yearned for, and literally dreamed about, but what then?

The thought of going to the university stole her appetite completely. Graduation had been something she'd looked forward to for so long, but now that it was right around the corner, the anticipation had devolved to dread. It wasn't that she feared the work university would require; she was smart, studious, the quintessential overachiever. What depressed her was the likelihood of abject loneliness. If she felt like a pariah among her own flesh and blood, there was slight chance she would feel accepted among total strangers.

For the first time in eight years, she realized that maybe she hadn't had it so bad living with guardians who didn't care about her. At least they threw her a party once a year, however minimal the enthusiasm they put into it. At university, no one would even know she existed.

"So," Maggie chimed with a put-on, chipper tone, "where'd you run off to earlier, Chlo?"

Chloe hated it when Maggie called her "Chlo," as if they were best friends.

"Someone gave me a one-day pass for the new museum, so I went," Chloe said, nonchalantly stirring her noodles.

Travis cleared his throat. "I heard about that on the news. Pretty nice gift, I'd say. It costs a pretty penny to get into that place."

"My friend works there," said Chloe. She waited for her brother to sing "Chloe and Ethan, sitting in a tree," but apparently he'd grown up. His eyes were glued to his cellphone, globs of cheese stuck to the corners of his mouth. So he'd grown up *slightly*...

"See anything noteworthy?" Maggie asked as she looked down at her watch.

Sure that her aunt was counting the seconds until she could turn on the TV again, Chloe thought back to the odd white building with its secret passageways, the ancient gryphon fossils, the scroll, and of course, Carya and the two walnuts still waiting for her in the bottom of her purse.

Confused, exhilarated, and scared at the same time, Chloe wanted to tell her family how *fascinating* the visit had been, but she knew that doing so would be risky. By law, all Petrodians were required to report anyone who displayed what the Fantásmata termed *paráxeno theáseis, or* "strange sightings." They were two of the most peculiar words Chloe ever had to memorize in school, but she knew their meaning well: "Any supposed encounter with the preternatural that one might associate with fantastical figures or myths from Petrodian lore. The Fantásmata must be notified of any individual who claims to have experienced such a sighting."

That was all that had ever been written or stated about *paráxeno theáseis*, but Chloe reasoned that whomever was guilty of encountering them and then squealed about it, or got caught would live to regret it for the rest of their life—if they lived at all.

The Fantásmata didn't appreciate anything that deviated from the status quo. Just last year, one of Chloe's teachers had been arrested during class after one of his students told the headmaster that Mr. Boulos had taught that historically, the Lycaea festival had honored Apollo, not the Unknown God. Because this sparked curiosity in a classroom filled with teenagers who questioned everything about everything, Mr. Boulos was accused of "corrupting the youth." By the end of the day, he was exiled to an undisclosed island "where he'd have no access to anyone to whom he could spread lies."

If a teacher could be hauled off to a deserted island for including unpopular, peripheral tidbits in his history lesson, Chloe didn't want to imagine what the Fantásmata might do to someone who purportedly conversed with an ancient being mentioned on a mysterious scroll. She decided it would be best to keep the details of her visit to herself.

"Not really," she said to Maggie. "Thank you for everything today. I'm going upstairs to get started on a research paper," she lied.

"What research paper?" asked Damian, but Chloe ignored him and took her dishes to the sink. It wouldn't hurt him to sweat a little over a made-up assignment.

(

Chloe took a seat next to her purse on the bed. She reached into it and scooped up the walnuts, wondering why Carya had given her two. She assumed one was a backup in case the other was lost. She placed one on the shelf above her and cupped the other in her hand, staring at it carefully; scrutinizing it like a jeweler does a diamond. It looked like a walnut, felt like a walnut, it probably tasted like a walnut...

"How do I open this thing?" she muttered before falling back onto her pillow and stuffing the walnut under it.

What in Hades was she doing? Was she really going to eat something given to her by some crazy, well-dressed urchin who just happened to fit the description of a newly discovered, next-to-unknown character named Carya? On the other hand, was she really going to chalk up the bizarre young girl—the "strange sighting," as the Fantásmata would put it—to a deranged passerby or obnoxious prankster despite what the girl knew about the scroll?

Chloe decided to do what she always did when she felt indecisive: make a pro/con list.

She sat up and reached over her desk for her diary and then its key hidden beneath an empty picture frame with the word *Family* painted in bold, multicolored letters around all four of its edges. It had been a gift seven birthdays ago, and she'd cried when she realized she'd run out of pictures of her parents to place in it.

She didn't have any photos of Maggie or Travis, but even if she did, she doubted she could bring herself to insult the frame by filling it with images of her dismal, substitute family. Following an unspoken sibling rule, which dictated that you mustn't let your brother or sister know you care about them, the pictures she had of Damian were kept in a shoebox under her bed.

It was the joyful-looking frame with its sad symbolism that inspired Chloe's first entry on the pro side of the list she labeled *Pros and Cons of Eating the Weird Walnut*.

She unlocked her diary, opened it up, and scribbled: *If I eat the walnut and something bad happens and I die, maybe there really is an afterlife and my parents are there waiting for me.*

She tapped her chin with the pen and looked at the rain dribbling down the windowpane. She'd never given much thought to an afterlife before. After all, she was eighteen, with fifty-seven years of life still ahead of her before her Coronation. And even after that, death would be no concern of hers; only rare, freak accidents caused death.

When Chloe and Damian were eight years old, their teacher chaperoned their class on a field trip to the Religious Council building downtown. Eight was the age at which Petrodian children learned about the birds and the bees, and life and death, from the religious elite themselves. Every day during one month of the year, no fewer than one hundred and fifty Petrodian children had their innocent eyes opened to the world beyond playgrounds, arithmetic, and grammar.

The most significant memory Chloe had about that day was how frightened she'd felt.

The teacher had led Chloe and her fifteen classmates into a titanium-plated dome that defined the Eirene skyline. The teacher didn't go inside but left the class with a bald, skinny man with a raspy voice and a nametag that read *Head Attendant.*

The only words the man had spoken were, "Come with me."

The class had followed him through enormous ebony doors into a rectangular room lined with columns, the likes of which Chloe had only seen in one chapter of her history book. Nothing so opulent still existed in Petros—at least that's what she'd thought. Her jaw had dropped at the spectacle of reliefs along the walls, each one depicting, with sharp detail, a scene from nature. There was a flock of geese flying over a frozen river, a lighthouse illuminating a ship at sea, a lone lion hunting through hills.

On the left and right sides of the room stood at least a dozen bronze cauldrons perched on tripods at least fifteen feet tall. Their white-hot flames cast eerie shadows on the ceiling, which itself was a canvas of swirling galaxies and glowing stars. A few feet above the tripods was a line of semicircular clerestory windows that splashed light throughout the hall.

In the center of the room, directly below the brilliant, painted sun, had been an elevated stone platform supporting three tiers of marble benches. Those were occupied by nine old men, the oldest in Petros, all adorned with deep-purple chasubles loosely cinched with golden ropes. Before them, on the mosaic tile floor, were three rows of small, white, square mats. When the unnamed head attendant gestured to them, Chloe and the other children had taken their seats in silence. They shuddered as a gavel was struck against a sound block.

"We welcome you, *paidiá*," the chief councilman had welcomed them, using a Próta word that Chloe assumed meant "children."

"Today is a most important day for all Petrodians. What you hear within these walls may not seem important to you now, but one day you'll be glad we afforded you this privilege."

That was the beginning of a day that had provided more questions than answers, more confusion than clarity.

First, they'd learned about sex. Chloe remembered, with some amusement, that it had been the easiest part to process. There were a lot of rules regarding sexual intercourse, and they filled an entire notebook on fertility and reproduction given each child, rules such as: "Sexual intercourse may be partaken of after the age of fourteen. At that time, every Petrodian is lawfully bound to visit the Fertility and Reproduction Center to receive a temporary contraceptive injection (TCI), the effects of which will last six years. Should citizens be prohibited by the Fantásmata from procreating, a TCI will be administered again and every sixth year thereafter."

Chloe's mind didn't linger long on those memories. Perhaps she'd revisit them in two years' time when she learned whether or not she was selected to be a mother. Surely she wouldn't be. The way she saw it, any potential she might have had to nurture a child had been quashed the day her own mother had been killed.

Chloe's thoughts were instantly wrangled back to the second subject taught that day before the Religious Council: death...and its non-existence.

CHAPTER NINE
CORONATION

Does anyone here know of a contemporary Petrodian who died prematurely?" the chief councilman had asked. No one's hand was raised. "Good. That's very good. As you know, it's very rare for a Petrodian to die before his or her Coronation."

Coronation. Chloe hadn't understood the word then, much less how it could be used to describe the ending of a life.

The councilman had continued. "Thanks to the marvelous advances in medicine and technology, it's been decades since our society has perished from illness or pestilence. Our highly trained doctors and surgeons treat all injuries sustained through accidents, and indeed can do anything, from erasing all manner of deformity and scarring to making dead hearts beat again. Have any of you known someone whose life was saved with the help one of our physicians?"

A burst of small hands shot up into the air. The councilman took a few minutes to indulge the children, listening patiently to their stories of mended limbs, reconstructed faces, and robotic hands and feet. Then, after every triumph had been recounted, the councilman turned to the head attendant standing at the back of the room and motioned for him to come forward.

"Paidiá, this is Acacius, a long-time friend of the Religious Council," he said, introducing the attendant. "He went to Limén when he graduated primary school and learned the trade of a custodian. He did so well that his overseer took notice and sent him here, where he kept this building and its surrounding premises spick and span for forty years."

The councilman rested his hand on Acacius' shoulder and gave him a proud smile. "When Acacius became an Elder, we promoted him to head attendant with the responsibility of facilitating and leading the various tours and conferences we host throughout the year."

He turned his smile on the children and eagerly scanned their faces. "Which of you bright young striplings knows what follows elderhood in the life of a Petrodian?"

Chloe had known the answer, but she'd been too timid to give it. Her eyes were riveted on Acacius, whose own gaze was on the floor. With his shoulders stooped and his long thin arms fallen in front of him, he reminded Chloe of a willow tree, curved and leafless in old age.

"I do, Your Eminence!"

Chloe hadn't been at all surprised to see it was Damian piping up.

"The cycle of Petrodian life goes from infancy to childhood, then to either child-rearing, labor or one of the noble arts, then elderhood and Coronation," he said proudly.

"Very good," the chief councilman said, leaning down to get a better look at the little brownnoser, who beamed back at him. "You will do very well at the university. Perhaps you'll be in my spot one day."

The councilman stood and faced Acacius. "And the Coronation. What does that word mean?" he asked the children, tapping his gray goatee with his pointer finger.

Not even Damian knew the answer to that. The children glanced at each other and shrugged, feeling quite sure they hadn't heard the word "Coronation" in a vocabulary lesson yet.

"A Coronation is a special ceremony. It celebrates one's graduation from average citizen to ruling sovereign. Every faithful, law-abiding Petrodian is given one."

Chloe could hardly believe her ears. Her peers oohed and aahed at such a splendid thought. They knew well what "sovereign" meant. Not only was it used multiple times in the ancient myths regarding Zeus and his fellow gods and goddesses, but it also described the most powerful person in Petros, the sovereign minister of the invisible and unknowable Fantásmata.

"What happens during the Coronation, Your Eminence?" asked one of Chloe's classmates, a bony redheaded girl named Agnes.

"Well, I'm glad you asked," said the councilman, now within a foot of Acacius. He reached out and put his hand on the man's shoulder, but Acacius remained still. "Acacius' seventy-fifth birthday is today, which means it's also his Coronation day." The hall echoed with handclaps until they were shushed by another council member. "What happens is very, very sacred, and only a chosen few are privy to its exact details. They are the ones who make all the appropriate arrangements, just like your parents do when planning your birthday parties."

"Where will Mr. Acacius go after his Coronation?" Agnes asked.

"That's the best part," said the chief councilman, smiling at them like a magician about to start his grand finale. "Wherever...he...*wants* to go."

Once again, the children stirred with excitement—all of them except Chloe, whose focus was on Acacius and his shaking hands.

"Acacius!" called a voice from above their heads. Chloe looked up to see a council member standing in the balcony before a giant stained-glass window. "Have you chosen your final destination?"

Acacius shifted his weight from one foot to the other and drooped his head even lower. The chief councilman clutched the man's shoulder and whispered something inaudible into his ear.

"I have," the old man said as loudly as he could, then he coughed into his sleeve.

"Come with me. We will send you there promptly," said the council member with a smile. He stretched out his arms to Acacius, beckoning the worn-out Elder to join him upstairs.

The councilman patted Acacius on the back. Every eye watched as the head attendant hobbled down the center of the hall, with each shuffle of his heavy feet wrenching Chloe's heart.

"Will he be young again?" Chloe couldn't help herself. The question popped out of her mouth before her mind could give it permission.

"Say 'Your Eminence!'" whispered the boy sitting beside her.

"Your Eminence!" It sounded more like she was demanding rather than inquiring, but the councilman didn't seem to mind. He turned to her and sauntered back toward the platform.

"I almost forgot to mention..." he began as he took his seat. He took a drink from the glass of water that sat on the podium before him, then interlocked his fingers and raised them to his chin. The children knew this was what adults did when they had something especially significant to say, and they leaned in with curiosity.

"During one's Coronation," the councilman continued, "one reverts to the peak of one's youth, twenty-five years of age. Old enough and young enough to enjoy the best of their final destination with the throngs of fellow Petrodians that have gone before them."

Chloe turned back toward Acacius as he finally made it out of the room and joined the two attendants who were waiting for him. The ebony doors groaned shut, and Chloe wondered why she didn't feel comforted. If Acacius were about to enter eternal bliss, wouldn't he be happier about it? Was he too decrepit to show any degree of joy over his Coronation? Was he too cold-hearted not to want to see his parents again, who'd had their own Coronations years ago?

The children startled as the room suddenly went dark. Chloe's eyes jumped to the windows that had sealed themselves with steel shutters. The flames of the tripods below them were nothing but smoke. Then a haze of soft blue light shone down on them, and every head tilted up to the painting of the cosmos, now transformed into a cloudless sky.

"In just a few moments," said the councilman from somewhere in the shadows, "you will see what Acacius sees when his Coronation is complete. Everyone's final destination is self-determined. As you will see, the sky's the limit."

Chloe and her classmates lay back and watched the blue dome fade to white, accompanied by the sound of whinnying horses. Seconds later, there appeared a sea of rolling, emerald-green hills that stretched across the ceiling, each of them dotted with purple crocuses and yellow daffodils. It seemed so real to Chloe that she thought if she could only find a ladder, she could climb up into it.

Horses of every shade and size galloped into view, their manes flowing in the wind regally, and their hind legs kicking playfully in the air. And then a young man appeared; he remained facing away from his audience as if he knew he was being watched. He meandered through the small herd, taking his time to feel the soft grass beneath his bare feet, examine each horse, and enjoy the breeze blowing in his wavy black hair. After a few minutes, he stopped in front of a golden palomino that shimmered in the sun. He swung onto the animal's back, kicked its flanks, and with an ecstatic yell, took off into the distance.

"There goes our Acacius," said the councilman as he stood, leading his fellow councilmen in the Petrodian salute.

Each man held his right arm out straight, palm facing the floor. They recited in unison, "We salute you, Sovereign. We honor the works of your hands. May you forever savor the fragrance of this new life."

☾

Looking out her bedroom window as the sun peeked over a cloud, Chloe wondered if Acacius really was somewhere basking in the sunshine of his own paradise. But more than that, she wondered what had become of her own parents who'd not lived to make it to their scheduled Coronations.

Chloe looked down at the walnut, the question of eating it no longer a question. Even if the nut didn't provide answers or reunite her with her parents, she could think of nothing more worthwhile than finding out for sure.

CHAPTER TEN
INTIMATION

Chloe had kept herself busy with homework until the house went quiet, save for Travis's abominable snoring. She'd reasoned it was best to avoid getting caught carrying a knife upstairs. Around midnight, she sneaked downstairs and scoured the kitchen drawers for a sharp knife and a cutting board.

She returned to her room and sat staring at the knife and nut on her desk as her mind thought of one unsettling positive in her list of pros and cons. She jotted it down in her diary. *I accidentally cut myself with the knife, scream, then Damian runs in here, asks me why in the world I'm trying to eat walnuts in the middle of the night, and then eats them himself or throws them away. He probably wouldn't even bandage my hand first.*

But as she stared at a cluster of stars twinkling high in the heavens, her mind conjured up those green fields and whinnying horses. Then the image was shattered by a much less pleasant one, that of old Acacius' shaking hands and spiritless, downcast eyes.

She tucked up her knees, rolled herself onto the edge of the bed, and slid the knife and walnut toward her. She held the walnut between the fingers of her left hand, pressed the knife into the crack in the shell, then wriggled it and twisted. The two halves split apart, revealing a perfectly normal-looking walnut.

"It looks like a brain," Chloe mused as she got a closer look. Then, before she could mull it over a second more, she popped it into her mouth and watched the edges of her room shrink to total blackness.

☾

The darkness remained and Chloe felt as though she were suspended somewhere in outer space. *But there was no oxygen in space*, and her breathing was easy. In fact, the air felt pure and pleasant in her lungs and on her skin.

Before she could see anything, she heard women's voices speaking a foreign language, and fell forward as the earth rose to meet her feet. She caught herself before hitting the ground, just as light sliced gently through the darkness, causing the gloom to roll up into its shadows and flee. The first thing she saw were her bare feet, since she'd almost tripped over them. They were standing on a sandy floor, and yet there was a mud wall a few feet in front of her. She was inside a room.

She turned slowly toward where the voices were coming from, the ones speaking in what she assumed was Próta, the first and only other Petrodian language; a dead language.

She saw two women, one who appeared to be in her mid-forties and the other her own age. The older one sat at a small wooden table holding a bone-colored reed in her right hand, and the younger stood over her shoulder, speaking softly. The young girl had curly, strawberry-blond hair that fell to her waist and wore a long, cream-colored robe that was draped elegantly over one shoulder.

The older woman's hair was the color of rich, red wine and was pulled back into a bun, which was intertwined with several braids and crimson strips of fabric. She wore a robe similar to that of her companion, only hers looked heavier, its excessive fabric gathered and joined together by copper brooches.

Where in the world was she? Chloe decided to find out.

"Hello, there. My name is Chloe Zacharias," she said as she took a step toward them.

The two women continued talking. The older woman stood and kissed the younger on her cheek and temple as she placed a rolled-up scroll in her hand.

"*Na prosécheis*, Charis," the older woman said.

Chloe approached the women, but still they gave no response. She tried to pick up the jar of ink that rested beside a stack of papyrus sheets, but it might as well have weighed three tons. She tried to shake the table to get their attention, but it felt bolted to the floor.

"*Naí*, Mama," Charis said, and kissed the older woman back. And then she vanished.

"What was that?" exclaimed Chloe as she took Charis's place beside the other woman.

The woman was facing her, but seemed to stare right through her, completely unaware of Chloe's presence. She turned toward an unlit hearth and raised a hand toward it. A small ball of fire, no larger than Chloe's palm, shot toward it, kindling it with a flurry of flames upon impact.

Was it the woman from the ship? The thought was like a hammer slamming down on Chloe's brain. Her heart began to pound. Where was she? Who were these people? How was she going to get home?

She pinched herself until the sides of her wrists were covered with rows of tiny crescents. She even called for Carya to get her out of there. She ran to the door, but as she pushed it open, the mud-brick walls melted around her, and the world went dark again.

Chloe was sure she was in Hades. Two thick walls of roaring fire enclosed her. Billowing smoke blocked out most of the cloud cover above. A circle of daylight was visible at the end of the tunnel, but Chloe sensed she'd be a heap of ashes before she got near it. And she doubted anyone nearby was a doctor, much less one with the knowledge and means to save her life.

Looking over her shoulder to search for any other hope of escape, she saw Charis and her mother. Their long robes were tucked into thick leather girdles as they ran breathlessly alongside a man and a grotesque-looking animal, which had the head and torso of a man, and the feet and hindquarters of a horse.

Chloe cringed at the sight of the mother's ashen face, strained and covered with sweat. Her eyes were squeezed shut, arms outstretched to either side, and palms erect as fire flowed out of them like gushing rapids.

"Why are you doing this?" Chloe shouted at her. But, again, no one knew she was there.

The man shouted something at the woman, followed by the name "Iris." They started to run faster, and Chloe had no choice but to join them. After just a few seconds, Chloe's sprint had decelerated to a lumbering jog.

It was time to find out if there was an afterlife or not. She felt more distressed at the thought of dying than she'd expected as her survival instincts began kicking in. She wasn't sure whether she'd die of asphyxiation or cardiac arrest, or if she'd just catch on fire. She picked up her pace and watched as Charis disappeared again.

"Take us with you!" Chloe yelled, her weak lungs retaliating with sharp stabs in her ribs. She'd never run so hard or so far in her entire life.

Not five seconds later, Charis reappeared a few yards in front of the others and stood still with her arms lifted, reminding Chloe of one of the marble goddesses she'd seen in her mythology books.

Iris closed her hands and doubled over to catch her breath and rest her arms. The walls of fire weakened until only dark gray whorls of smoke were left. Everyone, including Chloe, lay on the ground for a good while, gasping for air as drops of rain fell onto their parched tongues.

☾

Orpheus and Hermes stood over Chloe's bed, watching her closed eyes flutter rapidly as she tossed and turned fitfully. Then, with a final jerk, she stopped. Her eyes softened and her breathing slowed, and Orpheus noticed goosebumps rising on her arms and neck.

"The ichor in our veins makes the air get colder when we're around them," said Hermes.

"She's about to wake up," Orpheus said. "You're certain we're invisible?"

Chloe shivered and opened her eyes as she yanked the comforter onto her shoulders. Orpheus ducked beside the bed and watched as Hermes skipped around the room and clicked his heels together like a frolicking satyr.

"The only evidence of our proximity is the temperature change," Hermes said, "which they mostly attribute to fever, normal climatic shifts, or air-conditioning, which I don't have time to explain to you just now." He leapt onto Chloe's desk. "Their other senses cannot perceive us," he shouted as he stomped his feet.

"Shhhhh!" Orpheus scolded. But Chloe wasn't reacting to any of it; the little devil was right. "So this is the woman I'm to keep an eye on?" he asked.

"It's not so easy as that," hissed Hermes as he jumped down into a squatting position beside Orpheus. His copper eyes narrowed as he came within inches of the poet's face. "You have to do what your father trained you to do." He reached for the lyre in Orpheus's arms and plucked it with a long, curved fingernail. "Your mission, my charming nephew, is to charm her."

Orpheus laughed as he stood and walked toward the window. "I cannot believe it. I cannot believe I fell for one of your idiotic jokes," he said, shaking his head and turning toward the bed.

Hermes was crouched on the pillow beside Chloe. They watched as she sat up, rubbed her arms for warmth, and then hurried out the door.

"You won a friendly bet with my father, is that it?" Orpheus said. "And now he's permitted you to drag me on some ludicrous charade for your own twisted pleasure." His smile faded to a scowl. "Well, you've had your fun. Now take me back to the Vale."

Hermes shook his head and joined Orpheus at the window. "You, and all who dwell below, are ignorant of what has taken place in Petros," he said in a low, earnest voice. He untied a small satchel from his belt and pulled it open. "This will answer all your questions about this modern age," he said, flicking its side with his finger.

Orpheus smirked. "And what bedazzling sorcery is this?" He leaned in to catch a glimpse of the bag's contents.

Hermes turned the satchel upside down and out fell a smooth, round graphite stone, and green confetti of crushed leaves. "The laurel leaves will give you knowledge," he said. "That stone is the sacred Baetylus kept in the innermost sanctum of Hades' palace. It's what will imbue you with life and a youthful form. Every mortal will interact with you as if you were one of them; you *will* be one of them, as well as one of us, able to reenter Hades and communicate with me. But the most important facts are these. Are you listening?"

Orpheus nodded.

"First, you must have the satchel with you at all times." Hermes collected the items and returned them to the pouch. "You are not powerful on your own. But surely you know that better than anyone, considering all you've suffered."

Orpheus bit his tongue. He knew better than to exchange insults with Hermes; it would only encourage him.

"Second, every evening at dusk, you must go to Lake Thyra," Hermes said. "Again, the lotus leaves will educate you and orient you with your surroundings. Thetis, the sea goddess, will meet you there and bring you back into Hades until morning. Any questions?"

"Am I dull, uncle, or did you neglect to tell me what my actual task is besides wooing this homely maiden," Orpheus said gruffly as his lyre fell to the floor. He pounded the windowsill and pushed himself away from it just as the sun, the true sun that he had not seen in thousands of years, splashed the eastern sky with rosy foam. He was too upset, too confounded to gaze upon a beauty that might soften him. How could he possibly win back Eurydice if he had not the foggiest idea what Apollo wanted from him?

"All you must do is lead her to Psychro Cave and lure her into the pool therein. What waits on the other side shall take care of itself."

Hermes gave a mischievous wink, and Orpheus didn't even bother asking what his guileful mind was plotting. As long as it won him Eurydice, he didn't care.

"Now I must be going, nephew," said Hermes, patting his dog-skin cap and pulling it lower over his brow. "Be a good lad and fasten the satchel securely to your girdle. Your clothing will change shortly. Then you must hide the satchel inside what the Petrodians call a 'jacket.'"

Orpheus's ichor veins felt as though they were freezing over inside him. His anger was rising, causing his temperature to drop and his teeth to chatter. He'd never felt such a sensation in either life or death.

"Don't worry, Orpheus. Your blood will run hot soon enough. I'll see you back in hell."

Orpheus opened his mouth to object, but it was too late. Hermes was gone, leaving Orpheus with nothing but a pouch of flowers and a silly mortal to bewitch. He picked up his lyre, turned toward the sunrise, and couldn't help but strum a few notes. As he imagined Eurydice smiling at him in the blushing sky, he stopped playing and held the satchel to his chest.

"Bring me Eurydice," he prayed.

CHAPTER ELEVEN

METAMORPHOSIS

Orpheus didn't know how or when he had ended up on a bench within the courtyard of Eirene High School. Moreover, he wasn't sure how he even knew the place was called Eirene High School, or why he wasn't appalled by the boisterous teenagers rushing around him dressed in tight-fitting pants and vulgar shoes.

He stretched out his legs and looked down to see that he, too, wore dark denim pants, and that his sandals had been replaced by leather shoes the color of metal. Somehow he knew they were called "loafers." *Rather comfortable*, he thought, curling his toes inside them.

He glanced down at his arms and shoulders, covered by a fitted black "bomber jacket" made of wool. *Jacket...*

Remembering the satchel, Orpheus explored the outside of his new garment for pockets, but the few he found were no deeper than the length of his pinky finger. Then he found, on the inner right side, a small zippered compartment. He gave a sigh of relief when he saw the pouch safe inside it, still filled with the laurel leaves and the stone that was giving him life. He pressed two fingers to his wrist and relished the feeling of his pounding pulse.

As he sat there, enjoying the breeze and the chirping birds, he noticed that every student had attached to his or her back a load called a "backpack." He felt the tops of his shoulders, grabbed the straps that lay across them and slid them down. He carefully lifted the large gray backpack onto his knees, feeling the familiar weight of his lyre inside it. He zipped it open and smiled.

"Hello, old friend," he murmured.

☾

Chloe had been looking forward to lunch all day. Her stomach in knots after her nightmare—or time travel, or whatever it was—she'd skipped breakfast and laid on the couch with a cold, damp dishtowel folded over her forehead until Damian called her to the car. The last thing she'd wanted to do was go to school, but skipping without a doctor's note would land her in detention for a month. So she'd dragged herself to the car, all the while feeling the phantom presence of Iris's fire hovering close to her skin.

All day long, her mind had flashed with images of the mud-brick house and the blazing tunnel that had nearly engulfed her. She could vividly recall Charis's freckled face before the girl had disappeared with the scroll, and Iris's concentration as the woman had held up the flaming walls with her porcelain hands.

Chloe wondered why Iris was creating that fire in the first place; surely not to murder her own family. But as the hours ticked by and Chloe continued to think about it, her question became: what provoked Iris to create it?

Chloe had been a stress-eater for years. It was the first "condition" Aunt Maggie had reported to Chloe's doctor weeks after her parents' death, and ever since it had been tightly monitored.

The one time Chloe had tried out for the track team, she had been likened to a turtle, a sloth, and a pregnant mule for the slow and graceless way she ran. That was when she began to nibble insatiably on apples, crackers, peanuts, anything she could get her hands on. The headmaster told Maggie and Travis to lock up the pantry and refrigerator at night, giving Chloe the strict warning that "gluttony and lack of discipline shall not be tolerated."

A few years later, when she was nervous about the needle that was necessary to inject her contraception, she spent two weeks' worth of allowance on the school vending machine. That time, she received in-school suspension and had to attend counseling for a week.

For the past four years her stress-eating "condition" had been managed. Chloe had mainly accomplished this by avoiding all athletic endeavors and declining to dance at any festival; she could only imagine the less-than-flattering comparisons that would be made were she to sway and twirl and fall on her face. If she wasn't chosen to be a mother, and therefore had to receive another injection in two years, she was sure she'd have a relapse. She would just have to cope with the consequences.

Today, seeing as she'd scarfed down her chicken, potatoes, and bowl of raisins with the voraciousness of a lion, she feared she was going to crack. What were those breathing exercises the counselor had taught her?

Chloe took in a long, slow breath through her nose. She placed a hand on her belly and felt it rise, then held her breath and counted to three. Then she pursed her lips, relaxed her jaw, and released a smooth exhale. She repeated the process a second time, but on the third, she rushed the breath out as she noticed Ethan sit down at the table cattycorner to hers.

When she hadn't been preoccupied with replaying her visions over and over, she'd toyed with the idea of discussing all of it with him. What if he'd been given a walnut, too? What if he'd seen Carya in the museum, or knew if a half-man, half-horse creature had ever existed? At least then she could rule out schizophrenia for sure. But every time she resolved to scout him out and pick his brain, she remembered the law of *paráxeno theáseis*.

She had no doubt that having dreams of a mother-daughter duo with superhuman powers, and a man with a horse's body, would be deemed strange sightings. She'd be carted off to who knows where, no questions asked. Ethan would have no choice but to turn her in, even if he did know something. Perhaps he was keeping mum for similar reasons.

Ethan smiled at Chloe, and she realized she'd been staring at him as she reviewed the pro/con list in her head. There were definitely too many cons associated with talking to him, and so plan A was foiled. Her only plan B was to find Damian and see if he'd give her any leftovers. But before she could get up, she saw Ethan coming toward her, bringing his backpack and food tray with him. Chloe quickly spread her napkin over her tray to conceal the fact that she'd cleaned her plate before most of her peers had even sat down.

"Mind if I have a seat?" Ethan asked. Chloe nodded and took a sip of water. "Don't you normally sit over there with your friends?" he said, pointing to the far side of the cafeteria.

Chloe looked over. A group of girls were huddled close to their laptops; she assumed they were studying for a test that was two weeks away. All antisocial over-achievers like her, which made them friends.

"Yes," Chloe said. The rest of that answer was she didn't feel like conversing with anyone, no matter how antisocial they were. She couldn't risk disclosing anything sensitive. "Just needed some alone time." It wasn't really a lie...

Ethan set down his backpack and food, and took a seat across from her. "I understand that. I get plenty of alone time at the museum," he said. "A little too much, probably. By the time I get to school on Mondays, I'm actually looking forward to some human interaction." He put his napkin on his lap and started cutting into his chicken.

Chloe searched her purse for a mint to keep her taste buds busy. He'd come to the wrong human to interact with.

"I'm sorry we had to kick you out yesterday," he said. "My mom said the museum is closed today and tomorrow, too."

He had to pique her curiosity. "Really? Do you know why?"

"I only know that the Religious Council is meeting there with the Fantásmata. Why at the museum, of all places, is beyond me."

Chloe felt a spark of hope. Her hands might not be tied after all. Maybe if she was clever enough, and discreet enough, Ethan could provide her with a lead or two simply by answering a few questions. If she was lucky, she might get a hint as to whether or not he had secrets of his own. It was worth a try.

"Hey, can I ask you something?" she said.

"Sure."

"You might've been joking yesterday when you said it, but you referred to the Fantásmata as 'crazies.' What did you mean?"

Ethan sat back in his chair and pulled back his shoulders as he swallowed a piece of potato. "I shouldn't have said that," he said, looking at the end of the table. Then he took a swig of water and began biting a cuticle on his thumb.

Chloe pushed her tray aside and leaned forward as she whispered, "I'm not going to tell anyone anything you tell me, Ethan. I promise."

He relaxed a bit, but still avoided her eyes. She would have to open up, at least somewhat.

"I've been thinking a lot about the field trip we all took when we were kids. You know, to the Religious Council building." Ethan nodded. "Did your class see a Coronation take place, too?" He nodded again. She noticed he'd stopped eating. "Ours was for a man named Acacius. It's sort of been haunting me lately. The man didn't want to be coronated, or whatever the word is. He was scared. Why would he have been scared?"

Ethan shook his head and pressed his lips together. "Old people can act strange sometimes. Maybe he didn't even know what was happening. His meds might've been off. Who knows?"

Chloe wasn't buying it. She knew Ethan had more to say. He'd called the Fantásmata crazies for a reason. He'd said they didn't care if their decisions made sense. He knew how they'd treated his mother by kicking her off her site just as she was making headway. Why wasn't he talking? What was he afraid of?

"Chloe, maybe inviting you to the museum wasn't such a good idea." He was looking at her now, his leaf-green eyes filled with a mixture of pity and concern.

"Why are you looking at me like that? What you said in the museum...I thought you...I thought..." Her mind and heart felt like they were racing each other as her thoughts and emotions collided and swelled like a tidal wave.

"I don't mean to upset you." He placed his silverware on top of his half-eaten chicken. "I'd better go."

As she watched him walk away, everything in Chloe's body rushed to a halt. Every breath and cell and thought and heartbeat shook in its place as a fierce wave of loneliness swept through her.

She had no true friends, no family who truly cared for her; even her own brother was too embarrassed by her to admit he loved her. No bright future to look forward to. All she had was an experience that either proved she was clinically crazy or a criminal in the eyes of the Fantásmata. And neither prospect was favorable.

☾

After lunch, Chloe went to the school office and requested the use of her cellphone. She explained to the secretary that she needed to inform her brother, who was in wrestling practice, that she didn't need him to drive her home from school. When the secretary asked why, Chloe coolly replied that she needed the exercise and wanted to walk on such a lovely day. Satisfied, the secretary then handed Chloe a form and had her record her reasoning and sign her name.

This piece of protocol fell under Petros's law of vigilance, by which the whereabouts of all citizens were known at all times. Ostensibly this was for everyone's safety, but for the first time Chloe felt more threatened by the law than protected by it. Maybe it wasn't wise to deviate from her daily routine. She'd already been behaving strangely as it was. But changing her mind and erasing her name would only have drawn attention.

Chloe's walk home, which she'd intended to be her chance to center herself with deep breaths and mindfulness meditation, was only making her more distraught. It was even adding paranoia to the mix as she wondered whether Ethan had reported her questions to the headmaster. She could be arrested any second.

For whatever reason, Chloe kept on trudging. She followed a footpath formed by the cross-country runners until it reached the turnaround point at the bridge over the Maqor River. Her thighs were aching and her breathing was labored, but surprisingly, she was enjoying herself. It felt good to exert more than her mind for once.

She stopped in the middle of the bridge to take in the lazy turquoise river as it snaked its way down the mountain. It looked so inviting, so peaceful with the juniper trees and evergreen shrubs nestled around it. It was a shame it was against the law to swim in the river. She would have given anything to let it carry her away. She wouldn't have cared where it took her.

"Beautiful, isn't it?"

Chloe jumped at the voice coming from the far side of the bridge, closest to the mountain. She turned to see a young man her age she didn't recognize. He was tall, with dark, tousled hair that fell in loose waves around his face, touching the tops of his cheekbones.

Chloe nodded and stared back into the river, hoping he'd pass her and be on his way.

"I read that the river's named after an ancient spring," he said, walking toward her. "Two aqueducts fed its water into Eirene, to the temple that used to be there."

Chloe had never heard of any temple in Eirene. "I'm sorry. Do I know you?" Chloe asked, not caring whether she masked her irritation or not.

"No. My apologies," the man said as he joined her at the bridge's wooden railing. Chloe pretended not to notice. "I'm Orpheus," he said. He extended his hand, and after a moment's apprehension, Chloe took it and gave him her name. "It's a pleasure to meet you," Orpheus said.

Finally looking at his face, Chloe didn't know whether it was the water below or the sky above that made his blue eyes shine like sapphires. She wanted to stare and count the different shades of gold and green she saw scattered within them. His olive skin was even smoother than Damian's, except for the short stubble that lined his full lips and angular jaw. His nose, which was a tad long and slightly crooked, was the only flaw she could see. He was nice to look at, which made Chloe suddenly aware of how un-nice she probably looked, covered in sweat and splotchy makeup. She bent down and set her purse and backpack on the bridge so his eyes would move elsewhere.

"What are you doing out here?" she asked. Immediately, she regretted the question because she would inevitably be asked to answer it as well.

"Same reason as you, I presume," he said, and left it at that.

Chloe released her left hand's grip on the railing and realized she'd been clenching it; it hurt to open her fingers. *You're okay*, Chloe, she told herself. *He's not your enemy*.

"Are you a senior?" she asked as a gray heron swooped by and landed on the bank below. "I've never seen you before."

"I'm a junior, actually. My father was transferred here at the beginning of the semester." Orpheus smiled and pointed at the heron. They watched together as the bird spread its wings and plunged its broad bill into the water. "It was once thought that herons were messengers of the gods," he said.

Chloe marveled at the way he spoke, at how he enunciated every syllable perfectly and spoke so clearly. She had never heard a voice like his, so rich and deep, like thunder rolling quietly before a storm.

"You said there was a temple in Eirene," Chloe said.

He nodded. "Where a people called Eusebians worshipped, long before the city was burned to the ground, and all its people plundered and shipped away as slaves."

Chloe had heard Ethan mention Eusebians back at the museum. And another group called Alphas. How could Orpheus have known any of this?

"Do you work at the museum?" asked Chloe, eyeing him suspiciously.

"No. My father is a keeper, one of only a few who know the whole history of Petros." Orpheus turned back to her and lowered his head as if he were about to share a secret. "He's told me a few things about the past. Things that the Fantásmata prefer to hide from the population."

Chloe raised an eyebrow. "And you're allowed to tell just anyone about them?"

"You're not just anyone, are you? It isn't just anyone who hikes up here to get away from the world. Just anyone doesn't visit the Eirene Museum on the weekend."

"Wait. How did you know that?" Chloe asked as sweat dripped along her spine.

Orpheus looked down at Chloe's purse.

She picked it up, spun it around, and sure enough, saw the museum emblem still stuck to its side. "Oh." She lowered her purse as her cheeks flushed with embarrassment. "A friend gave me a pass for my birthday. It was sort of a disappointment. Except for the gryphon fossils. Those were unbelievable."

Orpheus laughed and then rolled his neck, popping it. "The Fantásmata won't allow anything too interesting. They don't want any 'rumors'," he said, forming quotation marks with his fingers. "They think rumors precipitate insurrection."

Chloe took a moment to think on his statement. "Why build a museum in the first place if they don't want people talking about it? The curator seemed to think only the elite ever visit it. But if that's the case, I wonder why there are only a few fossils and an old scroll. I doubt anyone will go if that's all there is."

Her mind traveled back to the brown-and-yellow pages inside the glass case. She remembered Ethan saying he hoped Iris had "sicked her doma" on her master, Acheron. Did Iris's doma have anything to do with the fire Chloe saw coming out of her hands?

"There's more than that. Much more," Orpheus said, as the afternoon sun sank into the trees behind them and a warm wind rustled the leaves. "At the museum, did you see anything regarding a woman named Iris?"

Chloe nodded. "She was mentioned in the scroll fragments. It was written in Próta, though. I couldn't read anything." *Play dumb. Act normal.*

"She's the reason the Fantásmata destroyed the temple." Orpheus leaned away from the railing and stood up tall. "They were afraid of her then, and they're afraid of her now."

"How do you know that?"

Orpheus paused as he looked at her skeptically, as if judging her trustworthiness by how well she held his gaze. "Are you sure you want to know?"

Chloe wasn't sure, but she nodded anyway, silently cursing herself for letting curiosity quash all common sense. For all she knew, this Orpheus guy could be an agent of the Fantásmata sent to ascertain whether she was guilty of experiencing *paráxeno theáseis* or not. But despite her better judgment, she couldn't stop herself. If Ethan wouldn't open up to her, she'd have to take her chances with someone who would.

CHAPTER TWELVE
STRATEGEM

At the beginning of his first day as a mortal reborn, Orpheus thought his father would have been better off finding a dead actor to woo this woman. Some venerated *hypokrites* from the stage. He'd always admired the way thespians could effortlessly stifle their own personalities and embody someone else's, like an oracle channeling a spirit. The way they could manipulate their emotions and cry artificial tears. Poets' tears were always genuine. As were their smiles and sobs, their fury and their fears. He hadn't expected it to be this easy.

The girl named Chloe seemed desperate for someone to talk to. It didn't seem to matter who he was or where he'd come from. She appeared to be attracted to him, or to his words at least, like a moth to a flame, and he hadn't even played a single note.

Throughout their hike, he found himself daydreaming about the first words he planned to whisper to Eurydice. Maybe he would be with her tonight. All he needed to do was get to the portal. Just a little farther.

"I'm sorry, what did you say?" he asked Chloe. His thoughts were in Elysium, where he was reclining beneath a poplar tree, tenderly kissing his wife as he strummed the first love song he'd written for her.

"I asked you how much longer until we get to the cave." Chloe dropped her bags to the ground and took a drink from her water bottle. "I have to be home in two hours or they'll send a search party. Won't they come searching for you?"

Orpheus shook his head. "It's another benefit of being a keeper's son. I'm free to roam wherever and whenever I choose." He was half tempted to stretch those words into a poem.

"I've never heard of such a privilege." Chloe shrugged. "But I guess there's a lot I've never heard of."

"Indeed," said Orpheus.

"Indeed," Chloe mimicked.

"Have I misspoken?"

"No, I wouldn't say that. You just speak very...*properly*."

He smiled. "I speak Próta properly, too."

Her head canted right and her eyes squinted at him with suspicion. "You're kidding. It's a dead language."

"Dead to *most*," he corrected.

"Show me." She folded her arms across her chest as she leaned against an oak tree that looked to be as old as he was.

Orpheus grinned. He was amused by her sass. "How about I teach you."

"And how are you going to do that in hour?" asked Chloe, putting her hands on her hips.

"They say the best way to learn a new trade or craft is through immersion. That is, becoming an apprentice so as to learn and observe. Am I correct?"

Chloe nodded as Orpheus fiddled with the collar of his jacket. He reasoned this was something an actor would do to project nervousness. "I'm not being completely honest with you, Chloe," he said, raking a hand through his hair.

Chloe pushed herself off the tree and stood completely still, like a hare that had been spotted in a meadow. She was afraid.

Orpheus cleared his throat and continued. "Part of why I know so much about Eirene and Iris and all the rest I've told you is because I've...well, I've *seen* much of it, with my own eyes. It's how I learned Próta."

"*Paráxeno theáseis,*" said Chloe under her breath. Her eyes widened. "You do know it's dangerous to tell me this, right? I mean you could be arrested if they found out."

Orpheus took a step toward her, and with his blue eyes pleading, said, "Please...you mustn't tell a soul." Then he spun away from her and shook his head toward the ground. "I shouldn't have told you." He pressed his palms into his temples and gazed up at the pale sky through the branches, another melodramatic pose he'd learned from watching plays.

"It's alright, Orpheus," she said, walking after him. She tapped his shoulder and he faced her once again. "I won't tell anyone." Then she paused, cuing him to look her in the eye. "I swear."

Orpheus's face softened. He found himself unable to separate his real self from his acting self as he noted the kindness in her eyes; were he to write a poem about her eyes, he would compare them to starlings' eggs. Her uninspiring brown hair, on the other hand, he would have likened to a starling's nest.

Watching Chloe progress back up the mountain, Orpheus had to remind himself that there was something poets valued far more than outward beauty, and that was truth. Orpheus knew Chloe was pursuing it, and if he had been anyone else he would have been tempted to help her.

The one piece of knowledge Hermes and Apollo had withheld from him was *why* she was to become a prisoner.

He knew she was special, but how could she be an enemy of Apollo? To her, Apollo was nothing but a myth.

"Thank you," he said. Then he commanded his mind stop to thinking and to instead envision Eurydice, her golden hair bouncing and her emerald eyes gleaming as she saw him racing toward her with open arms. He couldn't let himself feel or say or show anything but lies as long as he was in Chloe's presence.

They walked in silence to the shoulder of the mountain before it curved toward the summit. They admired the view behind them, the towers of sandstone and rocky spires interspersed throughout the woodland, and the cliffs of the Apokálypsi mountain range cloaked with shadows.

Orpheus noticed a mound of scree and four large boulders less than fifteen feet away. Like a migratory bird that instinctively knows its destination when it sees it, Orpheus knew that this collection of stones was his. It was the entrance to Psychro Cave, the place where he would play his lyre and lure his unwitting hostage to her holding cell. Then his job would be done, and he could forget tricks and spells and guile, and finally step into his fate as Chloe stepped into hers.

"I'm going to show you something I've never shown anyone," he said. *This is fate's decision, not mine.* He repeated the phrase in his head, forcing himself to believe it.

As Orpheus walked closer to the cave, he felt the air around him grow colder, and he was sure the temperature must have dropped twenty degrees. "I know you're here, Hermes," he muttered as he zipped his jacket up to his chin.

☾

Hermes sped over the rivers and fields of the Underworld like a meteor streaking across the sky. His brothers had been expecting a report for nearly a day. It hadn't been his fault that the poet's methods for charming the girl were less than expeditious. It *would* be his fault if he failed to convince them that the methods were proving effective.

He landed in front of the palace gate as the Chimera roared from the wall above. Hermes waved at the beast as the six brutes that stood guard stomped their spears in greeting and lifted the latch off the double doors.

Hermes strode into the throne room, and then, with the bravado of a clown, tossed his cap high into the air, and performed two flips and a somersault before jumping to catch it. He grinned at Apollo, who sat on the steps of the dais twirling the tip of his sword on the obsidian floor. His black cowl was pulled over his head, preventing Hermes from detecting whether Apollo's mood was fair or foul. *Why do I have to be the one ever at their mercy*, he thought.

"Do not dare try and distract me with acrobatics, you fool!" Hades' voice thundered from his throne. "If you were not our brother, I would have no greater pleasure than binding you to a spit and watching you roast over the Phlegethon River. But keep up your nonsense long enough and not even kinship will stay my temper."

"Yes, sire." Hermes secured the cap to his head and marched forward, all the while thinking how an hour in the sun above would do them some good. There was one thing he had over his brothers, and that was the coveted ability to leave this abyss any time he chose.

"You will deliver your message and then get out of our sight." Hades stood up, the sheen of his gilded panoply and the points of his charcoal horns now visible in the torchlight. It didn't matter how many times Hermes met with Hades, he always felt his innards coil and writhe at the sight of him.

Long before, the throne of Hades had seldom been occupied. Aside from Hermes, the Lord of Death had traveled more than any of the other rebel gods, for at any given moment he had been busy ripping souls from their dead bodies and dragging them down to the River Styx. But as the Petrodians became proficient at delaying death until they deemed its presence necessary—or advantageous—his errands became fewer and fewer, but Hades was not at all perturbed by this. He spent his days seated on his basalt throne, waiting to receive word of what the Petrodians called a Coronation, but what he and his consorts below knew only as glorious sacrifice.

"The metamorphosis is complete, My Lords," said Hermes as he bowed low and remained close to the floor.

"And the poet is cooperating?" asked Hades. "And stand up so I can see by your eyes whether or not you're lying." His voice vibrated in Hermes' chest and then echoed sharply off the concave walls, a harsh metallic cauldron that could sear the skin of a mortal man in seconds.

Hermes obeyed and rolled back his shoulders as the final echo faded. "Yes, sire. He'll soon have the Vessel convinced that he is an Asher, like herself. She trusts him completely." Apollo stopped spinning his sword. It seemed he finally liked what he was hearing. "They're entering Psychro Cave as we speak. He will leave her in Circe's company, and she will be taken care of. I have already given the witch her orders."

Hades threw back his head and laughed, his white fangs betraying the evil beneath his mirth. "Clever, indeed. The All-Powerful only said that we could not 'harm' her. Circe is nothing if not a gracious hostess." He erupted in laughter again and sat back into his throne. "Well done, brother. You may go. Return only when the Vessel is secure in Circe's care."

Hermes nodded and walked away from the bellowing merriment, pleased with himself for the scheme he had weaved. *All-Powerful*, he silently mocked.

"Hermes, stop."

Hermes was just outside the gates when he turned to see Apollo standing behind him. Apollo removed his cowl and placed a firm hand on Hermes' shoulder. Hermes tried never to stare at his brother's beauty, at his diamond-blue eyes and the crystalline flecks of light that skipped across his alabaster skin.

"You must forgive our brother's temper," Apollo said. "He can be quite insufferable, especially when there's much at stake."

"I know," said Hermes, and made to leave again.

But Apollo clenched his shoulder hard until Hermes buckled beneath his hand, fighting the urge to yelp. "I don't know if you know," he said, his diamond eyes darkening. "The All-Powerful knows what is happening. We would be fools to think he is sitting idly on his throne with folded hands."

"Apo—" Hermes began.

"Not a word, Hermes. You think you're clever, but if you don't keep your eyes open I will bind you over the fires of the Phlegethon myself. The All-Powerful has not commanded that you remain unharmed." He shoved Hermes to the ground and stalked back inside the palace.

CHAPTER THIRTEEN
PSYCHRO

The coolness of the cave was a welcome relief for Chloe, who, for the last hour and a half, had been perspiring profusely, either because the exercise was making her overheat or because her nerves were on edge since Orpheus had made his admission. Probably both, she decided. She'd been in an inquisitive and fairly amiable mood before he'd alluded to the fact that he had seen and maybe even spoken to Iris. Now she was about as talkative as the stone staircase she was walking down, though her mind was as curious as ever.

Should she tell him that she'd also experienced so-called strange sightings? Though she couldn't possibly fathom why, Orpheus had confided in her. He'd told her a secret that would likely reap grave consequences if the Fantásmata ever found out. Half her brain—or maybe it was her heart—told her it would be wrong not to tell him, while the other half, her common-sense half, hypothesized a worst-case scenario. *What if he told someone else as easily as he had told her? What if keeping it to himself had become a burden, and now he was trying to relieve himself of it by recklessly rattling on about it to random strangers? Whoever he had told would report him eventually, and when he was caught, what was to stop him from ratting on her?*

As if he could sense the discourse going on between her ears, Orpheus stopped walking and turned to her. "Are you all right?"

"Uh-huh," said Chloe with a smile. She pulled her cellphone out of her pocket and checked the time. "I've got an hour and twenty-one minutes."

"Good,' said Orpheus. "We're almost there." He took a flashlight out of his backpack and handed it to her.

Chloe tucked her bangs behind her ear as she stopped to shine the light around. She'd been inside of caves before, but never one this massive. The staircase kept winding down, down, down...until she wondered if there was a bottom.

Giant spear-like stalactites pointed down from the ceiling, while beige-and-brown flowstones overhung the walls in wide, spongy sheets. The ground was a forest of mud-colored stalagmites that smelled of peat and sand. She remembered being scolded by her parents for sneakily trying to touch one, despite the tour guide's strict orders to "keep your hands to yourselves." Even now, she fought the urge to reach for the intricate frostwork, a virtual coral reef in the heart of the mountain. Some of the stalagmites were tall and thin, reminding Chloe of skeletal fingers, while others were more conical and rotund, like coniferous trees turned to limestone.

"Beautiful, isn't it?" asked Orpheus over his shoulder.

"In a creepy sort of way, yes." But compared to the things she'd seen in her visions, Chloe thought this really wasn't so bad. "Are we going all the way down?"

Orpheus stopped abruptly beside a sump that was half the size of her swimming pool. She set down her bags, then kneeled and peered into it, a static pane of opaque glass reflecting the twisted clusters of helictites that clung to the walls like frozen worms. She grabbed a smooth white cave pearl and dropped it onto the surface, then watched the waves roll gently across the flowing mirror.

To Chloe, there was something majestic about this place. The way the formations, so alien and primeval, seemed almost alive, as if they were listening, observing, whispering to one another with every echo, drip, and ripple.

She jumped when Orpheus's contorted face entered the liquid mirror's frame. "This is it," he said. "This is where I come to learn."

Chloe stood up and backed away from the pool, suddenly fearful of its placid appearance. "They come out of here? Iris and whoever else?"

Orpheus laughed and shook his head. "No, no, silly girl. I go *in*."

"You what?" Chloe tried to appear dumbfounded, but she'd seen too much to label him a lunatic. If she could consume a walnut and be transported back in time thousands of years, why couldn't he dive into a sump and experience equally illogical things?

"I know it sounds crazy, Chloe," said Orpheus, his blue eyes now gray above the water. "But I can show you, if you'll just trust me."

Chloe sighed as she looked up at the fang-like stalactite over her head. She could think of no reason why she shouldn't go with him. He'd obviously lived through whatever was down there. And he definitely wouldn't be telling anyone that she'd gone with him, unless he had a death wish. She had only one concern. "How do you breathe?"

Orpheus laughed at the question, seemingly relieved that she hadn't written him off. "Just like normal. The water is simply the gateway to where we're going. I can't explain it, exactly..."

Oh, how Chloe understood. But how could she have explained to him that just last night she'd seen a girl disappear before her eyes and nearly die inside walls of fire, all because she'd eaten a walnut given to her by a girl who communicated only in rhymes?

"How do you know who we're going to see?" she asked.

"I don't. I've been going almost every day since I found this place a month ago, and the people and places have been different each time."

Chloe blinked at him, hoping he would add something about how friendly the people were, or how the flora and fauna were unbelievably docile and benevolent, but he only proceeded to slip off his loafers.

"So you just do a cannonball and down you go?"

"A cannonball?" His face scrunched with confusion, like she'd spoken a different language.

Chloe shook her head. Where was he from that he didn't know what a cannonball was? "Never mind. Are you going to keep your jacket on and take your backpack?"

"You never can predict the weather," he said, dusting off his sleeves. "And my backpack is precautionary as well. Any more questions?" He flashed a smile that told her he was just as anxious as she was, but just as excited, too.

Chloe took a deep breath and shined the flashlight on the surrounding city of stone statues one more time. Then she set the flashlight down, plugged her nose, and did a cannonball into the center of the sump.

☾

Chloe never felt the weightlessness of being underwater, or the rush of tiny bubbles cascading around her. One second she was in midair, her knees tucked to her chest, and the next she was standing on sand, in a place as primitive and unfamiliar as the cave she'd just trekked through. She could smell the unmistakable scent of salt and seaweed, and sure enough, the Great Sea stretched out behind them. *Please, no monsters this time.*

The afternoon sun felt like a laser boring its beam into the top of her head. She shielded her face with her hand and looked up at Orpheus as he made his way toward a small grove of trees, which, thankfully, were thick with leaves. She followed closely behind, wishing she'd brought her water bottle or, even better, a swimsuit.

When she got into the shade, she turned and stared out at the aquamarine waters. Sunlight glinted off the tops of the languorous waves, and a few gulls circled overhead. There were no clouds in the sky, and no ships or fishing boats on the horizon. She couldn't tell whether she and Orpheus had traveled across the centuries or were simply lost somewhere in their own time.

"What now?" Chloe asked, wiping the sweat from her lip.

"We wait." Orpheus reached up to the branch above him and pulled off several pieces of round green fruit.

"What are those?"

He juggled them for a few seconds, then tossed one to Chloe. "In Próta, they're called *karydiá*. We know them as walnuts."

Chloe examined the nut in her hands. "*Karydiá*," she repeated, thinking, *sounds like Carya.* She cleared her throat and handed the walnut back to him. "I'm allergic to nuts."

He smiled. "More for me, then. I'll remove the shells as soon as I find a stone to crack them on."

"Well, shouldn't we go explore or something? I don't guess there's a water fountain anywhere." She wilted to the ground like a sun-scorched flower and lay back against the tree.

"Look," said Orpheus, pointing toward the sea.

Before she could look, she heard the sound of dogs barking. She jumped up and hid behind Orpheus. She liked dogs, but she couldn't imagine wild, island dogs to be welcoming creatures.

Orpheus said something in Próta. Chloe peered around him to see a beautiful woman clothed in magenta robes standing before not just dogs, but cats, horses, and fluttering parakeets, too. The woman answered him and gave a ladylike bow, her jewel-encrusted tiara glittering in the sun.

Chloe stepped to Orpheus's side and smiled at the woman, trying not to think about how disheveled she looked.

"What is your name, young lady?" the woman asked in perfect Petrodian. She sank a hand into a pouch she was carrying, and scattered seed and fruit slices onto the ground. The small menagerie gathered around the food and grazed happily, not fighting one another or snarling as most animals would.

"Uh, Chloe, madam," she said, eyes fixed on a sleek, shorthaired hunting dog munching on an apple. "I didn't know dogs liked fruit."

The woman knelt down and stroked the dog's back. "These dogs are special. And very well behaved." She stood up, snapped her fingers, and pointed at Chloe. "Theron, go and greet our guests."

Theron swallowed his food and walked toward Chloe and Orpheus, his head drooping and his tail between his legs. Chloe bent over and scratched behind the dog's ears. He looked healthy enough. Why did he seem so sad?

Orpheus chuckled, and she looked up to see that a lime-green parakeet had landed on his shoulder. It began to squawk, and Orpheus whistled along to its animated tune.

"That is Erato," the woman said. "She fancies herself a muse."

"And may I ask who you are?" Chloe asked.

The woman tilted her chin toward the sky as she answered, "My name is Circe, the monarch of Aeaea, on which you stand." She lowered her eyes and looked at Chloe, though her proud chin remained aloft. "You've not heard of me where you're from?"

Chloe looked to Orpheus as she shrugged. "Uh, I'm sorry, but no."

"Forgive us, madam," Orpheus said. "We hail from the future world. And I regret to say that our scholars leave out much of the past from the history books."

Circe pursed her lips, and with a clap of her hands every animal stopped eating and pointed their ears toward their mistress. "Come! I'm sure you are famished from your journey. I was just preparing a banquet when Erato informed me of visitors. We shall feast, and I will give you the pleasure of learning what your daft teachers have neglected." She picked up her long skirts and walked toward the beach, her herd of pets trailing behind.

"Do you think she knows Iris?" Chloe asked Orpheus. She caught him staring at Circe, at the woman's suntanned arms swaying to her own melodious song, and her long, bleached hair blowing in the breeze. "Orpheus?"

"I...I don't know," he said. "But I'm hungry. How about you?"

Chloe took another look at the world around her: the craggy rocks that separated the shore from black, vertical cliffs; the lush copses of tamarisks and pine trees; the azure waves lapping onto the shimmering sand; and the complete quiet that encompassed it all.

She wanted to feel peace here. She wanted to feel a latent spirit of adventure taking flight inside her and then throw every grain of caution to the wind. As silly as it was, she wanted to be like Rhoda, her yellow-haired, hand-drawn friend who was afraid of nothing, nothing except the ordinary. But no matter how hard she fought it, she couldn't suppress the unease sitting in the pit of her stomach like a stone.

She wasn't hungry. She felt sick. And worse than that, she felt stuck.

"How do we get home?" She checked her phone, but not surprisingly it was dead, as worthless as the pebbles she was standing on.

"I don't know that, either," said Orpheus, already a few yards ahead of her.

Chloe wanted to scream at him. She wanted to scream at herself. She was stranded, for all she knew, on a deserted island with a boy she'd just met, and a gorgeous, egocentric animal tamer who probably knew nothing of Iris or Charis, much less why Chloe and Orpheus were the lucky ones traveling back in time to see them. But what could she do? Where could she go?

The stone in her stomach grew larger as her pulse quickened. She took three deep breaths and recited a mantra her counselor had taught her to say whenever she felt stressed: "Stay calm and carry on." It didn't help.

CHAPTER FOURTEEN
SEEDS

Circe led them through a stone gate into the courtyard of her home. Every animal fit comfortably inside it, and Chloe's eyes grew wide at the sight of myriad other creatures, some she couldn't name, napping silently beneath the colonnade. Even the birds, perched on the red tile roof, were quiet, their tiny eyes glued to their guests.

Chloe glanced at Orpheus to see if he found the scene as strange as she did. Startled by his pale face and glassy eyes, she followed his gaze to an enormous narrow frieze chiseled into the side of the courtyard wall, just below the triangular gable that formed the end of the roof. It depicted dozens of men, some young and beardless, others old and bald, but all of them with woe and torment etched into their marble faces. All of them were struggling, veins bulging from their arms and necks, their sandals broken, tunics torn, striving to break free. But from what, Chloe didn't know, and she didn't have the nerve to ask.

"Welcome to my Elysium," said Circe, her gold bracelets jangling as she spread her arms and spun in circles, the proud monarch of this otherworldly oasis.

"Who are they?" Chloe asked Orpheus, her eyes darting back to the frieze.

In response, Orpheus clenched his jaw.

"Perfect!" Circe exclaimed. She was standing beside a pomegranate tree, inspecting a piece of fruit. She strode under the covered porch and called for someone from inside the house.

Chloe gasped to see a half-man, half-horse hybrid step out, his golden head bowed submissively. Circe handed him the pomegranate as she pointed to the tree. Without saying a word, the man—or was he an animal—fetched a wheelbarrow from behind one of the columns, trotted to the tree, and began pulling down the fruit with his brown, muscular arms.

"We'll gorge ourselves on pomegranates and honey cakes for dessert," Circe said to Orpheus and Chloe. She motioned toward a round wooden table in between two long rows of blossoming Jacaranda trees, their branches bending to meet one another and forming a lilac canopy which sufficiently blocked the sun. "Sit," commanded Circe.

Orpheus and Chloe obeyed, each immediately eyeing the tiered fountain beside the wall, its water flowing from a stone ring of lions' heads crowning the top. Chloe was about to run to it and quench her thirst when yet another half-man, half-horse creature appeared holding a jar of red wine and three black terracotta cups. He poured them a glass, his eyes never looking up. Chloe could see that he was very young, her age or a few years older, with a clean-shaven face, full head of black hair, and a broad bare chest that had obviously done its share of labor. His legs and hindquarters were the same color as the hair on his head, and just as strong.

"Sir?" Chloe said. But the man disregarded her and quickly slipped out of the shade. "I was just going to ask for water," she said, and then took a gulp of wine. Orpheus laughed as she winced and shook her head wildly, as if doing so might weaken the taste. "It's awful," she rasped, her tongue and esophagus stinging.

"That was a generous drink for your first time." Orpheus raised his cup and swilled the wine, then breathed in its aroma with a smile. "You get used to it." He took a drink, sat back in his chair and let out a long, contented sigh. "And then you love it."

"Do you know anything about that?" Chloe asked, her thumb shooting back to the frieze behind them. "Who they are?"

Orpheus's smile evaporated. His eyes skimmed the purple blooms then fell onto his hands. He opened and closed his fingers as his lips parted a little. "Old heroes," he said, just above a whisper. His blue eyes, made violet by the trees, locked with hers. "Heroes to whom fate was unkind."

Chloe sat still, unsure whether she should probe him further. After a minute, she decided to change the subject. "And what about them?" she asked. "The horse people."

"They're called—"

"They are my centaurs," Circe interrupted, her magenta robes sweeping under the table as she sat down. She placed a loaf of dark bread and a shallow bowl of pomegranate seeds in the center of the table. "Very helpful boys, but very dull. They hardly converse, even amongst themselves. I apologize for their boorishness. But in their defense, we don't receive many guests for whom manners are required." She laughed.

"Are all centaurs like that?" Chloe's mind flashed back to the centaur she saw with Iris, Charis, and the other man, fleeing together in the fire tunnel. She'd been too distracted—and too afraid—to study him for any length of time. She only knew he was ugly, and Circe's centaurs were anything but.

"Do you mean brutish, or beautiful?" Circe asked, tearing off a piece of bread.

"Both, I suppose."

"All are brutish." Circe dipped the bread into a small puddle of olive oil and handed it to Chloe.

It was the best thing she'd ever tasted, crisp on the outside, fluffy in the middle, and every morsel warm and rich, with just a touch of sweetness. The pit that had been in her stomach was summarily mollified, filled with the decadence of a simple slice of bread. Her mouth began to water.

"But only mine are beautiful," Circe added, as she gave both Orpheus and Chloe more to eat. She placed two fingers in her mouth and whistled for a centaur. "More dishes!" she shouted.

The same black-haired centaur galloped to the table, set three plates in front of them, then bowed and retreated as quickly as he'd come.

"So skittish," said Circe, her mouth full of bread. "Like untamed horses, aren't they?" She giggled, almost wickedly.

As Chloe washed down another bite with a conservative swig of wine, it dawned on her that she wasn't as hungry as she was acting. She was stress-eating again. Of course, this island and its residents were unusual, and the circumstances of how she'd arrived there were mind-boggling, but there was something else, something in the animals' eyes and the dispirited way they carried themselves, in the centaurs' pitiable shyness, and in the way Circe controlled their every move with a snap of her ageless fingers.

Chloe could sense that Orpheus was uneasy, too. Ever since she'd asked about the frieze of men in anguish, the "old heroes," he'd been restless, shifting in his seat, cracking his knuckles, rubbing the back of his neck. What else did he know about them? What else did he know about Circe?

"Which is your favorite?" Circe asked, bringing Chloe's unspoken questions to a halt.

Chloe jumped to attention and forced a smile before taking another drink. "Excuse me," she said. "My favorite what?"

"Animal," Circe said, pouring herself a cup of wine.

Chloe noticed that every finger, save for Circe's pinkies, were adorned with rings, each one covered in jewels. How had she become so rich? It was a nosey question, to be sure, but it seemed utterly impossible for a hermit to have such wealth.

"I have more inside the house," Circe said. "Deer, wolves, boars, tortoises, leopards, all of them gentle as doves."

"In the world we come from," said Chloe, "we're only allowed to own one animal: a dog, a cat, or a fish. All the other species are kept inside of zoos and nature reserves. I suppose my answer would be a horse. I saw some a long time ago and since then I've always wanted to ride one."

Circe's eyes lit up then narrowed as she smiled. "Excellent answer." She stretched her arms wide over her head and stared up at the sky through the branches. "We shall go for a ride after our meal," she said as her arms returned to her sides.

"I'd love to, but I have to be home soon," Chloe said, her finger tracing the rim of her cup. "In a few minutes, actually. I'll be in very big trouble if I'm not." She took a sip, beginning to change her opinion on wine. Orpheus was right—it just took some getting used to.

"Oh, nonsense," said Circe, her smile widening. "There *is* no time here. You didn't know?"

Chloe shook her head and looked at Orpheus.

"Eat, drink, and be merry," Circe said.

Chloe felt a lump in her throat. Who was she to question how time worked? It was obvious, more now than ever, that she knew nothing of physics, or history either for that matter. The whole world was upside down and spinning, and it was all she could do to keep her balance. She downed the rest of her wine. It was the closest thing to stress-eating she could do without devouring all of Circe's bread.

"I will have the centaurs saddle the horses," Circe announced as she stood from the table.

If Chloe hadn't been so confused by the picture that statement evoked, she would have laughed.

"Do try the pomegranate seeds, my dear Chloe. They're one of the keys to everlasting youth." Circe winked and tossed a silky curtain of hair over her shoulder as she headed toward the house.

Well, now Chloe knew at least *one* of Circe's secrets. She placed her hand into the dish of seeds and watched them bleed onto her fingertips. She'd never had pomegranate seeds before and wondered if they'd be sweet or tart, and whether she'd feel any younger if she ate one.

She could feel Orpheus staring as she plucked one out and held it between her fingers. "Would you like some?" she asked, pushing the dish his direction.

He shook his head. "All yours," he said. "Excuse me. I'm going to go see if I might be of help inside. Enjoy." He rose, took his glass of wine, and left Chloe alone at the table.

It was then that the air got cold, though there wasn't any wind; the leaves and limbs were completely still, and the sun shined bright outside the trees. Chloe set down the seed and stared at the dish, the red seeds like eyes looking back at her. They reminded her of the myth about Persephone, how she had been abducted by Hades, ruler of the Underworld, and tricked into remaining his queen because she ate seeds just like these...

> *"There's just one warning you should heed:*
> *Do not eat of the enchanted seed.*
> *Take a lesson from Hades' wife,*
> *Who descended to hell, though she kept her life."*

Carya's words echoed like a bell in Chloe's brain. Her breathing became shallow as the chilled air seeped into her bones. She stood and went to the fountain, hoping the sun would warm her, but its rays felt like sleet against her skin. She gripped the edge of the first tier, leaned over and splashed her face with the tepid water until she could form one coherent thought: *the myth of Persephone was just that: a myth.*

Chloe cupped the water in her hands and took a drink as she thought back to the day before. The warning from the odd girl in her backseat had sounded so absurd that Chloe had let it go in one ear and out the other. But somehow—somehow—it had entered her memory before exiting her ear, because now it was the only thing she could think about.

"I can't eat those seeds," she whispered as she turned back to the table. "I won't."

She watched in stunned silence as the bowl of seeds levitated from the table and flew through the air like a discus until it crashed into the frieze ten yards away, smearing a man's marble face with blood-red juice. A calico cat in the nearest tree hissed and jumped down to the grass.

Chloe's hands got clammy as the pit in her stomach returned, this time joined with a burning acidity that climbed into her tightening throat. On her periphery, she saw the magenta hem of Circe's robes drawing closer.

"What have you *done?*" shouted Circe, both her hands raised toward the vandalized frieze.

"I didn't do anything," Chloe said, sweating now that the temperature had normalized to somewhere near ninety degrees.

"I show you nothing but hospitality, and you repay me with this barbaric act of insolence." Circe's white face swelled red with rage. "I used to know better than to fraternize with sycophantic humans. It seems that I've gone soft after these thousands of years."

"It lifted and threw *itself,*" Chloe said, frantic boldness mixing with her fear. "You must know *something* about the supernatural, Circe. That's why I came here with Orpheus." Speaking of Orpheus, she wondered where he was right about now...

Circe's sinister laugh sickened Chloe further. "You will *never* know about the supernatural, my dear, naïve girl. Unless..." She began to walk toward Chloe, her lovely features softening with every step. She reached into a pouch near her breast and pulled out a pomegranate seed. "Unless you eat this." She held the seed to the sunlight, smiling as it glistened like a ruby. "Eternal youth, unthinkable knowledge, impossible beauty, all yours."

Chloe stared at the seed, thinking of Persephone. If Carya's words were trustworthy, the tragic queen was somewhere below her feet in the Underworld, forever beautiful, forever immortal, forever wise. Yet it had all been against her will; all Persephone had wanted was to live her life like anybody else. Chloe, on the other hand, had been warned of the insidious trap, and evaded it. And still Circe persisted. Why? Hades already had his queen. And if he hadn't, he surely wouldn't have chosen Chloe Zacharias to marry.

Asking more questions, Chloe knew, would only encourage Circe to continue tempting her. According to Circe, she wouldn't know anything until she swallowed that infamous little seed.

Chloe reached out to Circe and opened up her hand.

"That's a good girl," whispered Circe as she dropped the seed into Chloe's palm and froze, waiting.

Before she had time to consider the repercussions, Chloe turned and flung the seed far over the wall. Circe screamed so loudly and so long that the dogs and wolves began to howl. Polecats, weasels, and red foxes that had hitherto been hidden scurried across the courtyard into the house.

Now that Circe's last drop of hospitality had drained away, she charged the table and grabbed the pitcher of wine. "Orpheus!" she shouted. "Hermes! Show yourselves!" With an ear-splitting shriek, she raised the pitcher over her head and started back toward Chloe. "Very well. I will have to do this the hard way."

And then there was music. Sweet, mellow notes rolled through the jacaranda trees to where Circe and Chloe stood, soothing and light as a summer breeze. Hearing the melody grow louder, Circe reacted as though she'd been stung by a hornet. She threw down the pitcher and covered her ears.

"What are you doing, you fool!"

Orpheus was approaching, playing a harp-like instrument Chloe had never seen before. She felt herself calming down and a sublime apathy taking over, erasing every shred of anxiety.

Circe was on her knees, rocking back and forth and groaning for Orpheus to stop, but after a minute her groaning ceased. Her hands collapsed to her sides as she, too, succumbed to the hypnotic song. Circe bent over and reached for the pitcher, but she faltered and fell to the ground, out cold in two seconds.

Chloe opened her mouth to speak to Orpheus, but he pressed a finger to his lips, and with his hand bade her sit down on the fountain. Then the music faded as she lay down and felt consciousness slipping away...

CHAPTER FIFTEEN
TRAPPED

Orpheus cursed himself as he emerged from the Psychro Cave sump, the mortal girl sleeping soundly in his arms. Why had he intervened? He should have let Circe strike the girl. The blow wouldn't have killed her. She would only have been knocked out so the seed could be forced down her throat. But Orpheus knew full well that he had acted for reasons that far outweighed merely keeping the girl unharmed.

It was Circe's frieze that had done him in. Though he hadn't lied when he'd told Chloe it memorialized old heroes, he'd kept the whole truth concealed, hoping in vain that if it was left unspoken, his pathos, his vexatious pity, would be repressed. But he'd been unable to repress the memory of the song he'd written, so very long ago, that lamented the marble men.

"Men of courage, men of renown, bound
    for adventure all your days,
You sailed the breadth of the wine-dark
    sea, for which Petros gave you praise.
When your ships found harbor on Circe's Isle,
    you feasted heartily, drank her wine,
And one by one, you each transformed
    into cattle, leopards, swine.
Never again to hear your children's laughter,
    never again to kiss your woman's face,
You are explorers made brutes, now trapped
    in time, in Petros's most wretched place."

Though Hermes hadn't divulged the details of the doom he'd planned for Chloe, it hadn't taken Orpheus long to see plainly what was intended. Chloe, this unremarkable Vessel—Vessel of what, Orpheus couldn't guess—would join Circe's collection of debased human beings.

Orpheus thought he'd had the strength to go through with his mission no matter what it entailed, that his love for Eurydice would overrule his sympathy, and silence any treasonous thoughts against his father. But his poet's heart had been rent, torn in two by the sight of his fellow men creeping along the ground, their intelligent eyes completely vacant, simply desolate black holes where hope of escape had once flickered.

He was a poet, not a heartless mercenary. He couldn't hand someone over to be turned into an animal, especially not an innocent.

Orpheus propped Chloe up against her bags and gently leaned her head against a stalagmite. *Innocent*, he thought, scowling. *You know nothing about this girl, you fool.*

He spat on the cave floor and kicked a cluster of cave pearls into the water. In a little less than an hour, the sedative effects of his lyre playing would wear off; he had to get Chloe home. But then, what of him? What of Eurydice?

A cloak of cold air wrapped around him. He waited a few seconds, and then watched as Hermes' golden wand materialized near Chloe's head and waved in circles around it. His dog-skin cap appeared next, followed by Hermes' torso, legs, and finally, his ruddy, devilish head.

"I could have put her to sleep myself if that was what Apollo required," said Hermes spitefully. His wand continued to wave, reinforcing the lyre's spell.

Orpheus winced at the rebuke and pressed his tongue against the roof of his mouth. He couldn't retaliate or try to defend himself. That would only dig a deeper hole.

Hermes pointed to the lyre poking out of Orpheus's backpack. "If I could play that piece of trash, the Vessel would be a little oinker by now, happily eating slop and rolling around in her own filth."

"She knew about the seeds," Orpheus said, hardly opening his mouth.

Hermes' eyes closed as he took a long inhale through his flared nostrils. "An irrelevant point, my dimwitted nephew." He lowered the wand and floated closer to Orpheus. "Whether she knew about the witch's wiles or not is no concern of yours."

"How did she know? Who is she?" Orpheus couldn't control the rising volume of his voice. "You've told me *nothing*." He shoved his hand into his jacket pocket and pulled out the pouch. "*This* has told me nothing."

A smile played on Hermes' lips as the gilded wings of his sandals fluttered like those of a hummingbird. Even when he was outraged, he appeared to enjoy the nuances of confrontation. "You've been dead for how long, nephew?" He tapped his chin with his forefinger. "Forgive me. That's an unfair question, more suited for a mathematician than a poet who must count with his fingers and toes."

Orpheus flexed his fingers. How he wished to show his uncle that his hands could do far more damage than lulling poor maidens to sleep.

"No matter the number," Hermes continued. "The point is, you existed in the Vale of Mourning as the world spun on without you. Meanwhile, Hades, Apollo, and the other rebels and I have been busy keeping things intact. Busy influencing, strategizing, observing, acting and reacting, making sure the Eusebian religion stays buried and their god unknown. I find it amusing that you think you're entitled to know *anything*."

The sides of Orpheus's head began to pound, more with frustration than offense. While in the Vale, he'd learned of the genocide that had wiped out a group of Eusebians who followed a religion called the Way, known in Próta as the Hodos. Various sects were suppressed and destroyed all throughout Orpheus's mortal life. It wasn't that knowledge that troubled him; it was his waxing concern for the girl he knew nothing about, this *Vessel*.

He looked at her dozing peacefully, her chest slowly rising and falling, her hands folded on her lap, and thought of Eurydice, how senseless it had been for her to die, killed by a viper at just eighteen.

"Perhaps if you'd told me why she's so valuable to you and the other *mighty* rebels, I wouldn't have taken pity on her," Orpheus said to Hermes.

He brushed past Hermes and reached down to scoop Chloe up, then lay her down again when he heard the discordant clanging of wind chimes and felt a violent gust beating against his back. He turned and saw Hermes hovering above the sump, his wand pointing down into the water that now roiled and churned as though afflicted by a squall.

"Come and see," Hermes said, with a cordial bow of his head.

Orpheus hesitated. He had a feeling he knew what vision waited for him in that pool, and just the thought of it caused a stabbing pain in his chest.

"You asked for revelation, did you not?" Hermes shouted. "Come and let me reveal to you all you'll need to do your duty."

Orpheus cocked his head to the side. "My *duty*? Why not just drop me back into the Vale? I've failed, haven't I?" His orotund voice echoed through the cave like a surging crescendo. His eyes flashed to Chloe, but she didn't stir.

"You think it's that easy, do you?" Hermes sniggered. "*You* are the one Apollo appointed. *You* are the one with the talent to charm. *You* are the one who will do this job." He floated higher above the water, and with a slight move of his wand, he calmed the waves. "She's ready to see you, nephew," he said, gesturing to the smooth black surface.

Orpheus shook his head, his teeth grinding. "I know what you're going to show me. It isn't necessary, uncle. Please." He would beg if he had to.

"Orpheus! Orpheus!"

It was Eurydice's voice, calling for him in panic.

"What are you doing to her?" yelled Orpheus.

He ran to the edge of the sump and stared in. He could see straight down into the same cell Apollo had shown him at Hades' palace. Only now it was completely bare. No dead flowers, no marble bench, no trellis of lifeless vines, just his darling wife backed up against the prison bars as snakes came slithering toward her. It was easy to see by the dark zigzagging stripe that ran down their backs that they were vipers.

Eurydice looked up to the ceiling, toward the portal through which Orpheus could see her. Her red, tear-stung eyes darted from corner to corner; she was searching for him.

"She knows you can see her," Hermes said, his tone nauseatingly blithe. "Do you insist on being shy?"

"Let her see me!" the poet roared, his right arm stretching up to Hermes, intent on strangling him. "And as my true self."

"You're certain?" Hermes said, wisely staying out of reach. He folded his arms, pointing the wand toward the wall behind him. "You know she cannot physically die again. She will simply be in pain for a very, very long time. The venom reacts quite nastily with ichor."

Orpheus watched as the army of snakes, no fewer than a hundred, flicked their black forked tongues and encroached on their prey; their hisses were almost deafening.

"Now!" Orpheus pounded his fist on the cave floor.

Hermes grinned as he lowered his wand and waved it until the murky water became clear as hand-blown glass and a beige tunic replaced Orpheus's jeans and jacket.

"My darling," shouted Eurydice, inexplicable happiness replacing sheer horror, if only for an instant.

"My love, I'm here," Orpheus called back. "Darling, sing to them. Sing and they shall be like lambs at your feet." He reached out and gingerly traced her face with his finger, wishing with everything he was that he could stand in her place. Why must she be tortured for his defiance? "The song I sang on our wedding day, do you remember it?"

"Oh, Orpheus, haven't you heard your wife sing?" said Hermes. "It will only speed them up."

"Shut up," Orpheus snarled out of the corner of his mouth so Eurydice couldn't see. He listened as she began to hum and softly sing the first verse, but alas, the vipers were not quelled. They hissed louder, encircling her as she spun and pressed herself against the iron bars.

Orpheus stood and looked imploringly at his uncle, who still hovered along the cave wall, looking on with perverse satisfaction. "What do you want," Orpheus said, hot tears welling as his hands and heart trembled.

"I'm glad you asked," said Hermes.

He flew to Chloe and squatted behind her, brushing her hair with his fingers. "All you have to do is make her trust you. Be her confidant." Hermes pulled a small book from his satchel and flipped through its pages. "The All-Powerful has already been working. He's shown her the past, and she has written all about it in here. She needs a friend, Orpheus. A teacher."

Orpheus looked back to Eurydice. The snakes were just an arm's length away, ready to strike at any moment. He could see slick tears trailing down her cheeks as she reached her hand up toward him, completely helpless, completely innocent.

"I'll do anything, just *stop* this," Orpheus pleaded as he dropped to his knees, joined his hands and bowed his head in supplication.

Hermes snapped the book shut and tossed it to the poet. "I am so pleased by your cooperation," he said, though there was only sarcasm in his voice. "I know your father will be very proud." He bounded to the sump and stirred the crystal water with his wand.

A weight that felt like a thousand tons lifted off Orpheus's chest as he watched the vipers shrink back and dissolve into dark ribbons of shadow. "All's well, my love," Orpheus cried out, as the water darkened and the cell seemed to descend to a lower level of hell. "I love you." He felt his heart breaking as she replied in kind, her flaxen hair fading into the void.

Hermes crouched beside the poet and clamped a hand on his shoulder. "Tell the Vessel who she is, and that you are like her. An Asher. Her doma could manifest at any moment, so it's of utmost importance, for your sake and mine, that you make quick work of it. I have no doubt that Apollo will give us Prometheus' fate to share if you don't."

For the first time, Orpheus noticed fear, raw and undisguised, slide across his uncle's face, overtaking it as a sheet of rain engulfs blue sky.

"I don't know who she is," Orpheus said, twisting himself free from Hermes' hand. "You're babbling on like a senile fool." He rose from the edge of the pool and punched a limestone column so hard his knuckles bled.

"Control your passions, Orpheus." Hermes waved his wand, transforming Orpheus's clothes once more. "I will teach you what is necessary. Nothing more, and nothing less."

"Where will the girl go if she cannot be killed?" Orpheus thought for a moment and then said with confidence, "I shall not take part in making her one of Circe's pets. Eurydice would rather suffer in the viper's den than learn that I ever came close to assisting such an abomination."

Hermes floated over to Chloe and picked her up. "You will leave that to me," he said as he placed her in Orpheus's arms. "Return her to her bed and then go to Lake Thyra. Once you're back in Hades, your education shall begin."

CHAPTER SIXTEEN
WARNING

Ethan Ross knew when he saw the Moonbow in the sky two nights before that it was no coincidence the Religious Council was hosting private meetings with the Fantásmata.

The sound of rain and a bright shaft of moonlight had awoken him just before dawn, and he held his breath as he went to his window and opened the blinds. In the southeastern sky there was a full moon hanging low, it's right half hidden behind a cloud. To the west was the deluge of rain the meteorologists predicted would arrive. What they did not predict—*could* not predict—were the seven arches that appeared over the colony for the first time in untold thousands of years.

Ever since his mother had deciphered the scroll, Ethan had been drawn to it, transfixed by the few scant glimpses of history they'd been allowed to study. He'd never heard of—much less seen—a Moonbow, the phenomenon Iris described in her letter. It seemed a rare thing for her time, too. What had it meant back then? And what could it possibly portend now?

Tonight, Ethan couldn't sleep. He was lying awake, watching the shadows of tree limbs sway and shake across the moonlit ceiling. He'd been to the window twice, but the skies were clear, and it was still too early for the Moonbow to form, regardless. Even the question of what it represented and how it might be connected to the Religious Council and the Fantásmata had dissipated somewhat, making room for an even more troubling question, a more personal one.

It wasn't even a question, really. It was a reality he had no idea how to handle. He'd proven that earlier when he sat in the cafeteria with Chloe and just stared at her, probably making her feel like a fool, as she spoke about things he'd pondered constantly since that day with her father.

In the dim light, Ethan could just see the faint white scars, below his elbow, where the beast had sunk its teeth.

And although it had been eight years, he could still recall, in sharp detail, all that had happened, even though at the time it had rushed by in a blur.

Ethan sat up, switched on his desk lamp, and walked to his closet. He pulled the stepstool from the corner, then climbed to the upper shelf and began rummaging through dusty boxes of old clothes and toys he hadn't touched in years.

When he was ten, he'd put the diary at the bottom of a box marked *Stuffed Animals*, figuring it was as good a hiding place as any. Plus, he'd reasoned that the word "animals" would remind him of the rhino-sized wolf he'd seen stalking the shores while his mother was digging pottery out of a hole. But that had proved an unnecessary measure to take; he always knew exactly where the diary was and had been tempted to open it countless times over the years.

After sweeping piles of hoarded papers and books onto the floor, and pushing aside box after box, he finally found the one he was looking for and carefully lowered it from the shelf. His breath caught in his throat when he opened it and spotted the diary wedged between two stuffed animals he'd received on Lycaea: tawny wolves with white chests and cheeks, not unlike the one he'd seen that day.

He hadn't planned it that way. At eight years old, he wouldn't have been clever enough to consider any association between the creature he'd seen and the festival that honored the Unknown God, and, for reasons unexplained and uncontested, paid homage to the wolf with costumes and trinkets. But now the images struck him like a hand to the face, waking him up to a clue, a confirmation: a signpost pointing him to the Moonbow, Iris, and Chloe.

Either that, or his active imagination was trying to make things more interesting than they really were, and the best thing he could do was pretend there was nothing to see.

Ethan carried the diary to his bed and flopped onto his stomach, holding the book out in front of him as if it might sting or bite. After the incident had happened, he'd scribbled everything down and stashed the diary away, knowing his parents would have to report his "strange sighting" were he to tell them about it.

As a boy, he knew little about the Fantásmata, but the fact that his mother's body tensed and her voice shook whenever she spoke of them was enough to dissuade him from ever mentioning anything out of the ordinary. Even his questions about how their world was ruled he mostly kept to himself. He'd had sense enough to keep secret what he'd seen, and how he'd been healed, and had left it in the past. Until now.

With a sigh, Ethan opened the diary and flipped through it until he found the section written in permanent marker, the entry he never wanted erased. Then, before he could talk himself out of it, he began to read.

☽

Today was vocation day at school. Every kid got to go to work with his dad all day, or his mom if she wasn't home taking care of a younger sibling. Since my dad works at the Religious Council, which is off limits most of the time, I went with my mom to the place where she does archeology in Ourania.

I was so bored and was glad I brought books to read. My mom doesn't get bored. Neither do the other people who do what she does. She says there's nothing she would rather do than uncover things from the past that can teach us about the present. One lady showed me an old broken oil lamp and some coins. Then we ate lunch. Then I walked around for a little while and took a nap under a tree.

After that, the page was nothing but doodles and random drawings. Ethan smiled and sighed through his nose, remembering clearly what his child's mind had been thinking as his pen had meandered aimlessly, sketching geometric shapes and animals. He had been debating whether to write another word. But eventually the doodling stopped, and two pages later the text began again.

☽

I go to school with a girl named Chloe Zacharias. Her dad picks her up from school every day, so I knew who he was when I saw him walking on the beach close to where I had just taken a nap. I don't know what he was doing out there. We're not supposed to leave Eirene unless we're told to or you're an archeologist like my mom. He looked like he was waiting for a ship to sail by or something.

I called to him, "Mr. Zacharias! Mr. Zacharias!" but it was windy, and he couldn't hear me. I started to walk closer and then heard growling coming from behind me, where the tree was.

It was a wolf, much bigger than any dog I've ever seen! It was a yellowish-brown color and had short hair and orange eyes that looked like they were on fire. It showed me its teeth and kept growling, louder and louder. The hair on its back stood up like cats' hair does, and its ears flattened backward.

I started to run for it, but it jumped at me and bit my arm. It would have eaten me, but Mr. Zacharias ran up to us and pulled the wolf off of me and onto him. I wanted to help him, but my arm was bleeding pretty bad and hurt a hundred times worse than the time I stepped on a nail on our back porch. The wolf was twice as big as him and took huge bites out of his shoulder and neck.

Mr. Zacharias didn't yell or anything, even though there were some people not very far away who probably could've helped. He tried to wrestle the wolf, but I knew he didn't stand a chance. Pretty soon Mr. Zacharias stopped moving. I couldn't even see his face anymore. He was covered in blood and guts.

The wolf left me alone. I guess it was tired, or maybe I didn't taste very good. It ran off toward the cliffs, and I called for help. And then Mr. Zacharias' leg jerked up in the air like mine does sometimes right before I fall asleep.

He gasped for air and then groaned a lot and started to move his fingers. I didn't know what to do. I tried not to cry, but I wanted to. My arm wouldn't stop bleeding and I was feeling dizzy. Mr. Zacharias noticed me, and then he used all his strength to rock himself up. Then the weird stuff happened.

Mr. Zacharias sat really still and his shoulders sort of slumped. I thought he'd passed out again. But then all the gashes and bloody openings on his body started to close up, starting at his head and ending at his feet, which were missing their shoes. Even the smaller scratches from the wolf's claws disappeared.

I was sure my mind was playing a trick on me, but then he crawled over to me and put his hands on my arm, right where the teeth had gone in. A few seconds later, the bleeding stopped. He took his hands off, and my arm looked like nothing had happened to it at all!

I asked Mr. Zacharias how he'd done that, but he just told me to keep quiet and not to tell anyone, not even my parents. He looked angry and scared at the same time, but I knew he wasn't angry with me. He took my hand and walked me back to the edge of the site where my mom was. Then he told me to be careful and left.

I didn't tell anyone. And I won't.

. And then Ethan's heart missed a beat, for just after his handwriting ended, a typed note that had been stapled to the page began.

Dear Mr. Ross,

On behalf of the Fantásmata, I wish to express both our gratitude and our disappointment. We are grateful for your disciplined diary keeping, as without it we would have lacked the necessary proof with which to apprehend Mr. Zacharias. We are disappointed because you chose to keep your experience private, despite your awareness that all paráxeno theáseis episodes must be reported to a Religious Council member. However, due to the significance of your unintended assistance, we have chosen to overlook your unlawful behavior and categorize it as easily corrected youthful indiscretion. We hope, for your sake, that you choose differently in the future, should you ever again be subjected to what we are certain was a traumatic experience.

If our note remains unseen, we can only hope that your conscience matures and guides you toward the path of unity and obedience, two tenets of our society that we proudly uphold and enforce with fervor.

Kind regards,
The Fantásmata

With chills spreading throughout his limbs, Ethan flipped through the rest of the diary to see if anything else had been left for him. Nothing.

His heart pounded as he hurried from the bed to the box of stuffed animals and searched it, too, throwing the toys over his shoulder until he reached the bottom. Nothing.

Whoever had taken the trouble to trespass onto his parents' property and sneak into his room had done so only to leave that note, that...warning.

Ethan leaned his head against the edge of the bed, closed his eyes, and made his heart rate come down as he thanked himself—his ten-year-old self—for not journaling the second part, the part he'd hoped he would forget, but never had.

CHAPTER SEVENTEEN
ASHER

Chloe's alarm began its staccato beeping at six thirty a.m. She rubbed her eyes as she turned and punched the snooze button. When she opened her eyes, she could hardly see. Her window, dresser, and reading chair were only discernible by the morning light that traced them. The rest of her bedroom was black space. It was as if she'd been lost in a cave and gone half blind.

The cave...

Chloe sat up and felt for the lamp on her desk and flicked it on, then winced as the brightness burned her eyeballs. She knew she was indeed at home, in her own bed, yet she felt so far away, as though her throbbing head was underwater and her body was detached from it, swimming around below it. She remembered a cave, though.

She remembered meeting a boy named Orpheus, who led her to the cave. And after a few minutes, she remembered the strange, sad animals, Circe and the pomegranate seeds, and falling into a deep sleep as Orpheus played a song on that odd little instrument.

Please let it have been a dream, she thought, as she stumbled out of bed and braced herself on the back of her desk chair to keep from falling headlong onto the floor. She shook her head, willing herself to feel normal again. If being drunk felt anything like this, she could understand why drinking wine had been outlawed. And then she turned to her wastebasket and vomited.

"Are you okay?"

Chloe peered at Damian's bare feet out of the corner of her eye. She groaned and retched again as she remembered the wine from her non-dream.

"I take that as a no," he said.

"Get out!" she shouted when she'd finally stopped heaving.

Damian backed out, then returned a few moments later and set a glass of water next to her knee.

"Thank you."

"I'll send this in to Dr. Leandros," said Damian, as he kneeled down and held out his phone to record her.

"You're going to make him sick if you film it this close," Chloe said, as the waves of nausea rolled again. But as she threw up a third time, she had a feeling that Damian was purposefully making the footage as detailed as possible.

"Awesome," he said. He patted Chloe on the back and stood up. "I'll text this to school and bring you some meds, k?"

Chloe gave him a thumbs-up as she drank the water and grabbed a tissue from her desk.

"Did you eat something bad last night?"

Chloe shook her head. She *drank* something bad. She crawled up onto her bed and curled into a fetal position. It was then it dawned on her that she was still wearing her jeans from yesterday, and they were filthy.

"I went for a walk after school yesterday and went into a cave," she said as convincingly as she could. "Maybe I inhaled something."

"Do you need to go to the hospital? I can take you as long as it's before wrestling practice."

"You're very kind, but no, I'll be fine."

Her brother gave her a long look. He actually appeared concerned. But then, it'd been ages since either one of them had been sick. And when they had been ill, it was because their bodies were responding to routine vaccinations.

"Damian, I'm *fine*," she said, managing a smile. "You can have my room if I die."

Damian raised an interested eyebrow and smiled as he scanned the room, which was much larger than his. "Thanks." Then he carried out the wastebasket and returned a minute later with a handful of pills.

"Finally." Chloe sighed when she heard Damian pull out of the driveway. Had he lingered any longer she was sure she would've said too much and given herself away.

She rolled out bed and sat down at her desk. Where was her diary? She always kept it in the same spot, squeezed in the middle of her bookends between her favorite dictionary and the first volume of Mythologica she'd received in her first year of primary school.

Who would have taken her diary? Maggie and Travis never came upstairs, much less took interest in their niece's private life. Damian, on the other hand, had stolen her diary plenty of times when they were young; it hadn't mattered where she'd hidden it. But ever since she'd placed it in plain sight and removed the challenge, he couldn't have cared less about it. Plus, he was too busy being popular to pester her anymore. And what did she have to hide over the past few years?

Chloe's mind retraced her steps from two nights before, the night she'd eaten the walnut and written all about it. She hadn't left the room, nor would she have slipped the book into her backpack, though she rummaged through it just in case. Her stomach had finally settled, but now there was a hammer pounding away at her skull.

She went to the bathroom and refilled her glass, then plopped into her desk chair and stared at the single walnut atop her mesh penholder.

"Carya," she said, as she lifted her chin to the ceiling, "I need some help here. If someone has my diary, they'll report me to the Fantásmata, and I don't want to know what they'll do when they find out."

Chloe thought of Mr. Boulos, her history teacher who had been exiled for teaching about the true origins of Lycaea. She thought of Acacius, whose countenance alone had been proof enough that his Coronation was not what it seemed. And she thought of Ethan Ross, the classmate who'd never crossed her mind a single time before he'd given her the most unusual birthday present she'd ever received.

What are the odds that on the very day she visits the museum, Carya pops up, gives her mystical walnuts, and prophecies about Circe and the pomegranate seed? She pictured the look on Ethan's face when she sat across from him at lunch and needled him about the Fantásmata. He was agitated, that was for sure, but it wasn't because she sounded nuts. It was because he was afraid to act as though she wasn't.

It wasn't just a coincidence that he'd invited her to view those gigantic fossils and fragments of Iris's scroll. He wanted her to know something, but didn't know how to tell her.

Chloe took the walnut and held it between her fingers, eyeing it cautiously, as if it might crack open any second and deliver a rhyming message from its previous owner. She waited, almost wishing it would move.

Chloe, you are ridiculous. She set the walnut in the empty gap of her bookends where her diary had been. She didn't need her diary anyway. The walnut would be the only memento she'd need if she ever wanted to reminisce about Orpheus and the Isle of Aeaea. But the question of where it was and who had read it made her feverish blood run cold.

She had to find Ethan. She had to make him talk.

((

Please meet me at Astrolux after wrestling practice. CZ.

Ethan got out of his truck and removed the note from under the windshield wiper. After he ripped it to shreds and dropped the pieces into his pants pocket, he got into the cab and dropped his head onto the steering wheel. Then he lifted it and dropped it again with a careless thud. He never should have given her the one-day pass. He'd wanted her to figure things out on her own, not recruit him for help.

He sat up in the driver's seat and thought back to the seal at the bottom of the note left from the Fantásmata.

The Próta form of the letter F was bold in the center, with a black circle around it and a thick red column splitting it down the middle. Surrounding this was a black-and-red serpent wrapping the perimeter, swallowing its own tail.

Ethan shivered. He'd been given a clear warning never to withhold anything from the government again. But he wasn't in danger of doing that, was he? He hadn't seen anything, nor had he heard anything escape Chloe's lips that could incriminate her. The only thing he knew that would be of interest to the Fantásmata was the last thing Mr. Zacharias had told him just before a car accident took his life. It had been one of the few premature deaths in Ethan's lifetime.

Ethan restlessly tapped his hands on the wheel, wishing he could go back in time, back to the day he'd seen Mr. Zacharias walking on the beach. He would have made himself stay put and mind his own business. Then the wolf never would have attacked him, Mr. Zacharias never would have healed him, and Ethan never would have written in his diary the words that got Mr. Zacharias arrested, and—Ethan couldn't help but think—murdered.

Still feeling chilled, Ethan started his truck and turned on the heat. How could he live with himself if he ignored Chloe's note or, worse, lied, telling her it must have blown away? He might have been innocent, but he still had her parents' blood on his hands. And for all he knew, hers might be next.

Ethan opened the center console and pulled out a small leather bag, the one Mr. Zacharias had given him. Ethan had placed it there after discovering the letter inside his diary, planning to mail it to the Fantásmata with a note expressing his apologies for remaining silent as a boy. Perhaps they would consider it an olive branch and he could sleep a little easier at night.

But now, holding the pouch in his hand, he didn't feel fear, but inexorable shame. Was he really going to just roll over and hand the bag off to the Fantásmata so they could "apprehend" Chloe as they had her father? He could forget sleeping altogether if he buried his head in the sand without at least telling her what he knew.

He had to meet her. It was the least he could do for the man who'd saved his life.

☾

"He took his time deciding," said Orpheus, as he watched Ethan's truck pull out of the school parking lot. "What do you think he'll do?"

Orpheus had spent the night in Hades' palace, watching the past literally unravel before his eyes while mists, created by Hermes for the occasion, rose from an ephemeral stream. Scenes of the life of the woman named Iris flickered within them, and even glimpses of her gifted predecessors paraded across the gossamer-like screen. He saw men and women with astonishing powers, ones that put his talent for music and poetry to shame, and each one aligned with a color of the Moonbow.

The first man he saw, the one called Asher, had turned ochre earth into a bright red tablet on which he wrote his prophecies. Asher could make tablets from any part of nature he wished, be it grass, or sand, snow, or salt. And with them, he obediently recorded what the All-Powerful told him to for the rest of his days.

Another, a man named Icarius, had Herculean strength combined with superior combat skills. He'd used them to singlehandedly slay an Alpha phalanx when they'd laid siege to Eirene; the indigo arch of the Moonbow was represented by the veins of his massive arms. Icarius's daughter, Erigone, was a builder of siege engines the pale yellow color of the Moonbow's third arch and the desert sands they rolled upon, weapons that had routed the finest Alpha armies.

But not all Ashers were glorious. Iris's aunt, Corinna, had a doma that transformed her into a fearsome gryphon, a destructive weapon in and of herself. But she'd run away from home as a child, well before her eighteenth birthday, the year the gifts manifested. And with no one to guide or teach her, she fell prey to one of Apollo's men. She became assassin of her own people. The color of her doma was blood red, as was the doma of the last Asher, the one called Mania; Próta for "fury."

Iris had the ability to create fire with her hands, whether a minuscule spark or a blazing inferno. With it, she'd killed the man who'd corrupted Corinna, wounded the monster that tried to steal her child, and led her people through a fiery tunnel to escape Mania the day she razed Ourania to the ground.

It was Iris who had provoked Apollo's wrath. It was she who had lived to see the fulfillment of the prophecy about Phos, Duna's son, who had been sent to free the Eusebians from evil and tyranny. It was she who had tried to outrun the Moonbow, the symbol of hope that was now appearing once again, calling to the Vessel named Chloe.

Hermes nudged Orpheus's arm. "I wager that the boy will side with the Vessel. I've observed men long enough to know which are noble and which are spineless, and this one has a mild obsession with the heroes of long ago." Hermes looked away and filled his immortal lungs with the fresh fall air. "Beat him there. I'll fly you to meet her."

"And what of the boy?"

"If you do your job well, he'll back off," said Hermes, every word an admonishing jab. "He may have a spine, but he has a heart, too. He won't want it broken."

"He has romantic feelings for the girl?" Orpheus asked.

How much did Hermes and the other rebels know about the personal lives of mortals? Was childish eavesdropping how they spent their time when they weren't scheming and carrying out Apollo and Hades' plans?

Hermes smiled. "He's wisely kept his distance from her. But if it weren't for his past, I imagine he would give her at least one of those saccharine sonnets he's written about her."

Orpheus felt a twinge in his human heart. He couldn't help but feel sympathy for a youth in love, even more so when the love was kept secret, shut up in the solitary crevices of Ethan's own soul.

CHAPTER EIGHTEEN
DOMA

Hermes landed Orpheus on a street corner amid a crowd too busy to notice a man appearing out of nowhere. Orpheus felt warmth rush into his skin as the last trace of invisibility lifted away. Nearly everyone, he noticed, held a brown paper coffee cup. He followed his nose and walked into the Astrolux café just one block away, where he spotted Chloe waiting at the end of the line.

"Good afternoon," he said softly, so as not to startle her.

But her shoulders jumped to her ears anyway. She darted out of line and hurried toward the door.

"Where are you going?" he said as he followed her, smiling at the group of teens filing through the door, blocking her way out. "Chloe, I need to talk to you. Please, just give me five minutes."

With a sigh, she let the door close, but not before glancing up and down the street. "I'm waiting for someone."

"Please, Chloe. I know you have questions about what happened last night. I want to tell you." He moved closer and whispered, "I want to *help* you."

Chloe turned and gave him a look of disgust. "*Help* me? You mean lead me into a secluded cave and introduce me to a psychopath? You mean watch me intoxicate myself, and then lull me to sleep with your stupid music?"

"I only wanted to put *her* to sleep," said Orpheus. "Not you."

Seeing that his words did little to appease her, Orpheus pulled off his backpack and set it on the empty table beside him. He unzipped it and slid out the lyre, just enough so she could see its crossbar.

"I found this in that cave during a hike a few months ago," he said. "I've always had a flare for music, but this... this is supernatural, Chloe. I play it, and wild animals creep out of their holes and sit at my feet. My own family walks about in a halcyon daze. And if I play something particularly

177

pacifying, even the most highly strung become comatose, as you saw for yourself with Circe."

Chloe folded her arms, looking at him as though he were speaking gibberish. "So I owe a thank-you to a harp?" She laughed and pushed the door open.

Orpheus snatched his backpack from the table and followed her onto the sidewalk. "It's a lyre, actually. One of the most well-known instruments of the ancient world."

Chloe sat down at the outside table farthest from the door and eyed Orpheus with a skeptical smile. "You know, I'm wondering if I wasn't drugged last night and hallucinated everything."

She looked down at her nails and began to pick at them. "Your father is a keeper, correct?" Orpheus nodded. "He's definitely a man of many secrets. And he's obviously taught you a lot about Petros's past. Why should I doubt that he's also taught his son a few handy life skills, like how to deceive and debilitate his fellow man?"

Orpheus took the lyre out of his backpack and sat down in the corner. "The only way to debilitate my fellow man is with this," he said, holding the lyre by the arms that had been made from the horns of an oryx. He pulled his plectrum from his pocket and began to strum.

The melody was soft at first, blending into the buzz of conversation and the whir of traffic. Still, after just a few seconds, Chloe was leaning forward on her elbows, her eyes staring intensely at the six strings as they vibrated with irresistible euphony. How would he prove to her that the lyre's power was authentic if she was transfixed by his playing?

Orpheus set the plectrum down and watched as Chloe's brows furrowed, the last note fading into the noise around them.

"Are you going to play, or what?" Chloe said.

Orpheus had to laugh. "I just did." He pointed to the crosswalk at the end of the block. "Go down there and watch."

"Your magic instrument only works within a certain radius?"

"Are you always so snide?" he asked, finding himself, once again, more amused by her backtalk than riled by it.

Chloe grumbled something unintelligible and scooted back her chair. "Make it quick." Then she stuffed her hands into her jacket pockets and strode down the sidewalk.

Orpheus rolled his eyes. When he saw that Chloe was a safe distance away, he began to play once more.

Two canines were the first to be lured. The smaller one, long-bodied and short-legged, wriggled out of a woman's sizeable tote bag at an adjacent table and jumped into the chair where Chloe had been sitting. The second dog, much larger and resembling the shepherds' dogs Orpheus knew as a boy, refused to continue walking beside its master. It sat on its haunches in front of Orpheus as its petite owner whistled and tugged at its leash; even a treat from her purse couldn't coerce the animal to move. It just sat there, looking at Orpheus as its fluffy tail fanned back and forth.

The children were next. Breaking free from the hands of their parents, they joined Orpheus at his table, dragging unused chairs from other tables to be as near to the music as possible.

Orpheus laughed to himself, remembering how his friends once joked with him that he'd be the happiest of papas one day, so long as he held onto the lyre that could turn rowdy children into stoics. He counted himself fortunate that he and Eurydice hadn't yet had children when she'd died. He couldn't imagine raising them without their mother. But then, with children, he would have had a piece of her always, little reminders, perhaps, of what made her laugh, how she carried herself when she was blissfully happy, or how green her eyes were in the spring.

Orpheus jumped in his seat when a young towheaded girl pushed her tiny freckled face to the glass window behind him and tapped her mother's shoulder. A few seconds later, she, her siblings and every other café customer were crowding the sidewalk, completely mesmerized by the buoyant lilt flowing from the strings. Not a single person spoke; they all smiled contentedly as though they had just woken up from the sweetest of dreams.

The poet eyed Chloe leaning against a traffic signal, her arms folded in that defiant, unimpressed way of hers. He decided to change his tune.

Little by little, Orpheus slowed the upbeat cadence, letting the melody gradually fade from a jubilant benediction to a sober ballad, one he'd written about the Pleiades when studying the constellation on a winter night.

The children began to yawn. The shepherd dog beside Orpheus lay down and rested its head on its paws. The smaller one was already fast asleep, curled up in a furry chestnut ball, its pink tongue sticking out. After a minute, everyone, adults included, was sitting on the concrete at Orpheus's feet, nodding off as steam continued to rise from their forgotten cups of coffee and cocoa.

The only active body was Chloe's, as she walked back towards Orpheus, a patronizing smirk on her face as she applauded him. "You've proved your point," she said. "Now let the poor pedestrians go and explain to me how you're doing that."

As Orpheus rose from his chair to obey, he took a quick survey of the audience that had congregated. He was pleased to see that Ethan was not among them. What had Hermes done with him? Pushing the question from his mind, he gave a gracious bow and thanked his captive listeners for their attention, though he knew they were still too stupefied to hear him. Slowly, however, the trance wore off, and the dogs began to sniff and circle each other as the humans helped each other to their feet.

Orpheus put the lyre back into his bag and went speeding down the sidewalk to join Chloe before people had time to scratch their heads and wonder what had occurred.

"Now talk," Chloe said as they turned the corner. "How do you do that?"

"It's a gift," replied Orpheus. He lowered his head and whispered, "A *doma*, to use the ancient word."

Chloe gave him a wary sidelong glance. "And where, pray tell, did you receive this *doma*?"

She stopped in front of a shop with a small chalkboard outside the door that read: FLAVOR OF THE DAY: POMEGRANATE PUNCH. She pointed to it and turned to stare at Orpheus. "If what happened on that island was real, do you realize how traumatized I'm going to be for the rest of my life? I couldn't eat the ice cream of the day without imagining Circe coming at me with a bronze pitcher." She opened the door and motioned for Orpheus to go in.

"What are we doing?" he asked as he gazed at a giant display case filled with small troughs of colorful globs. *People eat this?*

"I'm hungry." Chloe's eyes danced across the bizarre offering of pabulum set before them. Then she looked down at the phone she now held in her hand and frowned. "I'd better go back to Astrolux. I was waiting for someone before you showed up." She shook her head as she sighed and tilted her chin to the ceiling. "I can't believe this is happening."

"Is the person you were there to meet tall and a bit gangling?"

Chloe nodded.

"And does he have short dark hair? Pale?"

"Yes..."

"He showed up," Orpheus lied. "But when he saw the audience I amassed at your behest, he left before the lyre could affect him."

Ignoring him, Chloe marched up to the counter and gave her order to the cashier. "What do you want?" she asked over her shoulder.

"I'm not hungry, thank you."

"And one chocolate brownie," she said to the cashier.

Orpheus watched as the man took a silver scoop and filled a pink paper cup to the brim with a brown heap of what the esteemed poet could only compare to cow manure. The cashier stuck a tiny wooden spoon in it, handed it to Chloe, and then proceeded to stuff another cup, this time with a creamy-white variation of the unappetizing sludge in the first cup. Oh, what he wouldn't do for a plate of sausage or a bowl of Eurydice's lentils. He began to salivate.

He sat down at the furthest two-person table and Chloe joined him. Without a word, she dug her spoon into her cup and pulled out a mound of white goop, the whole thing covered with pastel specks and dripping with a dark, honey-like substance. After a while, when the cup was half empty, she lifted her head. She stopped eating when she saw the Orpheus staring at her, a look of repulsion still etched onto his face.

"Here, have some," she said, pushing the untouched cup of brown mush towards him. "I got it for you in case you changed your mind."

"Or in case you're not satisfied after you've finished masticating your present portion of florid excrement," he said flatly.

"My what? Have you ever even had ice cream?" His silence answered for him. "You are the strangest person I've ever met."

"And you are the *rudest* person I've ever met," he countered.

Unfazed, Chloe licked her spoon before dunking it back into the cup.

"I'm sorry," he said, reminding himself that it would be infinitely more difficult to win her trust if they were enemies. "Let's start over, shall we?"

"Fine by me. You said this would take five minutes, and so far it's been almost twenty. And all I've learned is that you and that Circe woman are wackos, and that you're a fool for thinking I won't report this to the Fantásmata." She let her spoon rest against the rim of the cup, anticipating his reaction to her words.

"You swore you wouldn't." His voice broke and he lowered his eyes with flawless dramatic effect.

"Name one good reason not to." She was clearly unmoved by his show of self-pity.

"Because you and I are the same," he whispered.

This got her attention. She sat back in her chair, her eyes locked with his.

He didn't move a muscle as his thoughts refocused on Eurydice and what he must do to join her.

Chloe's body relaxed as she pulled her chair forward and cleared her throat. "What...what exactly do you mean by 'you and I are the same'?"

"I mean I'm not the only one with a doma."

Chloe laughed and pulled at the cuffs of her long-sleeve shirt. "I'm afraid you're mistaken. There's nothing special about me, unless you count the fact that I'm one of the only orphans in Petros."

"You *are* special, Chloe. You just haven't been given your gift yet. But when you have it, everything will change."

Chloe nodded toward Orpheus's backpack on the floor next to his chair. "I'm sorry if this offends you, but I have a hard time seeing how anything could change if all I have is a lyre that knocks people out."

She doesn't know what she's saying. She doesn't know you. Orpheus felt anger and, yes, offense swell inside him. His lyre was his entire life—*had been* his entire life. And it had changed everything by bringing him his one and only love.

"You don't have to worry about receiving a lousy lyre as your gift," Orpheus said finally. "Every doma is different, or so I've been told."

"Told by whom? And where did you get your *doma*? And what if I don't want one?"

Orpheus closed his eyes, replaying her questions in his mind. Why did she have to be so inquisitive? "Told by Iris," he said at last. "As for your other questions, I'm afraid I don't have the answers. I was hoping our little adventure in Psychro Cave would have provided more insight, but we both know it was a disappointment."

"That's a bit of an understatement, don't you think?"

Orpheus laughed. She was inquisitive and had a dry wit, two qualities that weren't making his mission any easier. He wished he could loathe her.

"The thing is," Orpheus said as he recalled the lines Hermes had told him to memorize, "I only know that your gift and mine can answer those and thousands of other questions that the powers that be don't want answered. We just have to work together."

Chloe looked out the window, squinting in the low, late-afternoon sun. She considered his words. "How do you know I'll receive a doma any time soon?"

Orpheus pointed at the clouds. "Have you looked up into the night sky lately? The Moonbow appeared three nights ago. And you also just turned eighteen, like me. That's when Iris says it happens. Approximately, anyway."

"The Moonbow?" Chloe picked up her cup and slid her spoon into a smooth corner of the ice cream.

Orpheus shrugged. "I'm just the messenger." He'd heard that line from Hermes at least a thousand times. "But now that the Moonbow has returned, Iris says she will meet us and answer all our questions."

Chloe finished her ice cream, then sat in silence as more customers began filtering into the shop.

Orpheus's knees bounced nervously. He pressed them down and started to hum the calming ballad he'd played out on the street. He had until sunset to take her to Lake Thyra, the portal to Hades, and time was slipping away. The more minutes that passed, the greater his chances that something would go wrong and he would be back in the Vale of Mourning, or worse, suffering in some forsaken corner of Tartarus, the uttermost sphere of hell.

"Okay," Chloe said. "I accept the message, and I'll give you another chance. But if this Iris you're talking about is anything like the seed lady, I'm out."

"Deal," said Orpheus, using every ounce of self-restraint he had to keep from smiling like a buffoon.

"And one more condition."

Orpheus slouched in his chair and ground his teeth. Maybe he could loathe her after all.

Chloe moved his cup of muddy-brown ice cream in front of him. "You have to try this." She scooped out a spoonful and handed it to him.

Suppressing his gag reflex, Orpheus raised the spoon to his mouth and forced it between his lips. Instantly, he sat straight in his chair, his tastebuds flooding with the sensation of rich, velvety sweetness. "It isn't excrement," he said in surprise as he took another bite.

"It's chocolate," Chloe said, pressing a finger to her lip to stifle a laugh.

For the first time since he'd been alive again, Orpheus felt at ease. Freedom and happiness were so close, he could taste them, just as well as he could the delectable chocolate ice cream.

CHAPTER NINETEEN
JASPER

After waiting twenty minutes for Chloe to show up at the café, Ethan finally gave up and made his way back to his truck. He wasn't sure if he felt relieved or disappointed that she hadn't come. On the one hand, the last thing in the world he wanted to do was risk putting himself and his family in danger by revealing his long-held secret to Chloe. But on the other, he'd sensed a surge of adrenaline flowing hot in his veins as he'd considered what might happen, what might change, if Chloe knew her father's last words to him.

He'd begun to look forward to throwing caution to the wind, to telling her the truth, come what may. It was reckless, to be sure, but it was a thought that thrilled him. But she hadn't shown up, and he felt stupid for thinking that confiding in her could possibly be a good idea.

And there was a second reason for his disappointment, one he couldn't ignore. For thirteen years, since he'd first sat next to Chloe in grade one, Ethan had harbored feelings for his distant classmate, the girl who always kept to herself, speaking only to him when the subject pertained to their studies.

As a young boy, it had been her long white-blonde hair that had first caught his attention. He'd often play with its ends when they stood in line in the hallway or when she leaned over her desk while writing. But as she got a little older and her hair became darker, he began to be interested in much more than her outward appearance.

He admired the intensity with which she listened to their teachers, and the way she chewed on her pen cap when she was momentarily stymied during an exam. He had to stop himself from staring at the soft curve of her neck, and the rose blush on her cheekbones as she read during study hall.

It wasn't that she was beautiful—it was that she was lovely. It was that she stood out like a radiant white lily among an amber field of barley. It was that, despite her quiet confidence and her preferred detachment from social groups and pastimes, there was a sad loneliness that he could see clear as day when she thought nobody was watching.

But Ethan had been watching for years. And had he met with her at the café, he would have been one step closer to gaining her friendship; giving her two ears eager to hear anything and everything she needed to say, starting with how much she undoubtedly missed her parents.

Ethan felt a drop of rain splash onto his forehead. He looked up as a dark gray cloud passed over the sun and released a few sprinkles, with the promise of an imminent downpour. He saw the sign for his favorite ice-cream shop a few yards ahead and picked up his pace before anyone else around him got the same idea to wait out the rainstorm with two scoops of strawberry swirl.

Standing in line behind an indecisive gaggle of preteen girls, Ethan looked around the shop for a place to sit and do his homework. And then he saw them, sitting by a window in a far corner: a guy he'd never seen before, and Chloe.

Ethan felt his heart sink like a stone. Before he let himself feel anything else, he was out the door, walking in the rain, not bothering to pull out the umbrella stowed in his backpack.

Thunder boomed, shaking the glass storefronts as he walked past them. Twin bolts of lightning ripped through the sky just over the parking lot at the end of the block, followed by another deafening thunderclap. The wind picked up, sweeping the rain into Ethan's face and body, pricking his skin like needles.

He didn't care. The louder the storm and the stronger the wind, the less his mind could entertain feelings of heartbreak, or thoughts of shame for having tried to help Chloe despite the Fantásmata's warning.

Take it as a sign, he told himself.

It wasn't just a sign to keep Mr. Zacharias's words to himself, but to let Chloe go—from his thoughts, from his cares, from his heart. She'd had her chance to speak with him. But Ethan knew that one thing would continue to eat at him, and that was the question of who the guy was. Chloe never went out with anyone, much less someone she hardly knew.

He shook his head, laughing at himself as rain whipped his cheeks. Chloe was a private person. If she had a boyfriend, she certainly wouldn't tell Ethan about it.

He sat down on a bench beside a bus stop just as the wind and rain began to die down. He took out the leather bag from his coat pocket, the one he'd intended to give Chloe. Opening it, he pulled out the gold chain and held the smooth red rock attached to it in his palm. Ethan had seen several such stones before, while working in the museum with his mother, but this one was different. There was no patterning on it, no rinds from weathering, no orbital rings, no banding. Its simplicity is what made it beautiful. It was as if it had never been touched by water or wind, or mingled with sediments or ash; it was completely pure.

The stone was small, no bigger than the tip of his finger. He had to stop himself from imagining how good it would look around Chloe's neck, granted the Fantásmata wouldn't take an interest in it; he had a feeling that they would.

"Mind if join you?" asked a gruff-sounding voice.

Ethan looked up to see a middle-aged man with horn-rimmed glasses, a white goatee, and windblown copper hair that showed no signs of thinning. He wore brown corduroy pants and suspenders over a wrinkly button-up shirt, all of which were quickly becoming drenched.

"Not at all," replied Ethan. "Are you a fan of rain?" He zipped his coat to his chin and slipped the necklace into the breast pocket.

"Oh yes," the man said, lifting his head up to the sky as droplets splashed onto his glasses. "A cold front is moving in too, I hear. Winter might be arriving early."

Ethan nodded and rubbed his hands together as chilly air replaced the rain. "I guess it's a good thing I didn't get ice cream."

"Indeed. A nice hot tea with Miss Zacharias would have been better."

Ethan's heart beat like a drum inside his chest. If this man worked for the Fantásmata, it wouldn't do him any good to play dumb. But what would happen to Chloe if Ethan gave the man the stone?

He grabbed his backpack and had risen halfway from the bench when the man said, "I don't mean to cause alarm, Ethan. I just thought I'd better prove who I am straightaway so you'd believe the rest of what I have to say."

Ethan sat back down, though as he did so, he grabbed his keys from his jeans pocket. If things went south, he knew he could at least outrun the man, hop in his truck, and take off. It was a pathetic plan, but better than none at all.

"I'm not a part of your government," the man said, "if that's what you're thinking."

Ethan felt himself relax a little. "Who are you, then?"

"A helper," said the man, as if his response needed no explanation.

"I don't need help." Ethan stood again and slung his backpack onto his shoulder. "Have a good evening."

Ethan had run halfway to his truck when a blood-red sphere the size of a star appeared in the smoky sky and slowly began to trace a curve upward. It was as if a hand were painting it, a perfect ribbon, onto the slate canvas of clouds. He turned back to the man on the bench to see if he was watching it, too, but he had gone.

"May I see the stone?" The man was right beside him.

Ethan's eyes darted from the man to the bench, then back to the man. "How did you do that?" The man couldn't have run; he wasn't even out of breath.

"I'm quicker than I look." The man smiled. "Katsaros is my name." He extended his hand and Ethan shook it firmly.

"And something tells me you already know mine." Ethan took the bag out of his pocket and handed it over.

Katsaros untied the bag and gently tugged on the golden chain until the necklace hung from his fingers. He removed his glasses, his squinty eyes widening as he admired the red stone. "Jasper," he whispered to it, as though it were a long-lost friend.

"Would you mind telling me just how much you know about me and that rock?" Ethan asked. Then he looked up at the red arc in the sky, just as pristine as the stone, and added, "And how much you know about that."

"I know all there is to know." Katsaros held up the stone, beaming at it like a father would his newborn child. "It's been so long since I've seen it. Two thousand years, give or take."

Ethan eyed the man suspiciously. He must be crazy, a vagabond, perhaps, whom the authorities hadn't sheltered yet. That would explain his delusions, but not his knowledge of Chloe and the rock.

"Let's see if I remember," Katsaros said, and began to recite.

"Jasper, red as blood and the
Moonbow's highest band,
Carry Jasper with you in your
heart and in your hand.

Remember the bow still shines after
   darkest days are done.
Remember hope will follow you into
   bright orange desert sun."

He lowered the stone and gazed pensively into the crimson arch. "Iris loved to recite the little songs of Carya."

Ethan watched the arch begin to bend and contort as charcoal streaks of cloud crashed into it. A bolt of lightning sliced down the center, leaving flashing red sparks where the bow had been.

Katsaros knitted his brow; his reverie was shattered.

"You knew Iris?" Ethan asked. Now he *knew* the man wasn't a loon. Nobody knew about the scroll except his mother—and the Fantásmata. "You know what, that's a stupid question." Ethan kicked some gravel across the pavement and blew hot breaths onto his hands. "I can't believe I'm talking to you. Of course you work for the government. How else could you know about that scroll?"

Katsaros gave a resigned sigh. Ethan couldn't help but think he looked more like a bookish librarian than a devious, undercover agent representing the Fantásmata.

"You can't take me at my word?"

"I'm afraid not," said Ethan.

"It's as good as gold. Or should I say 'as good as amber'?" Katsaros's eyes twinkled as his inflection rose.

"Someone got himself killed for fabricating an amber scroll," said Ethan. "I suppose you know that."

Katsaros's eyes filled with sadness as he clutched the jasper stone in his fist. "The Alphas have done everything in their power to erase every shred of the Eusebian oracles. Real or otherwise."

"Is that stone a part of the Eusebian oracles?" The question felt funny coming out of Ethan's mouth, like he should be reading it from a fictional book, not talking about it so seriously.

"It's one of the only four parts left they haven't destroyed yet. But they will." Katsaros turned, scanning the dreary world around them as the rain fell once again. "They will if they have their way."

"Four parts? What are the other ones?" But Ethan didn't have to wait for Katsaros to answer. "Chloe's one of them, isn't she?"

Katsaros dropped the necklace back into its bag and handed it to Ethan. "Ethan, I've been sent here by Duna. I could prove it to you, but you may not be prepared to process what you see."

Duna. The "one true God" the Eusebians worshiped. A myth, just like every other outrageous tale Ethan had learned in school and been told were parables concocted merely for philosophical purposes. He had concluded that mythological creatures such as the gryphon, two fossils of which were now housed in the museum, inarguably *had* existed and served to inspire the grandiose—and fictitious—stories weaved about them.

As a child, he had secretly wished the myths were true, that warriors like Achilles and commanders like Odysseus really had fought endless wars and sailed treacherous seas, things no modern Petrodian could ever imagine witnessing, much less doing themselves.

But Ethan had long since done away with senseless wishing, and with writing his own made-up stories. The artifacts in the museum, including the scroll, were nothing more than old rocks, with no relevance to the world.

"I've processed more than one might guess," said Ethan, as images of the monstrous wolf, his bleeding arm, and Mr. Zacharias' miraculous healing flashed through his mind. Feeling his body tense, and his palms perspire in the cold air, he focused on Katsaros, waiting for him to get on with proving who he was.

"I said I *could* prove it, boy. I didn't say I *would*." Katsaros removed his glasses and looked Ethan dead in the eye. "There's a little something called faith that Petros has been without for far too long. I intend to help restore it. Starting with you."

CHAPTER TWENTY
THYRA

S unset was well over an hour away, but the storm
had brought an early end to the day. Every business
and street in downtown Eirene had closed normally due to
the five-p.m. curfew, but the still-open playgrounds and
picnic areas were totally empty, save for the white-suited
custodians raking the leaves and picking up trash.

Damian had thought that finding Chloe under these
circumstances would be easy. She often went to Olympus Park
to read or study, but when she he found no sign of her there

he searched the hiking trails behind the school, the cemetery where their parents—and few others—were buried, and even the hospital in case her condition had worsened.

Now he was sitting in a faded yellow swing, twisting its metal chains around and around, tighter and tighter like he used to do as a boy, winding himself up before spinning in reverse, out of control. He was on his tiptoes, ready to release the swing and twirl into oblivion, when what he'd been subconsciously waiting for all afternoon began to creep across his mind.

At first, all he saw was wet grass and Chloe's ratty white sneakers covered in mud. He let the swing go and closed his eyes as the images sped up: a big gray backpack on a man he didn't recognize; a narrow avenue lined with cypress trees; stray cats scampering out of sight; the ancient olive tree standing on the bank of Lake Thyra.

When the swing came to a stop, Damian leaned over and pressed his hands into his head. The sixth and final picture appeared: a cloud of mist rising out of the lake, and the silvery form of a woman hovering within it.

Damian stood and sent his hundredth text to Chloe's phone, though he was positive it was either dead or still in her room. Then he sent another to Maggie, briefly explaining that Chloe had checked herself into the hospital and not to worry. It was risky to lie, but he was willing to wager that neither she nor his uncle Travis would trouble themselves to visit Chloe if she ever was actually hospitalized. They probably thought he and Chloe were up in their rooms, even now.

But regardless of his guardians' indifference, he had to find Chloe soon. Otherwise, the police would send a search party for them both the second Maggie and Travis finally noticed their absence.

Despite what Chloe probably thought, Damian *did* care what happened to her, but he had to admit that that was largely because she was his twin sister and their parents were dead. He felt pity and responsibility. He felt obligation. Lately, however, he'd been feeling something different, something shapeless, vague, and brooding, like a sinister presence in the dark that can't be proven exists. Although it was frightening and unfamiliar, it didn't scare him; he'd had premonitions before.

After the car accident, he would regularly hear his sister sobbing when she was in a restroom stall on the other side of the school. Other times, he would be playing with his friends at the playground and, in his mind's eye, he would see her sitting on her bed, hugging the stuffed lion their dad had given her and repeating, "Daddy, Daddy..." over and over.

He would start to cry, sprint straight home, and sure enough, there'd she be, just as he had seen her in his head.

The visions had become so overwhelming that Damian had felt compelled to see his counselor, who assured him telepathic bonds between twins were not unheard of and would likely subside in a few years, after they'd spent enough time apart. This had proved true, as the only time they were together now was during their ten-minute drives to and from school. So why was it happening again?

He didn't have time to psychoanalyze anything right now. Maybe after he found Chloe he'd make an appointment with his counselor and take her with him. He knew that if she also had this psychic ability she'd never let on, but he needed to know; he needed to end it.

All he'd ever wanted was to be a normal kid with a normal life, and not to let the fact that he was an orphan with a weird, reclusive sister get in the way of that. If it took moving to another colony to make the premonitions stop, he would do everything in his power to do that. It would be best for both of them.

((

Damian parked his car a half-mile away from the lake and put on an old pair of cross-country cleats he kept in his trunk for rainy days. He rolled up his jeans a few inches from the ground, zipped up his windbreaker then took off across one of Eirene's condemned vineyards, parallel to the road. If anyone happened to ask what he was doing out there he would say he was just getting in some extra exercise.

A few minutes later, he slowed his pace near the top of a hill overlooking the valley and lake below. Using the camera on his cellphone, he zoomed in and scanned the white-sand beaches, which were much broader than usual due to the low rainfall that summer, and spotted the massive, gnarled trunk of the olive tree on the opposite side.

On his side of the lake, he saw two figures walking across a stretch of land that jutted into the lake. One was a tall man with dark hair, wearing a black jacket and the gray backpack Damian had seen in his vision. Though their backs were to him, he knew it was his sister beside him.

Damian pocketed his phone and dropped to his belly. What was his next move? Was the guy dangerous? What if he was just her boyfriend? How stupid would he look if he interrupted their romantic, albeit illegal, jaunt around the lake? But every premonition he'd ever had had portended something dark, depressing, or disturbing, never something as innocuous as a date.

He didn't hesitate a second longer. He jumped up and ran down the hill, skipping onto and over boulders, brushing past the brambles, not caring whether they heard him coming. He was halfway down the hill when a long stick shot out from behind a rock. Before he had time to stop, he stumbled over it and fell onto his hands and knees.

He quickly rocked back onto the balls of his feet, grabbed the stick, and crawled around the back of the rock ready to beat whomever had tripped him.

Two hands rose into the air, followed by an orange tuft of hair and the face of a forty-something man with thick black glasses and a bulbous nose. As he waved for Damian to come closer, none other than Ethan Ross poked his head out from behind another boulder further uphill and pressed a finger to his lips.

Stick still in hand, Damian crawled over to the orange-haired man. "What in Zeus' name is going on?" he whispered, trying his best not to yell. He pulled out his phone and pointed to the round, red button on the bottom. "Hurry up and talk or I'll press it, and the police will haul you off to Enochos."

"Calm down, Damian," said the man. He adjusted his glasses with one hand, and with the other he pulled the stick from Damian's hand and threw it behind him.

"How do you know who I am?" Damian glanced down at the man's ample belly protruding between his suspenders and saw that his whole body looked soft and lumpy, like it was made of dough that needed kneading. He could take him out easily, with or without the stick.

Ethan, on the other hand, would be a different story. He would have to use his cleats on him.

"There's no time to explain now." The man turned and looked down at Chloe, who now stood just a few feet from the edge of the lake. "You're here now. You'll learn soon enough. Just stay put."

"Why is Ethan here?" Damian asked.

A shadow cast itself across the hill and darkened the valley below. Damian looked up to see a dense, low-hanging wall of clouds spinning straight over their heads like gears inside a machine. Directly across, just above the mountains, the pale full moon was rising.

"This is ridiculous." Before the man could stop him again, Damian jumped onto the rock they were crouched behind, sailed over his head, and let momentum carry him down the hill, accompanied by a rumble of thunder.

He reached the lake edge and shouted, "Chloe, let's go!"

Chloe and the man she was with both spun around.

Damian gave a relieved sigh when she saw she was unharmed; in fact, she seemed perfectly calm, but he had to obey his gut. "I'm not asking questions," he said. "I really don't care. We have to go home *now*." His heart was racing, and it wasn't from running; he wanted to get out of there and pretend the day was nothing but a bad dream.

"No, *you* have to go, Damian," Chloe answered. "I'm staying here."

The strange man beside her turned and gave him a curt, dismissive nod.

Just then, a column of mist appeared on the surface of the lake where the water met the sandbar, rose to the height of the olive tree, then froze. It looked like nothing more than a vertical patch of fog at first, but Damian knew it was something more; he'd already seen it in his vision.

"Chloe, come on." He took a deep breath and threw back his shoulders, ready to grab her and haul her off against her will if necessary. "What are you doing?"

She was ignoring him now, her gaze fixed on the mist, which was now aglow with glittering specks of platinum and bronze. The man reached out his hand and rubbed her back, then drew her closer to him.

"There's a woman inside it, Chloe. Do you see her?" Damian shouted as he clenched his fists, nails digging into his palms. Maybe if he could prove his clairvoyance, his own unwanted strangeness, she'd listen to him.

The man jerked his head toward Damian. "Everything will be fine, Damian. Listen to your sister and leave it alone." He took off his backpack and set it on the ground, and Damian could sense that was his way of warning him to back off.

"She's beautiful..." Chloe said.

Damian's eyes jumped to the fog as its hazy edges fell away, carving out the silver silhouette of a woman. "Chloe!" Damian shouted. "Look at me!"

As a long, luminous arm reached out of the metallic cloud toward Chloe, the man bent down, unzipped his backpack, and pulled out a small, stringed instrument. He faced Damian with a soft, inviting smile, and began to strum.

Too confused to speak, Damian stood silent as the music trickled toward him, each note sweeter than the last. He finally took a step forward, but both knees collapsed beneath him. All his muscles tensed, and then relaxed into useless noodles as he rolled onto his side.

His ear pressed against the damp earth; he could hear his heartbeat slowing. His eyelids felt like bricks as he fought to keep them open.

The last thing he saw was Chloe joining hands with the woman, and stepping into the mist.

CHAPTER TWENTY-ONE
HADES

J ust as when she'd dived into the sump in Psychro Cave, Chloe felt nothing—no heat, no wind, no sense of time—as she moved from one realm to the next. She had, it seemed, simply stepped into the cloud with one foot, and with the other, landed seamlessly on solid ground. Although this time she had traveled from light to darkness instead of the other way around, and her eyes were taking their time adjusting from the luminosity of the mist.

As she listened to the echoes of dripping water, she was sure she was in another cave. It wasn't the least bit chilly, but it was unbearably humid.

When her vision returned, she saw Iris standing before her, still glowing with what looked to Chloe like starlight pulsing around her silver robes. Iris's long pewter hair curled up toward her naked shoulders, as though she were suspended in water. In fact, her sandaled feet were levitating half a foot above the ground and softly fluttered back and forth, sending small strings of bubbles, like ocean pearls, into the air.

Iris's eyes, oval-shaped and violet, were the only features that were clearly defined. The rest of her face was blurred by a mask of light that Chloe found almost too bright to look at. Was this what all the dead looked like? Why had Acacius looked so different after his Coronation?

These questions and dozens more raced through Chloe's mind. She would know the answers soon enough. That's why she was here.

Iris floated down to Chloe and stood at her side as the sound of an oar sliced through water.

"Where's Orpheus?" Chloe asked Iris, but her purple eyes just stared ahead into the darkness.

"Aspádzomai!" shouted a man's voice, the steady rhythm of the oar growing closer. "Do an old man a favor and light up the river, will you?"

Iris lifted off the ground and raised her hands overhead, pressing her palms together. Then, with a whoosh of sound and a streak of light, she swung back her arms. Then she lunged forward. Her arms went rigid and her extended fingertips pushed a giant ball of fire toward the voice.

After a few seconds, the ball broke apart into smaller spheres. Then, one by one, they rushed to the dripstones above and the crystals below and stuck to them like miniature lanterns fixed to a wall.

"Thank you, goddess," the man said as the form of his torso and small boat sailed into view. "This is the one?"

Iris settled back down to the floor of the cave and placed her hand on Chloe's shoulder. Turning to her, she whispered, "It is time for us to part."

"Wait, what?" Chloe said, as Iris floated like a specter toward a foamy halo of light at the other end of the cave. "Iris!" She watched as Iris disappeared into the ring.

The man in the boat let out an abrupt guffaw.

"What's so funny?" Chloe asked him as she started after Iris.

She only went a few feet before she collided with an icy, invisible wall. As she rubbed her nose and forehead, the wall began to move outward, slowly pushing her toward the water. Pressing against it did nothing to impede it. Racing to one end to slide around it proved futile, too, as blasts of freezing air shot out of a crevice at breakneck speed, causing her cheeks to flap and eyes to water. She strained to step forward, but it was no use.

She retreated back to the center of the cave, and before long her heels were hanging over the water. It only took a slight tug from the man for her to fall in.

"I can't swim!" Chloe shouted, as her arms thrashed and beat desperately against the water. She reached out to the man, but saw not a hint of compassion in his steel-gray eyes. "Please help me!" she screamed, as briny water spilled into her mouth.

"I didn't know the Vessel could be so dumb," the man grumbled as he extended his oar to her.

She latched onto it and climbed into the boat, coughing and shivering while the man chuckled and dropped the oar's blade back into the water.

"The river is only five feet deep." He stroked his long, hoary beard, then balled up a blanket beside him. "For the dainty Vessel," he said, throwing it at her.

She quickly dried herself as well as she could, and wrung out her socks. Then, with teeth chattering, she said, "Who are you? And where are Orpheus and Iris?"

"I hate to be the one to tell you this," he said, as his lips curved up into a toothless smile, "but you've been made a fool." He stood, plunged the oar into the water, and pushed off from the riverbed. "You mustn't feel too bad about it. Immortals have an unfair advantage, what with all their tricks and centuries of experience."

Bracing herself on the wooden rail, Chloe rose and considered jumping back into the water. There had to be a way out of this situation.

"Ah-ah-ah," the man warned as he began rowing backwards, turning the boat. He pointed at the river as a row of red fins pierced the surface, followed by a black, fan-like tail. "It seems the woman you call Iris has sent her pet to serve as your guardian." The fish, or serpent, or whatever it was, circled the boat, its long silver body forming a fence around it. "Not that you could escape even if Cetus were absent. It's impossible for humans to ascend to Petros without the aid of an immortal."

"Why?" she asked, then moved to the center of the boat and hugged her knees to her chest. It actually made her feel a little safer.

"You have no idea where you are, do you?"

Chloe just stared at him, then flinched as the creature's tail pounded the water.

"You're in Hades, girl. I'm Charon, ferryman to all the cursed shades who have crossed the threshold upon which you find yourself."

His words echoed as they passed under a low archway and entered a narrow stream or tributary of some kind, every inch of it lit by walls of fiery magma. Chloe could see nothing—nothing but the monster swimming nearby, its sharp fins bobbing in and out of the water as its tail swished and whipped violently against the boat.

"I must say that it's good to be at the helm again," Charon continued. "It's been weeks since my last crossing." He looked at her with curiosity and scratched his chin. "And I can't remember the last time I ferried someone as young as you."

Tears welled in Chloe's eyes. Her breaths became short and shallow. The tip of her nose burned as she fought the impulse to cry. "Are my parents here? They died eight years ago. Their names are Damara and Nicholas."

She scooted toward him and waited until he acknowledged her with a sideways glace, a glance that gave her the answer, whether he wanted it to or not. "Take me to them, Charon, please!" But he hung his head and shook it slowly. "I'm not the Vessel, I *promise*. Listen to me. I don't even know what the Vessel is."

"Don't look to me for pity, girl," he rasped. "The only vessel I know is the one I'm sitting in. I only do as I'm told. I learned to cooperate with the Fates a long, long time ago." He leaned forward, stopping mere inches from her face. "And *you* should do the same."

Chloe stared at the infinite blackness above as tears slipped out of her eyes. *Where are you, Carya?*

((

Damian jolted awake as ice water splashed across his face. He opened his eyes to see Ethan and the other man from the lake kneeling over the couch he was lying on, their own faces moist and smudged with dirt.

"What happened?" He looked around and saw that he was in a strange house. He could hear the spurting and crackling of coffee brewing in another room. "Where's Chloe?"

"Orpheus charmed you to sleep," said the man. "I'm Katsaros. We met earlier."

"I remember," Damian said as he tentatively shook the man's hand. "Thanks for your help earlier." He rolled his eyes and swung his legs around to a sitting position.

"We had to keep our distance, Damian," said Ethan. "Or we would've been affected, too."

Katsaros lowered his head and peered over his glasses. "I told you to stay put."

Damian shook his head back and forth, as if rattling his mind would bring clarity. "So you know about this stuff? You're friends with this guy?" He looked to Katsaros. "Who are you, anyway?"

"I'm learning as I go," Ethan said, then stood and handed Damian a plate of cheese and sliced apples from the coffee table.

"I'm not hungry."

Ethan shrugged and took the plate for himself as Katsaros sat on the couch. "We're here to help your sister, Damian," said Ethan. "We're on the same side."

"What are you talking about? Has everyone lost their minds?" Damian sprang off the sofa and drew back the curtain behind it. His jaw hung agape as he saw, centered high in the midnight-blue sky, the biggest, brightest rainbow he'd ever seen. He looked down at his watch: 4:16 a.m.

"The meteorologists say it's called a Moonbow," Ethan said. "Apparently it's only the second one in recorded history. The first was three nights ago."

Damian brushed sand out of his hair. "And?"

"Damian, there's one thing you must realize about your world," said Katsaros, his hands folded neatly on his dirty lap. "It's ruled and run by liars."

"What does that have to do with a stupid rainbow?" Damian asked, giving the Moonbow one more glance before closing the curtain and plopping back onto the couch.

Damian waited for Katsaros to offer an answer, but he remained silent and looked to Ethan, who was fiddling with something in his coat pocket. A few seconds later, he produced a tan leather pouch and loosened its drawstrings.

"Damian, I know you don't know me that well, or Katsaros, but you just have to trust us," Ethan said as he leaned forward, propping his elbows on his knees.

As if anticipating Damian's next question, Ethan looked at the portly stranger with equal parts reverence and bafflement, as if he still wasn't sure what to make of him. "I trust Katsaros," he said, turning back to Damian, "because he's the only one who's been able to explain things that haven't made sense to me my whole life." He let out an easy breath as he upended the pouch and let a thin gold chain fall into his hand.

"Like what?" Damian asked.

"For one, he knew who the guy with the lyre was, the instrument that sedated you. He's an ancient musician who's been recruited by Apollo to lure your sister to Hades, in case you're curious. For two, Katsaros told me what this means." Ethan shook the jasper necklace out of the bag and handed it to Damian.

"Whoa, whoa, whoa," Damian said, letting the necklace hang from his forefinger. "Did you just say Chloe's been taken to Hades?"

"I should probably jump in here, Ethan, if you don't mind," Katsaros said.

Ethan sat back in his chair and nodded for Katsaros to continue.

"There's far more to your world than anyone could possibly fathom." Katsaros took a sip from a delicate teacup that looked like it might shatter inside his large, puffy hand. Although it was never intended to be this way." He looked into the teacup and shook his head. "No, no this won't do," he muttered, then set the teacup on the end table and tapped his goatee. "There's no time for a history lesson."

"But Hades exists?" asked Damian. His brain had stopped registering words after the phrase "lure your sister to Hades" had stampeded through it.

"Oh yes, I'm afraid so," Katsaros said, a smile spreading across his eyes, " but so does heaven."

"How do you know?" Damian asked. He noticed that Ethan was smiling, too, clearly convinced that this man wasn't stark raving mad.

"Because I know. I have friends who have been there." Katsaros said it so casually that Damian wondered if they were talking about the same heaven. Katsaros's brow wrinkled with no-nonsense sincerity. "Your questions will be answered in due course, Damian. I give you my word. But time, though it is an obsolete dimension in heaven, is running away from us." He reached up and pulled back the curtain; instantly, his face and arm were splashed with the lustrous colors of the Moonbow.

"Wow," Ethan and Damian said in unison as they watched the colors slowly undulate back and forth like sunlight reflecting off a swimming pool.

Katsaros closed the curtain, though a diaphanous streak of ruby-colored light still lingered on the tips of his fingers. "The stone," he said, pointing to it. "It represents the precious blood of a deity who sacrificed his life to save Petros. It was handed down through the generations, for thousands of years. It belongs to you, Damian. And to Chloe."

Damian placed the red rock on his knee and stared at it blankly, waiting for his gut instinct to set off his alarms and bring him to reason. Waiting for common sense to kick in and send him straight to the authorities to turn this man in for *paráxeno theáseis*. Waiting to stop wasting his time.

But he couldn't. Despite himself, he refused to just walk away. How could he run back to "normal" after learning that normal was all a sham? And if Katsaros *was* crazy he wanted to find out firsthand.

Damian grabbed the rock and squeezed it in his fist. "Will this help me get my sister back?"

"That," Katsaros said, "is up to you."

CHAPTER TWENTY-TWO
VESSELS

C hloe's eyes flew open as the reverberations of a booming bark rocked the boat like a gale-force wind.

Charon stood above her and planted his oar in the riverbed. "Sweet dreams?" he grinned, his brown teeth almost black in the shadows.

Chloe pushed herself back into the corner and shuddered as the sea monster's dorsal fin made a threatening pass, then slid into a cleft in the only part of the wall not glowing red with lava. She was glad the thing never showed its head; her nightmares had enough material to haunt her for the rest of her life...or the rest of her death.

"So," Chloe began, not believing she was actually asking this question, "am I still alive?"

When the ferryman didn't answer, she turned, following his eyes, and made out a mossy haze fifty yards ahead, and within it, a three-headed dog the size of an elephant, stalking back and forth, the thunderous barks growing louder and more frequent as they drew closer.

If I'm still alive, I won't be for long. But what could she do? She was trapped, lost in the bowels of Petros with a shark-like python beside her, a ferocious hound up ahead, and a heartless old man who would have no qualms about feeding her to either one of them.

"You still got a heartbeat?" Charon asked.

Chloe pressed two fingers to her wrist and nodded.

"Your body's still warm?"

Beads of sweat were rolling from the nape of her neck to the small of her back. *Who wouldn't be warm in this place?* "I'm burning up," she said, fanning her face with both hands.

"Then you're not dead." Charon waved toward the shore. "Cerberus, my handsome friend. Save an old man's shoulders, will you, and bring us in?" He sat down and rested the oar across his lap. "Do you like hounds, girl?"

Chloe winced as she heard the splash of the dog's giant paws stomping into the water. "Please don't do this," she whispered, her voice trembling.

"Do what?" said Charon, tightly wrapping his cloak around him.

"Please don't kill me."

Chloe could hear Cerberus grunting and snorting as he neared the boat. With three heads, at least it would be over quickly.

Charon threw his head back and laughed. "You're the Vessel, girl. I couldn't kill you if I wanted to. Neither could that old cur."

He motioned for Chloe to move closer, then stepped around her and extended the oar into the water. She watched as the second of Cerberus's three heads gently took the oar blade in its teeth and with a guttural growl began dragging the boat backwards toward the shore.

Each head of the beast was surrounded by a lion's mane, but in between black locks of hair there were clusters of red-bellied snakes, all writhing and hissing as they darted and struck at one another. Cerberus's long gray tail was sinuous and thin, itself like an enormous snake as it slithered in and out of the water. He snarled and bared his teeth when she looked at his eyes, six yellow, vacuous orbs with white-hot pupils that dilated each time he growled.

Chloe placed her shaking hands on the sides of the boat, closed her eyes, and squeezed as she took in three full breaths, just as her counselor had taught her. It had always proven a futile exercise, but now, its uselessness was almost laughable. How could one's nerves be calmed or stress quelled in a literal hell?

Chloe opened her eyes and tried to take comfort in Charon's assurance that she couldn't be killed.

Cerberus picked up his pace, grunting as he pulled the boat out of the river and slung it across the sand.

"Stupid dog," Charon huffed, as he yanked the oar from Cerberus's mouth and slid it into the oarlock.

Chloe was struck by how starkly different the shore was from the black, volcanic river. She stepped out of the boat and looked out into the labyrinthine void she had traveled through, the convex walls foaming with magma, the soupy, sulfuric air nearly suffocating. The climate here, just a stone's throw from the other, was tolerable, even balmy, and though there was no sun, she was glad for the additional light.

Up ahead lay gentle slopes of vibrant, green grass, and a gray mountain range in the distance carved from a crystal-blue slate of sky. She could even detect the faint chirping of birds and a mellifluent lyre like Orpheus's playing along to their melody.

Just another trick, she told herself. And then she thought of the old man Acacius and his Coronation, which she and her classmates had witnessed a decade ago: the rolling, emerald hills bursting with yellow and lilac flowers, the majestic herd of horses, and the golden palomino on which he'd loped away. That might as well have happened here, thousands of miles beneath Petros's surface, if she really was in Hades.

Chloe watched Cerberus slink away toward a wall of solid marble, at the center of which were iron gates as tall as the Folóï oak trees that grew outside of Limén. The creature turned clockwise, then counterclockwise, and collapsed into a formidable heap of muscle and teeth, all three sets of jaws gleaming like brand-new knife sets as he panted and yawned, his eyes fighting to stay open.

"Can you tell me what I'm doing here now?" Chloe asked as she turned back toward Charon.

But the ferryman was already inside his boat, rowing away and waving until he rounded a bend and disappeared, unwelcoming whirlpools eddying in his wake. She wouldn't try to follow him anyway, not with that monster swimming around.

"I will oblige, dear Chloe."

Chloe spun around to see a young redheaded man floating four feet up in the air. He was wearing an indigo, knee-length tunic secured with a rope around his waist and was holding a short gold staff by his side. On his head was a furry brown hat, and on each of his sandaled feet fluttered a golden pair of wings.

He grinned and crossed his arms, dimples deepening the longer he looked at her. "Have a nice journey?" he said.

Chloe hated him already. "Who are you? Why am I here? Where's Orpheus, and who was the woman that brought me here?"

She heard Cerberus bark and saw his heads shoot up, alerted by the commotion. But Chloe didn't care. If she was going to die—or if, as Charon said, she couldn't die—she at least wanted to know the reason.

"I am Hermes, humble messenger of lords Hades and Apollo. Come, and I will answer all of your useless questions," he said, smiling amiably despite his insult.

"I'm not going anywhere with you." Chloe sat down cross-legged and folded her arms like an obstinate child.

The man sighed and scratched his head with his staff. "I swear, there is never a deviation from mortals' insistence on being complete imbeciles."

He started making circling motions with the staff, but before Chloe could ask what he was doing, she, too, was hovering in the air. "I thought perhaps you would be an anomaly, but I see you're just the same." Chloe was being pulled toward him, though every muscle in her body strained with resistance. She slammed into the man's chest and he took her wrist, swinging her out to his side. "I don't recommend letting go," he grunted, squeezing her hand so hard she was sure it would break.

In three seconds, they were a quarter-mile above the wall, speeding toward the jagged mountains, into the lands of the dead.

(

Ethan thanked his mother as she poured his new friends and him a cup of coffee. They'd been up all night and were still talking, still processing all that Katsaros had told them.

If it didn't make such perfect sense, Ethan would've mistaken the past twenty-four hours for a stress-induced dream, something he could take a pill for and forget all about. And if Katsaros hadn't been able to answer every single one of their questions without fault, Ethan would have dismissed him as a lunatic or a liar and reported him to the police. Certainly, if his path hadn't crossed Mr. Zacharias's all those years ago he wouldn't be in this situation in the first place.

He looked at the clock on the kitchen wall. It was a quarter to eight, time to go to school and act normal, but there was still something he needed to do before courage abandoned him.

"Damian," he said, in a voice so serious his mother stopped washing dishes and leaned against the sink to listen. "Your father gave the jasper stone to me, just before he died."

"Oh, honey." Lydia Ross put a hand to her heart. It was clear she wanted to say more, but she pressed her lips together and waited for him to continue.

He wondered what secrets she could be keeping, what secrets anyone could be keeping but were too scared to reveal. For the first time in his life, Ethan realized that every statute, law, and stringent regimen, while they gave the illusion of facilitating a safe, well-oiled utopia, were nothing so honorable. Everything the Fantásmata had established, from the curfews to the Coronations and every edict in between, was meant to foment fear, to keep every Petrodian silent, submissive, and utterly controllable.

But why? Why didn't the government condone people talking about "strange sightings?" Why didn't they allow his mother to continue excavating just as she was making progress? Why did they find it necessary to search a little boy's room for clues about a perfectly good man? And why did that good man have to die?

They had to be afraid of something themselves. But what?

Damian took the jasper stone from the table and set it in his hand, regarding it as something different now. Something dearer. Then he shook his head, questions replacing sentiment. "Why did he give it to you? You're not related to us...are you?"

Both Ethan and Lydia shook their heads.

Lydia pushed the dishwasher closed, turned it on and took a seat at the table. She turned to Damian and laid a hand on his arm. "You can trust me, Damian." She turned and nodded lovingly to her son. "So can you."

"You know about all of this?" Damian asked.

Lydia shook her head. "I've had my suspicions that something alerted the Fantásmata, ruffled their feathers, shall we say. It started eight years ago, right before your parents were killed."

She cracked her thumbs and placed a long strand of brown hair behind her ear. "I'd seen your father walking along the beach where we were digging. He never told me how he was allowed to be in Ourania, and I didn't ask. He was always curious about what we found, but usually I had nothing interesting to show him. Until one day..." She closed her eyes and lowered her chin toward her shoulder, her mouth tugging downward, her chin quivering.

Ethan's breath caught in his chest as the wolf, the blood, and the closed-up gashes flashed across his brain. Did she know what Mr. Zacharias could do, that he could heal people with his touch, even bring himself back to life?

"Take your time, Mrs. Ross," Katsaros said. He folded his hands on the table and closed his eyes, then whispered softly to himself.

Lydia pressed her lips together and squeezed her eyes a moment as she drew a deep breath through her nose. "One day your father approached the team and seemed a little bit flustered. He asked for me. He said he wanted to show me something." She swallowed hard and eyed the stone in Damian's palm. "He led me about half a mile inland, to the limestone hills we'd excavated years before and found nothing in except some ceramics."

"He'd found something else?" Damian asked.

Lydia nodded as she rubbed the diamond in the center of her wedding ring. "There was a fissure in the northernmost cave, cave one, we called it. It was barely wide enough for a person to walk through sideways. None of my team had noticed it before." She pushed her chair from the table and stood up. "I'll be right back."

Ethan leaned back and clasped his hands behind his head. "Katsaros, we have to go to school in a few minutes. What will they do when they find out Chloe's missing?"

"They'll search, of course," said Katsaros. "But they won't find her. It's impossible."

"Because she's in Hades." Damian almost laughed as he said it. It was, without a doubt, a ridiculous-sounding notion.

But Ethan had seen too much to laugh off anything anymore. "If—when—we get her back," he said, "what will the Fantásmata do?"

"You're asking the wrong question," said Katsaros. "The question is: what will *she* do?" The boys exchanged glances, then waited for the sage to stop philosophizing and start expounding. "You two mustn't get ahead of yourselves. One step at a time."

Lydia reentered the kitchen, rolling a nondescript suitcase behind her. She hoisted it onto the table and tapped it on the side closest to Damian. "Open it," she said to him.

Damian hesitated a moment, pushing his tongue into his cheek. Ethan was tempted to open it for him, but finally Damian reached forward and slowly unzipped the luggage from end to end. Inside were seven small, ordinary amphoras lined up in a row; they were all alike save for a faint arc of color painted onto the bottom of each one. The jar farthest left was marked red, followed next by orange, yellow, green, blue, deep purple, and violet.

Ethan and Damian both moved closer, warily eyeing the jars. As they reached out their hands to pick one up, the sound of a rushing wind filled the suitcase, scaring them so badly they nearly tumbled out of their seats.

"What is *that*?" Damian shouted.

"This has never happened before," Lydia shouted back, her hands muffling her ears.

Ethan's eyes shot to Katsaros, but he sat calmly, staring at the jars as they rumbled and shook, louder and louder, harder and harder, until even the table legs rocked off the floor and crashed back down again.

Ethan hopped up and helped his mother take the coffee cups and saucers to the counter. When he turned around, Damian was leaning over the table, gripping the suitcase on either end, his entire body shaking furiously as the Vessels roared and rattled against each other.

"Damian..." Ethan started. But before he could finish his question, the wind went silent, and the jars stilled. Damian's eyes widened as he stared into the suitcase. "What is it?" Ethan asked.

Damian's hands relaxed as a thin red bolt of lightning shot out of the suitcase, disappearing just inches from the ceiling. "Whoa!" He yanked his hands away and backpedaled toward the wall.

A rosy cloud of smoke drifted down to the table. Next, six more flashes of light erupted out of the suitcase, following the color sequence of the jars, orange all the way through to violet.

After they'd waited for the onset of any further surprises, Katsaros walked over to Damian and watched with him as the last misty swirls of blue and purple dissipated. "It seems your sister isn't the only Vessel."

CHAPTER TWENTY-THREE
IDENTITY

That's what he meant," Ethan said, his hands pressed against his cheeks as he leaned against the counter and stared at the suitcase, dumbfounded. "He had a doma, like Iris."

"Who? My dad?" asked Damian. Ethan nodded. "What did he say? Who's Iris?"

Ethan turned on the faucet and splashed his face in the sink. All of this was fitting together like pieces in a jigsaw puzzle, and his brain felt hot, firing on all cylinders just to keep up.

"Your dad saved my life, Damian." Ethan looked to his mother, but her expression was placid, as if this was the most normal conversation in the world.

Anticipating Damian's next question, Ethan continued. He might as well reveal everything he knew; it was too late to turn back now. "It was on vocation day in grade three. I was with my mom at the ocean and had wandered off to the north shore to take a nap."

For the next few minutes, Ethan recounted the entire episode with the wolf and Mr. Zacharias. When he finished, he rolled up his shirtsleeve and showed Damian the chalk-white scars below his elbow.

Damian turned to Katsaros. "Is this possible?"

Katsaros pointed to the jasper stone gleaming on the kitchen table. "I told you it was passed down, generation to generation. You should know that the generations you come from are unlike any others in history."

Back at the museum, Ethan had come so close to telling Chloe about Iris and the power—the so-called doma—she had, power he thought was purely mythical. He'd had the opportunity to tell her what her father had said hours before his death, but he'd waited too long. He wouldn't miss his chance now.

"A few days after the incident with the wolf," Ethan told Damian, "your dad came up to me during one of our track meets. I was benched because my elbow was still hurting, but I'm pretty sure it was all in my head. I was still a little shaken up." Ethan caught himself rubbing his elbow even as he spoke. "He asked me how I was doing, how school was, all normal stuff. And then he told me I was the only one who knew his secret, and said he wanted to know if he could tell me one more."

Lydia wrapped her arm around his waist and squeezed her encouragement into him.

"'When my kids turn eighteen, tell them this,'" Ethan said robotically, concentrating on reciting the words verbatim. "'The Moonbow is the warning and the way.'" He paused, then looked away from Damian to the stone. "Then he gave me that. Told me to give it to one of you after you turned eighteen. I'd planned on giving it to Chloe. I guess I thought she'd take it better." He gave a little laugh as his mother patted his back.

Damian didn't crack a smile, or react at all, for that matter. He just stared at the checkered linoleum floor, and Ethan couldn't blame him. In a matter of hours, Damian's whole world had been turned topsy-turvy. Before, his biggest problem had probably consisted of applying to various programs at the university. Now it was figuring out what it meant to have a supernatural gift, not to mention retrieving his sister from hell.

"Damian," said Lydia in a soothing, maternal tone as her arm slipped from Ethan's side. "Why don't you take a look inside the first amphora, the larger one on the left."

Damian gave her a distrustful sidelong glare, then stared down at the suitcase as if daring it to come alive again.

Katsaros fetched the amphora for him and set it upright on the table. "Come see," he said, flicking its side with his finger. Then he bent over and peered into the opening. "Ah, yes," he said, smiling at whatever was hidden inside.

"Look at it, Damian," urged Ethan as he glanced at the clock. "We have to go to school."

Damian frowned. He parted his lips to speak, but then closed them again and scratched his neck. Like Ethan, he seemed to be realizing that returning to the status quo wasn't an option.

"Fine," he said. Then he strode over, grabbed the amphora by its neck, flipped it over and shook it, sending a huge chunk of charcoal onto the table. "What is it?" he asked, carefully picking it up.

"A scroll," said Lydia. "It was preserved in amber originally, or so we think, based on the ancillary fragments we found."

"A scroll? It's a *rock*," argued Damian, holding it out for her to see.

"Take a look at the end," she said.

Ethan walked over to Damian to examine the object himself. The ends did indeed look like rolled-up pages that had been petrified somehow. "How did it go from papyrus to this?"

"I suspect it has something to do with whatever catastrophe destroyed Ourania two thousand years ago," said Lydia. "Fire would've been involved, that's for sure."

"Have you opened it?" asked Damian.

"It would fall apart," Ethan answered before his mother had a chance.

"I have, actually," she said.

Ethan took the scroll from Damian's hand and studied it closely. It looked like a fireplace log, charred and dented, with deep grooves winding around it. It was incredibly dense. He was sure that prying it open would shatter it into thousands of useless pieces.

"In ordinary circumstances," Lydia continued, "something that old would be too fragile to handle, much less to study with your bare hands. It would require X-ray imaging, a particle accelerator. But its integrity has been preserved. It's quite remarkable."

"You've never taken this to the lab, or recorded it?" Ethan asked her.

Lydia shook her head.

"Very wise," Katsaros chimed. "The Fantásmata would love nothing more than to burn it to a crisp."

"Why?" asked Damian, taking the scroll back from Ethan, his fingers circling the rigid, bark-like curl of the pages.

"It was written by Iris," said Lydia, "who it seems was one of your ancestors."

"Here, man," said Ethan, handing the scroll back to Damian as goosebumps popped up on his arms.

Damian sat down and gently began to unroll it, revealing immaculate sheets of papyrus, inch by inch. "That's not possible," he said.

Soon, the whole thing, no more than a single page, was laid out flat on the table, almost glistening under the modest chandelier above it.

"Would you like me to read it to you?" Katsaros asked Damian as he pushed his glasses onto the bridge of his nose.

"Do I have a choice?" said Damian.

"Of course," said Katsaros, the facetiousness obviously lost on him. "We all make our own choices."

"Damian wants you to read it," Ethan assured him.

Katsaros took the scroll by its rough, black edges and lifted it to his face. Then he looked down at Damian, prompting him to object before he proceeded, but no objection was made.

"Red, the highest band, color of blood and vice,
I have learned to see within you
     redemption, sacrifice.
Orange, like the healing flower, and
     the burning desert sun;
Both have power, both hold brilliance, but
     none compares to the Promised One.
Yellow for the amber scrolls, prophesying
     salvation amid our strife;

Your shimmer is a just shadow in
*   the light of eternal life.*
Green for the stone I carry, a symbol of
*   forgiveness, growth, and mirth;*
But nothing can bring as much happiness
*   as a dying soul's rebirth.*
Blue, the color of Carya's sword that
*   cut us free from prison;*
But the greatest freedom I have felt flows
*   from faith that Phos has risen.*
Indigo, hue of an opaque void, the
*   barrier between Petros and glory;*
Its power has been stripped away by
*   the Finisher of our story.*
Now violet: triumphant, royal, reflecting
*   clouds in this bathing place,*
I will emerge boldly from these waters, an
*   orphan found and saved by grace."*

"The first symbol." Katsaros picked up the jasper stone by its chain and placed it in Damian's hand. "'Color of blood and vice...redemption, sacrifice,'" he said, repeating the words of the poem. Then he reached into the suitcase and removed each of the remaining amphoras before turning them on their heads.

Ethan and Damian flipped the jars upright as Lydia neared the table, her eyes marveling at the odd assortment

237

on display: five bright orange petals, a small block of amber, an emerald, a dagger surrounded by a thin film of light that glowed electric blue, an indigo strip of cloth, and a tiny, iridescent vial closed with a cork.

"Maybe now I can know what all this means," she said.

Katsaros lay the indigo cloth across his hand and stroked it tenderly. "They were all part of Iris's path. And now," he said, turning to Damian, "the path has intersected with yours and Chloe's."

Damian shook his head slowly as a hard line appeared between his eyebrows. "This doesn't make any sense. How would my father have known about this?"

He grabbed the emerald and placed it side by side with the jasper stone. Then he stood up and jabbed his forefinger into Katsaros's chest. "And how do you know about this?" He stepped forward, aggressively pushing Katsaros back until the bewildered man stumbled against a cabinet filled with china.

"Hey hey hey," said Ethan, hurrying to Katsaros's aid. He pulled Damian off of him and shoved him back toward the table.

"You boys better get to school," said Lydia as she returned the objects to their respective jars. "You can resume this conversation later."

"And what about my sister?" Damian fumed, kicking the leg of the nearest chair. "I'm just supposed to go on about my day like everything's just fine, like my sister isn't missing, isn't in Hades like you all say she is?" He spun around to Katsaros. "How do I know you haven't kidnapped her or something?" Then he took a step toward Ethan and pointed his finger at him. "How am I supposed to trust *any* of you?"

"Damian, calm down," Ethan said. "This is a lot to take in, but you ju—"

"But nothing." Damian threw the jasper stone to the floor. "You can have your rock back. I'm reporting my sister as missing. I've had enough of this."

With that, he rushed into the entryway and let himself out, slamming the front door behind him.

Katsaros straightened his suspenders and dusted off his pants. "I told you, we all make our own choices."

☾

Damian was turning the corner onto his street when he remembered his car was on the side of the road near Lake Thyra. He glanced down at his cellphone to check the time, but—no surprise—it was dead. He sighed and pulled his keys from his pocket, then jogged toward the garage to see if his bike had air in the tires. He couldn't be late. He really wasn't in the mood for detention, or an interrogation from the headmaster.

As he turned the key in the side door leading into the garage, he heard a car pull up behind him, followed by two doors shutting and footsteps coming toward him.

You should have gone straight to the police, he thought.

"Damian Zacharias?"

Damian turned to see two hulking police officers in hunter-green uniforms standing in the driveway, each holding a hand to the holstered Tasers on their hips.

"I.D." said the shorter, broader of the two. His arms were twice the size of Damian's and all muscle. Damian pulled out his I.D. card and handed it to the officer. "You want to tell us why your vehicle was found nine hundred meters from Lake Thyra?"

Damian gritted his teeth, debating whether he should tell them the truth, tell them everything, like he told Ethan and Katsaros he would. His sister couldn't really be in hell. Hell was a myth, a legend invented by ignorant, uncivilized people.

His mind flashed back to the jasper stone and the suitcase, and Ethan's story about his father... All of that could easily have been fabricated, too. Why Katsaros and the Rosses would conspire against Damian and Chloe in such an outlandish manner was beyond him, but the Fantásmata could get to the bottom of it, and Damian would certainly be rewarded.

And then he remembered the Moonbow, how its seven colors had streamed through the window, covering Katsaros's arm and face, and how the red light had lingered longer than the rest, symbolizing "blood" and "vice" and other things he couldn't remember. That much had been real, and for that reason alone he couldn't tell them the truth.

"I went running through the old vineyards after school and my car broke down," he said.

"Funny," said the taller officer. "It started just fine for us."

Damian shrugged. "It has a mind of its own."

"Uh-huh. And where were you all night?"

Damian looked down at his damp, dirty jeans and wrinkled shirt, then picked at the grime on the back of his ears and neck. He put on a shameful face and looked up at the policeman with bleary, apologetic eyes. "I slept by the lake. I was too tired to walk home."

"You could've called someone or alerted the precinct with the alarm," said the short one. When Damian showed him his dead cellphone, the officer grunted and took a few steps back to confer with his partner.

Damian's heart thumped nervously in his chest. He forced down a lump in his throat as his hand began to sweat around his keys. They were sure to find a hole in his story, or come up with more questions that would stump him. He'd be cornered eventually. Why delay the inevitable? No one fooled the Fantásmata, at least not for long.

The stocky officer walked back to Damian as his partner returned to the car. "We'll have your car taken to the school. Now clean yourself up and get to class."

"Yes, sir," said Damian with a respectful nod.

"And kid," the man snapped, "keep your phone charged. It's for your own safety."

"Will do, sir."

Damian's knees went slack as he watched them drive away. He grabbed onto the doorknob, leaned against the wall and exhaled hard, as if he'd been holding his breath for minutes. He was off the hook, although for how long he had no idea. It was only a matter of time before they noticed Chloe was missing, and when they did, he wouldn't get off so easy.

CHAPTER TWENTY-FOUR
EPIPHANY

Orpheus extended his arm in salute to the guards at the palace gates, but they continued staring straight ahead without so much as a twitch to acknowledge his presence.

"Open the gates." Orpheus stepped between them and placed his hand on the iron latch.

"Remove your hand, bard," one of them growled, "or I'll cut it off."

"I'm here to see Apollo," said Orpheus, backing away, "with news of the Vessel."

"He's heard your news," said the other man, turning to Orpheus with an indignant sneer. "Your uncle will be here shortly to escort you back to the cesspit you came from."

"This is *outrageous*!" Orpheus shouted. "My father and I had a bargain!"

He lunged toward the guard closest to him, and in one swift motion ripped the spear from his hand and angled its tip toward the man's throat. Two seconds later, he perceived the blade of the other guard's sword poised next to his ear. He could fool no one pretending to be a soldier.

"Stand down," said the armed guard coolly. "Sing us a song if you like, then get out of our faces until Hermes arrives."

Orpheus did as he was told and handed the guard his spear. His face hot with both rage and humiliation, he pivoted fast and plodded down the black, basalt hill from which he'd come. Sing them a song? Never. But he would *play* them a song...

He hopped over a wall of red scoria rocks and leaned against it as he pulled the backpack off his shoulders. He kissed the lyre's crossbar as he dragged it out and tickled his fingertips on six smooth strings. "Bring me luck," he whispered.

He began to play a Delphic hymn, one of the first songs he'd ever composed, in honor of Apollo. Though each note made his insides seethe, he knew it was the perfect choice for subduing the loyal sentinels, half-witted souls who bowed blindly to the prince of Hades.

"Cover your ears!" he heard one of the guards yell.

Orpheus shook his head. Not even balls of beeswax, like Odysseus used against the Sirens, could stop the melody from trickling into their thick skulls and enchanting them. He stood up and strolled leisurely up the hill, swaying to the music as the guards spun in circles, banging their weapons together and spitting out gibberish at the top of their lungs.

"I wanted to spare you your dignity," Orpheus intoned. "But you've forced my hand." He knelt down and began the song again, this time slowing the rhythm. The guards' spears fell to the ground as their voices faded and their eyes glazed over. "Watch me turn Apollo's trusted sentries into worthless house cats."

The guards groaned and sank unceremoniously against the gate, their chins drooping onto their chests.

"Sweet dreams," Orpheus said.

He removed the men's swords from their scabbards, kept one for himself, then flung the other down the hill toward a multilayered outcrop of pumice. When he heard the guards' snores and saw their limbs twitching, Orpheus kicked them onto their sides, lifted the latch, and let himself into the palace.

☾

Orpheus's stomach lurched at the smell of blood permeating the throne room. The last time he'd stepped foot in it had been the day of his death, when Hermes led him to the three judges of the dead who resided in the sweltering heart of Tartarus. He recalled that it had smelled intolerably of rot and brimstone, but this...this was the smell of death, of open tombs and decomposing flesh.

The air was thick with the stench, a putrid blanket of smoke pervading the atmosphere as he coughed and choked against it. Unable to see two steps ahead of him, he hugged the lyre to his chest, fearful it might fall into a blaze and be carried off into the Phlegethon River.

"Apollo!" he shouted, the rotten smell latching onto the roof of his mouth. He gagged and picked up his pace, anxious to exit the cloud of plague before he fainted.

Whisperings floated to his ears, and finally the smoke tore apart just enough for him to make out the great black throne and two figures standing beyond it. Before them, a fall of murderous red magma roared as it cascaded from the igneous stratum above. The noxious scent persisted. He zipped his jacket to his chin, pulled it over his nose and mouth, and continued.

"Apollo, the mission is done." As he called out, waves of a tar-like substance gushed down, masking the magmatic tide.

The figure wearing a glinting horned helmet—Hades, no doubt—raised his arms to either side. Apollo motioned for Orpheus to come forward.

Orpheus gripped his sword, chuckling nervously. What good would a sword do him here? He'd have better luck with his lyre, although neither wounding his father nor rendering him unconscious would bring him closer to Eurydice. He removed his hand from the sword and tossed it aside, resolved to see how far civility could get him.

"Where is Hermes?" asked Apollo as Orpheus approached.

"I couldn't say. With the Vessel, I presume." Orpheus stood at Apollo's side, mere inches from the precipice, just a nudge away from the volcanic cauldron below. He took a step back.

"How did you get here?"

Orpheus held up his lyre. "There was some confusion with the guards. I thought a good long nap might clear their minds."

"Ah, and what was the confusion?"

Before Orpheus could respond, Hades' gilt armor clanged as he dropped to a knee and fell onto his back, a twisted expression of both agony and ecstasy etched into his sunken gray face. He closed his eyes and began to squirm and jerk, a dark red cloud wafting toward him from the inferno.

A shiver snaked up Orpheus's spine as he saw the amorphous cloud take shape, spinning and shedding its vapor as it carved itself into dozens of outstretched arms and fingers, all scratching for Hades, hideous faces calling his name.

"What is all this?" Orpheus asked Apollo, pointing first to the wall of flowing magma and then the phantom mist now descending upon Hades, encircling him.

Wailing and emitting earsplitting screams, Hades' chin was tilted back, inviting the crimson brume to enter his open mouth. And enter it did, curving up in an exaggerated arc before it nosedived down, nebulous faces and flexed fingers shrinking to fill his nostrils and blow through his parched parted lips.

But Orpheus didn't have to ask again. The laurel leaves secure in his satchel were still feeding him knowledge of the modern world, including what the mortals knew as *Coronations*. "So the Coronations are sacrifices," he said.

He could now see that the tar covering the magma was not tar at all, but fresh Petrodian blood.

Apollo glared at him out of the corner of his eye while Hades sucked in the last misty sinew and puff of cloud.

"Where are the dead?" Orpheus asked. "Where are their bodies?"

"Don't be daft," Apollo said. "The bodies are in their graves, being devoured by insects and worms like any others. "Their souls bypass the Styx and fly to the judges. You do remember, don't you?"

Orpheus nodded slowly and thought back to the Vale of Mourning. He wondered how many there had been sacrificed. How many lives had been cut short in order to sate the appetite of reprobate deities? How many, like Eurydice, had not been ready to leave the brightness of life for the shadows of death, even death spent in Elysium?

In all his countless years spent languishing in that woeful plain, Orpheus had never once approached anyone and asked to hear their story. He'd thought that doing so would only wrench his heart all the more, and besides, he only cared to speak to one person, the woman who lived on in his memories, and in his songs.

"Where is Eurydice?" he said, gritting his teeth as Hades groaned, still supine on the floor of smooth, volcanic glass. "I've done what you asked. Thetis took the girl into the portal last night."

A smile tugged at Apollo's lips as the cascade of blood weakened to a trickle. "She isn't here."

Orpheus shook his head, frustration pounding against his temples. "Of course she isn't here. She's in Elysium. Take me to her!"

Apollo placed a cold hand on his shoulder, the yellow pupils of his cerulean eyes radiating like the noonday sun. "You have made me very proud, son. In return for your loyalty, I'll intercede on your behalf before the judges and persuade them to reassign you to Elysium."

The living blood in Orpheus's veins began to boil as his hands started to tremble, shaking uncontrollably until they loosened their hold on the lyre and let it fall to the floor. He should have kept the sword. He shouldn't have hesitated to find out what happens when a deathless god's head goes rolling.

"Where is she?" he yelled, jerking his shoulder free of Apollo's hand.

Hades stood up and charged at Orpheus, driving him toward the throne as he kicked the lyre over the cliff's edge. With Hades' fist in his stomach, Orpheus watched in horror as the instrument spun down, down, down until it pierced a spitting red bubble and sank into the fiery torrent.

"Enough!" Hades shouted, his breath a freezing, rancid mist against Orpheus's face. "Your father is generous with his own offspring, but I am not so patient."

He picked Orpheus up by his collar and, with one arm, held him out over the crag. "Your choices are these, and these alone: you may follow after your precious lyre and have that pitiful mortal frame you're wearing eaten away by fire, after which you return to the Vale. Or, you may ascend to Petros again as you are, still pitiful and as wretched as ever. And when your time comes, you, too, shall have a Coronation."

He lowered his arm, black eyes staring down at Orpheus as his pale lips curled into a snarl. "Make your choice."

Feeling the heat of the fire on his soles, Orpheus looked down at his feet and the black stone altar rising up from the burning sea, overflowing with blood. He wasn't afraid; he'd died before, at his own hand. It hadn't been so different then, hanging from the fig tree where he'd first kissed Eurydice. His feet had dangled there just the same, hovering helplessly above the pit of death. There, the last flicker of hope had died, just as it was dwindling now.

But something was undeniably different. A gnawing feeling in his gut was urging him to survive, an unexpected burst of adrenaline rousing the instincts he'd repressed for so long. He wanted to live. He *needed* to live.

For once in his unfortunate existence, he wasn't going to let death win.

"I choose to live," he said, carefully articulating every syllable so Hades couldn't misunderstand.

Hades grunted and tightened his grip around Orpheus's throat. He pulled the poet closer to him, a blue vein bulging down the broad center of his forehead as he whispered, "I look forward to watching your blood fall when they pierce you with the needle and suck your life away." Then he twisted fiercely and threw Orpheus at Apollo's feet. "Any final words for your son, brother?"

Apollo peered down at Orpheus with an unfeeling scowl. "The All-Powerful took your Eurydice. Not I." His words were tinged with both hatred and discomfiture, as if he were admitting a weakness. "It is impossible for you to get her back. Tell me, why torture yourself by continuing to try?"

Orpheus coughed and felt his neck where Hades' hand had squeezed. "I was born for torture, was I not?" he rasped.

After a few steady breaths, he stood, squared his shoulders, and searched Apollo's face. Could this man—this monster—

truly be his father? He could see no resemblance in his marble face, no trace of himself in the arrogant way he walked or in the merciless manner with which he devised lie after lie, scheme after scheme. The only similarity between them was their mutual love for music.

"What being," said Orpheus, "with your blood running through him, is not destined for anguish all his eternal days?"

The glowing centers of Apollo's eyes flared wide as he stiffened his neck, chin tightening as Orpheus waited for him to speak, or run a sword through his heart. This could be Orpheus's last opportunity to speak to his father; he wouldn't hold anything back.

"Is that why you've always defied the All-Powerful?" Orpheus asked. "Why you've made Petros forget him? Because his disciples served him willingly and rejoiced over him, and yours are trapped and chained?"

Orpheus paused as the clearest of epiphanies whispered within his heart. "So that's why you loathe me so," he said, "and detest the mere thought of our reunion—because Eurydice chose to follow the All-Powerful before her death. Everything I've seen of her—the mission to retrieve her from hell, the vision in the Vale, the brood of vipers in her cell—was all an illusion, a perverse ruse meant to satisfy your sadistic need to see me suffer."

Orpheus's heart beat powerfully, freely, emboldened by the truth of the words ringing within his veins. "You will drink the bitter cup of justice, Father. The All-Powerful will see to it soon enough."

Apollo's eyes blazed obsidian as thin red capillaries traversed his face, masking it with fury. He grasped the ivory hilt of his sword, sorely tempted to ignore Hades' judgment and decapitate him now, then feed his head to the fire. "And what do you know of the All-Powerful?" he said behind clenched teeth.

Orpheus stepped forward and regarded his father with a wry smile. "Only that you fear him. And that you fear the Vessel and his plan for her."

"I fear *nothing*." Apollo's chest was heaving. "It is *you* who should be fearful. I would gladly cut your throat this second if it weren't for the anticipation of your blood draining onto the altar from whatever unmarked hole they throw you in."

"Does a man fear death again after he has already tasted it?" Orpheus asked. "Is it any more bitter a second time?" He felt his face softening, his smile fading as the revelation alighted upon him, like a lark landing gently on his shoulder. "I don't fear you, neither do I fear Hades and his vile ritual. If it's my destiny to be dismembered now or become entangled later within a bloody haze of spirits, so be it. I only fear not finding out why the All-Powerful has led me this far."

"The All-Powerful is *dead*!" Apollo screamed, unsheathing his sword.

A strange peace settled on Orpheus, wrapping around him like a cloak, clinging tightly, comforting him as he caught his reflection in the bronze blade. A draft of cool air spiraled down from the ceiling's pointed pendants, carrying with it a faint *ting* sound. It was completely foreign at first, but as the sword was lifted, the sounds became a song, dulcet notes floating on the air, soft as butterfly wings. It was his ode to Eurydice, sung on his happiest days as well as his darkest.

And then he knew. He would be with her again.

"No he isn't, he is very much alive," Orpheus whispered. "And Eurydice with him."

With one swift thrust of the sword, the song faded, and blinding light consumed him.

CHAPTER TWENTY-FIVE
ASPHODEL

Chloe held her breath as Hermes shifted his weight forward until their bodies were parallel to the ground. He pointed down at the silvery meadow rising toward them and a slow-moving sea of people.

"The Fields of Asphodel," he said, his voice falling through the windless air, alerting only a handful of curious souls. "Your new home."

When they were still a few feet from the grass, he pulled her toward him and shoved her onto a hillside, knocking the air out of her.

She flipped onto her back, gasping for breath that wouldn't come, then scooted backwards as fast as she could as Hermes weaved his wand in a figure of eight above her, turning her clothes into a sleeveless, coarse brown bag. He held a hand over his mouth, snickering at her as she wheezed and slowly stood up.

This can't be happening, she thought. She'd eaten the other walnut and forgotten about it. That was the only explanation. She would get home—or wake up—just like last time; she just had to know how.

"Where's Carya?" she said at last. "The girl who gave me the walnuts."

Hermes tapped his chin with his wand and lowered himself to the ground. "Carya, you say?"

What was she thinking? She couldn't expect him—whomever he was—to tell her the truth. And for all she knew, Carya was never on her side to begin with.

"Never mind," she said. "At least tell me why I'm here."

"I take orders from no mortal." Hermes bent over and plucked a white flower from the parched earth, then began twirling it in his fingers.

"You told me you'd answer all my *'useless'* questions, remember?" She looked around at the people nearby, who were all dressed in sackcloth as they picked flowers and dropped them into wicker baskets on their arms. They couldn't have seemed less interested in the girl who'd just dropped from the sky.

He placed the flower stem between his teeth and crossed his arms, eyeing her with disgust. "You're far too gullible, my dear." He spit out the flower and tucked the wand into his belt. "No matter. Even if you had your questions answered, they would do you no good here, I'm afraid."

"So why won't you tell me if doing so won't help me anyway?" She narrowed her eyes at him. "What if you're holding back because you're afraid you'll reveal something I can use?"

Hermes' nostrils flared and his fingers twitched around the wand. "What if you're a fool, trapped in the belly of hell, still holding onto the moronic notion that escape is possible? You're helpless here. Is your feeble, mortal mind incapable of grasping that?"

"So I'm not dead, then," Chloe said, placing a proud hand on her hip. "You just answered one of my questions. Stick around any longer, Hermes, and you might be in danger of answering more."

"What's better? To be dead in hell, or alive in hell knowing that when time runs its course your heart will stop and your spirit will reenter the Styx a second time and be flown here once again?" He shook his head in mock pity of her.

Pretending to ignore his question, Chloe noticed an old man and woman leaning against a dead olive tree, asleep, their baskets overflowing with flowers. She began walking toward them.

"Go ahead," said Hermes. "See if they can help you."

Chloe slowed her pace and turned toward him.

He howled with laughter as he rocketed into the sunless sky in the direction they'd come from. "Farewell, Vessel!"

Refusing to let tears form, Chloe filled her lungs with the dry, stale air and continued toward the resting couple, though she had a sickening hunch that Hermes was right and they wouldn't be able to help her.

The man's eyes fluttered open as he heard her footsteps. He yanked his basket toward him, guarding it as though it were filled with gold.

Chloe lifted her hands. "I'm not going to steal from you, sir. I just wanted to talk to you." From his blank look, Chloe knew he didn't understand a word she was saying.

"He doesn't speak Petrodian."

Chloe turned to the old woman, her small brown eyes like pits stuck inside a shriveled date. "My name is Chloe Zacharias," she said.

The woman tapped the man's arm reassuringly and glanced at Chloe as she said something in Próta. "I'm Anastasia," she said to Chloe, "and this is my friend Calix."

"How do you know Próta?"

"Most of us speak both languages. We've been here long enough to learn them." She nudged Calix's elbow. "This one's never been much for conversation. I'm the only one he lets keep him company. Zeus knows why."

The old man hacked and spit carelessly into the grass, then tipped his head back and closed his eyes.

"May I?" asked Chloe, motioning to the ground. Anastasia nodded and moved her basket, making room for Chloe to sit beside her. "I like your flowers. What kind are they?"

"I don't know." Anastasia took a handful, arranging them into a small bouquet. "They're all that grows here, though. They're very precious to us."

Chloe forced herself to smile, still fighting the thick feeling of imminent tears tugging at the back of her throat. "They're beautiful."

Anastasia held the flowers to her faintly whiskered chin and breathed them in. "No fragrance, really. But sometimes my nose makes one up, and I smell..." She frowned and laid the bouquet on her lap. "I don't know what I smell, probably just nonsense. That's all we speak, anyway."

"Do you know anything about Hermes?"

Anastasia cocked her head sideways and began fiddling with the frayed ends of her frizzy white hair. "Hermes?"

"The man who flies." Chloe pointed to the sky. "He just brought me here."

The old woman's eyes widened with understanding. "Ah, the Free One. That's our name for him. He carried all of us here. Never someone as young as you, though."

Anastasia paused a moment, her wrinkled mouth agape as she examined Chloe's face. She reached out with her knobby hand and stroked the side of Chloe's head, then smiled and touched her cheek.

Chloe winced at the cold palm on her skin.

Anastasia pulled away and tugged on Calix's collar, speaking again in the old language. Then she whipped back around to face Chloe.

"Why are you warm-blooded? You're hot like...like..." she stammered, waiting for the word.

"Like fire?" said Chloe. "Because I'm not dead." She paused, unsure how that revelation would be received. But when Anastasia closed both her hands around one of Chloe's, she continued. "Hermes called me 'the Vessel.' Do you have any idea what that means?"

The old man smacked his lips and muttered, his beady gray eyes boring into Chloe's.

Anastasia translated for Calix, and his tan face washed white as his basket fell from his hands, toppling onto the ground.

"What's wrong with him?" Chloe asked. If it weren't for the fact that he was already dead, she'd swear he was having a heart attack.

Anastasia's joints popped as she turned and crawled closer to him. "Speak up, Calix," she said gruffly. "What's troubling you now?"

Calix pointed a bony branch of a finger at Chloe, his eyes shifting to Anastasia. "Asher," he whispered.

Chloe placed a hand to her chest. "Chloe," she said. "My name is Chloe."

Frustrated, Calix shook his head and latched onto Anastasia's shoulder, using it to struggle to his feet. He pulled the old woman up after him and dragged her backwards, out of Chloe's earshot.

"It's not like I can understand you anyway," Chloe uttered under her breath. She leaned against the rough, denuded tree and held her stomach as it rumbled. The last thing she'd eaten had been the cup of vanilla ice cream with Orpheus.

Her appetite vanished at the thought of him. It was his fault she was here, his fault for thinking domas were toys to be played with. But deep down she knew it was her fault, too.

How stupid she'd been to trust him, to blindly follow him to Psychro Cave and then to Lake Thyra. Chloe had always wondered why the Fantásmata required that all strange sightings be kept secret and reported, but now she knew. It was because they led to hell. For all she knew, Orpheus would be joining her any second—if he hadn't already been arrested for questioning regarding her whereabouts.

Chloe jumped away from the tree at the touch of Anastasia's cold hand on her shoulder. She turned to see Calix digging on hands and knees in the hard, cracked soil beneath the tree.

"What's he doing?" Chloe asked.

"Chloe, Calix seems to think that you're an Asher," said Anastasia.

"Is that good or bad?"

"You don't know what an Asher is?"

"I have no idea. Maybe Calix is a little, you know..." Her finger did circles around her head. "Senile, maybe?"

"He said you have something called a 'doma.'" Anastasia rubbed her colorless lips together as she peered down at Calix, still digging like a madman. "Normally, I'd say that he's speaking nonsense, but all nonsense here comes from what we know and remember. And we remember nothing of life or the world we came from. I've even forgotten the *name* of the world." Her voice cracked as she stared up at the bare, desiccated branches.

"Petros," Chloe said.

Anastasia's eyes lit up with recognition. "Petros, yes. Our own names are all our minds have retained."

"What happened?"

Anastasia lowered her head, eyes anxiously scanning the dirt as she wrung her hands. "The river," she grimaced, as if the word tasted sour. "The second we drank from the river, our minds, our memories, were erased."

Chloe gazed toward the horizon, then spun in a circle. She didn't see a river, only endless hills that appeared snow-covered in flowers. "What river?"

Anastasia took Chloe by the hand and led her up the hill. When they reached the top, she pointed to a large gully, at least fifty feet wide, cutting through a hill directly across from them.

"It fills up with water four times a day." Anastasia grabbed Chloe by the shoulders and shook her hard, her long nails stabbing her. "You mustn't drink from it. You *mustn't*."

Chloe didn't have to ask her why. Anastasia had stated the answer plainly. One drop of it would mean the closest thing to bodily death. What could possibly be worse than existing as a veritable shell of your former self, devoid of memories, passions, secrets and dreams, without even the slightest idea where smells come from, what fire is, with no remembrance of your family...

"I won't." Chloe knew she would have to die before allowing the faces of her parents, and Damian, to be ripped from her mind. What about her parents? Were they imprisoned down here, too? Would they know her if she saw them? Did they even know one another?

Hunched over and huffing up the hill, Calix made his way toward them, his bald speckled head facing the ground as he held a hand to his ribs.

"He must have found what he was looking for," said Anastasia. Then she went to him and put his arm over her shoulder, helping him along.

Chloe noticed a silver object protruding from Calix's skeletal fist. He babbled something to Anastasia and placed the item in her hand.

"He says this is for you," Anastasia said, "from a messenger by the name of Carya."

"Carya?" Chloe's heart skipped a beat as hope gripped it like a vise. She held out her hand. "May I see it?"

Calix spoke again, much more rapidly than before, repeating the words "Asher" and "doma" as Anastasia scrunched her brow, trying to keep up.

Anastasia gave him a wide grin, revealing black gaps where teeth used to be. "The messenger was sent by the All-Powerful, he says. She entrusted him to be its keeper until you arrived. A wise woman, this Carya, for choosing the soul who has but one friend." She handed the cylinder to Chloe.

Chloe flipped open the cylinder's sandy lid with her thumb and slid out a crisp, off-white scroll. She hastily unrolled it, only to find that not a single word had been written on it. "Is this some sort of joke?" she said, incipient tears stinging her eyes.

Calix cleared his throat to get her attention then tugged on his earlobes. Chloe shrugged helplessly, sure by now that

he was nuts. But then the sound of a soft inhale ruffled the
scroll's edges and lifted its center, as if breathing it to life,
and a girl's familiar voice began to speak.

The realm you stand in as I speak
    was never meant to be,
The brothers who rule it changed
    forever the course of history.
Their pride rose up against Duna, seeds
    of sin made them scream, "More!"
With their free will they chose a path
    of treason and cosmic war.
Petrodians were tempted, polluted and deceived,
They fled the All-Powerful's shelter,
    and a new plan was conceived.
Asher was the first to write the oracles down,
Prophecies pointing to a savior king
    who never wore a crown.
Phos, his name, for he was light,
    sent from Duna's throne,
Battled Apollo in the heart of the sea,
    where he bled and died alone.
Though it seemed that all was lost,
    his death marked victory,
For he broke the chains of darkness
    and set the captives free.

A new age dawned for all mankind; a
  time for Petros to believe or deny,
Many accepted and followed the Way,
  while others let truth pass them by.
The Ashers—your family—were tainted by
  one whose sin-sick heart turned black,
Who was corrupted in youth, deceived and
  seduced, all part of Apollo's attack.
A new wave of evil washed over the world,
  all traces of Phos were destroyed,
Man's connection with Duna was completely
  erased, replaced by Hades' void.
The Moonbow, bright sign of redemption,
  placed long ago in the night,
Has appeared again to signal an ending
  to hell and Petros's plight.
The brothers foresaw a coming Vessel,
  for Iris's prophecies they read,
How quickly they forgot: Duna is
  always ten steps ahead.
And so they've plotted and prepared, poised
  to pounce should an Asher rise,
For although they cannot kill you, they
  can corrupt you with their lies.
There is a way, there always is, to
  escape the enemy's snare,

But you must seek it first with a
  single, heartfelt prayer.
Your doma is not enough, for to
  faith it must be tied,
Strength and wits can save no mortal,
  nor heaven's gates be pried.
You have never been alone, despite
  your many years of sadness,
Duna's eyes have been upon you; he
  can fill your soul with gladness.
The old man and those around him who
  wander through these vales of dust,
Can be restored with all of Petros, if
  in Duna's might you'll trust.

The scroll jumped to the grass from Chloe's fingertips and curled closed on its own accord. With all feeling draining from her limbs, she shrank onto the ground in frozen silence while Anastasia interpreted the message for Calix.

Carya's words swirling thick in her mind, Chloe watched as the pair locked arms and began to dance, pure joy shining through their eyes and infusing their faces with youthful euphoria. She marveled at the miraculous way hope could transform people, even if it was founded on nothing but delusion.

"You believe this?" Chloe snatched the parchment and crammed it back into its container.

Anastasia stopped dancing and held a hand to her collarbone as she caught her breath. She kneeled beside Chloe and tucked her blond hair behind her ear. "Sometimes it takes falling into the pit of Petros to start believing in the impossible." Her eyes welled with tears as she leaned in closer. "I wish you could meet all the men and women here who have been praying for centuries to an unknown, unknowable god, pleading with him to help us." She smiled at the sky, her moist eyes twinkling. "And he heard us. He heard us..."

CHAPTER TWENTY-SIX
NIGHTMARE

Chloe awoke to the wetness of saliva pooling around her chin. Rolling onto her back, she noticed a constellation of green, glowing stars stuck to the ceiling. She then realized that her head was supported by an abnormally squishy down pillow—*her* pillow. The sheets she clutched were teal with white polka dots, and at her feet was folded a patchwork quilt—*her* quilt.

Her antsy eyes darted right, where a shaft of warm light shone through the window, illuminating dust particles in the air.

She threw off the covers and ran to it, hardly registering that the plush carpet had been removed and replaced by a surface that was hard and scalding hot against her soles. With a yelp, she scampered toward the window on her tippy-toes, desperate to see the sunrise and hear the morning birds.

Behind her, something fell to the floor with a clear ringing sound then skidded toward her. She held her breath and turned around, cold beads of sweat beginning to trickle beneath her sackcloth tunic. She looked down to see Carya's silver cylinder glinting up at her.

"Carya?" she whimpered, but she knew, by the malevolent presence she could sense drawing closer, that Carya was nowhere nearby. In the darkness that filled the rest of the room, she could see nothing except the outline of the bed, just another trick.

"I'm afraid not."

The voice sounded as though it were made up of many voices, some grating and shrill, some breathy and childlike, and others low-pitched and gravelly, all with a mechanical, almost robotic, undercurrent running through them. It sent a chill straight through to Chloe's bones.

"Did you sleep well?"

"Where am I? Where are Calix and Anastasia?"

Chloe leapt to the window and seized the iron bars, using them to pull herself up off the scorching floor. She sat on the narrow stone ledge and pressed her nose through the bars, straining to view her surroundings. There was nothing but fiery red sand dunes as far as the eye could see, and a sky tinted a nauseous shade of green, the color of mold. It was a scene from a recurring nightmare she used to have after her parents died, one a drug from Doctor Leandros had banished. *I'm dreaming*, she told herself.

"No such luck," called a young man's voice.

A bolt of neon-red lightning flashed past Chloe's ear with a terrifying roar, striking behind her with a deafening crash. She jerked back as the bars began to buzz with an electronic hum, closing together no matter how hard she pulled against them. She gave up trying when her knuckles were within centimeters of each other, seconds away from being smashed.

Thick trails of smoke filtered in from outside, and with a cough, she sprang back down to the floor, only to find more smoke billowing, forming a dense cloud around the conflagration that used to be her bed. She wondered which would make her pass out first: the fumes or the pain of third-degree burns on her feet. The part of Carya's message that said she couldn't be killed was of little comfort to her; she would rather die than be tortured and toyed with.

"Don't fret yourself," said the first voice, or group of voices. "We let your friends be after we forced the poppy capsule down your throat. Now tell us, what was in the Vessel, *Vessel?*"

The floor turned to ice beneath her feet, which promptly sizzled and stung with relief. She picked up the cylinder and emptied the rolled-up parchment into her hand. "Could you not see for yourselves?"

"Watch your tongue, or I'll slice it in half."

Out of the smoke stepped the owner of the voices: a tall, wild-eyed man a little older than Chloe, with bulging black eyes and two-inch-long fangs protruding from his mouth. From neck to ankles, his body was covered in what appeared to be lion's fur, and his feet were cloven hooves. His hands were humanlike, save for the tawny curved talons he had for fingers; Chloe realized he *could* slice her tongue in two. She also discovered the reason for his strange voice: he was four, perhaps five, animals in one.

Just as she was about to speak, the other being leapt in front of her on all fours, a leonine tail swishing against her shoulder and cheek. He began to unfold upwards onto his human feet, and her gaze rose along with him, meeting his slanted, green feline eyes.

He, too, was a hybrid creature, half lion, half man as far as she could tell. His lion's head was framed by a short, shaggy mane, and his furry arms and legs were covered in brown rosettes, indicating to Chloe that he was young as well. His extremities, however, were completely human, as was his adolescent voice.

"Speak politely, Deimos, or let me change the scenery. She'll not talk if she's scared out of her wits." He pivoted toward Chloe, his round pupils dilating. "What's it like to be living in your own nightmare?"

"She isn't scared, she's stupid," said Deimos's horrid harmony of voices. "Some Asher you are." He began to stalk the width of the room, his tasseled tail swooshing violently back and forth. "What's your doma, anyway?" He turned to his brother. "Phobos, I think there's a very real possibility that our overlords captured the wrong mortal."

Phobos dropped to all fours and lunged forward, taking deep whiffs of her through his muzzle. "I don't sense any power in you." He yanked her hand toward him and flicked it hard with his finger. "No fire in those palms, like your ancestor, Iris?"

"You're right," said Chloe, pulling back her hand. "There's nothing special about me. This has all been a mistake." It was a lie she'd believed as truth until Carya's message had arrived. And still she had no clue what to do with it.

"Duna doesn't make mistakes," said Deimos. "We know he sent you the message. There's no other means by which it could have entered the Fields."

"We intend to find out what it said." Phobos's hot breath reeked of sulfur. He spat at the cylinder in her hand before backing away. Then he lifted his hands and began chanting something in Próta.

A faint squeaking noise followed, and Chloe's eyes caught movement from a crevice in the corner of the limestone ceiling. The squeaking grew louder as a pair of wings flapped open.

"We heard that you like bats." Deimos smiled, clicking his talons against each other.

Chloe felt herself beginning to panic. How did they know she had a fear of bats? Ever since she'd been to the zoo and learned that a species of bat subsists on blood, she'd been terrified of them.

She turned and hugged the wall, squeezing her eyes shut and breathing as deeply as she could to keep her anxiety at bay. She heard the bars on the window beside her groan, and then watched as they were snapped like twigs and ripped out of their bracket by an invisible force.

A black cloud of rushing wings flooded the empty space and descended upon Chloe, the bats' tiny claws scratching through her tunic, their harsh squawks and high-pitched squeals piercing her eardrums. She crumbled to the floor and covered her head, feeling the bats pull and tangle her hair. After a few minutes, she began to scream. A few seconds after that, she began to cry.

"Enough," she heard Deimos say. He was standing close, apparently looking on her torment with pleasure.

Phobos chanted once more in Próta, and the bats disappeared in an instant, though their echoes still grated inside her ears.

"If you won't cooperate with us," Deimos said, "I assure you we have plenty of methods that will get you to talk."

Chloe pressed herself up and sat against the wall, her tear-drenched hair stuck to her face. As a salty teardrop entered her lips, she was overcome with thirst...and immediately remembered the River Lethe. How long until she begged for water and forgot everything—and everyone— she ever knew?

She could see no harm in telling them what Carya had said. They already knew she was the so-called Vessel. She was already trapped in a simulation of her utmost fears, surrounded by devils that would love nothing more than inventing new ways of making her suffer. Nothing could get worse.

"She told me I was the Vessel," she said. "That's isn't news to you."

"And what of your brother?" Phobos said, his mouth pulled back tightly in a snarl, revealing black gums, and every one of his canines and sharp incisors.

Chloe's heart pounded. She thought of Damian standing behind her at Lake Thyra, pleading with her to go home with him. How had he known she was there? Why had he been so concerned? Normally, Damian couldn't care less about what she was up to. He must have known something. Maybe he'd had strange sightings of his own. Whatever the case, she couldn't risk getting him involved in this, even if she ended up drinking from the Lethe and forgetting she ever had a twin.

"She didn't mention Damian," she said flatly.

"That's not what we heard the fat man tell him," said Deimos, the high register of his voice overpowering the others. He pawed impatiently at the floor with his hoof. "He told him he's the Vessel as well."

"What fat man?" They'd truly lost her this time.

"Your brother has befriended someone with some sensitive information," began Phobos as he waved a hand toward the wall, beckoning the bars to return to the window, "which would greatly interest our masters if we prove it to be true."

"I don't know anything about that. All I know is that a jerk named Orpheus told me we both had domas and promised we would meet a woman named Iris who'd answer all our Asher questions." She couldn't help but laugh at the ridiculousness of her words. It was more preposterous than anything she could think up for her cartoons. "I never met a fat man."

"A decoy, perhaps," murmured Phobos. "She's the Vessel," he said, louder. "Duna wouldn't have prevented us from observing her the last few days if she wasn't. The brother is meant to confuse us."

Chloe shrugged and started picking at her cuticles, trying in vain to get her mind off her parched tongue, which was presently glued to the roof of her mouth.

"We'll keep our eye on you," bellowed Deimos's baritone. He nodded to Phobos. "Wine."

Phobos cupped his hands together and whispered into them a conical gold cup, the shape of a donkey's head.

"Should we learn of your deceit," Deimos said, "I will hold your head under the Lethe until it empties itself of every memory, leaving black weepy holes where images of your sweet mother and loving father used to be. And then I will waste no time securing an identical fate for your cursed twin. Seems appropriate, does it not?"

Phobos laughed uproariously and handed the red wine to Chloe, purposefully sloshing some onto her tunic. "I have a better plan," he said, as a long string of drool broke away, falling into the cup. "Just because there's never been two Vessels at once doesn't mean it couldn't happen." He knelt beside her, an amber eye reflecting the dying firelight behind him.

"Pray tell, what is your plan?" said Deimos.

Phobos continued to stare and sniff at Chloe, as if her scent or body language might give something away. "We act preemptively. We go to Apollo and deliver our concern. He will dispatch Hermes to go and lure the brother, just as his shrewd sister was lured."

Chloe set the wine aside as she turned her face away. But Phobos grabbed her chin and jerked it toward him, pinching the skin. "You'll be reunited with your brother after all."

Chloe wanted to scream at them, to plead with them to uncover whatever decency, whatever shred of compassion they might have, buried deep beneath their callous words and heinous exteriors. But despite herself, she couldn't speak, nor cry, nor move.

Then she was overcome with a feeling of stillness, an uncanny quiet falling like snow, spreading from her heart to the top of her head. An inner voice, like a ray of sun through a wintry sky, whispered through it: *Call to me...*

Phobos sneered at her silence, then skulked away from the wall and stood beside Deimos.

"A good plan," Deimos said, nodding to his cohort. He turned to the burning bed. "Phobos, be a good host and give our guest a new bed. The dirty floor won't do for the blessed Vessel." His myriad voices erupted in a chorus of sardonic laughter.

Phobos raised his hands and waved them through the air, conducting a symphony of dark magic as he incanted another spell. Seconds later, a new bed appeared over the debris of the last. The comforter folded back and the pillows fluffed all by themselves. "Get your rest. We'll throw a welcoming party when your brother arrives."

Then Phobos snapped his fingers, and the tormentors vanished, leaving her alone, yet somehow not feeling so.

"Duna?"

As she whispered the name, a soft haze of light poured in through the iron bars, stretching into the cell, suffusing it with the golden gleam of moonlight. Chloe froze as the wine beside her evaporated from the cup, making room for water bubbling into it like a spring.

She took the cup and drank, cautiously at first, just a drop to note its effects. When nothing happened, she tested twice more, and still she felt just the same. Finally, she gulped it fast, only to see it refill again, and then once more until her thirst was slaked.

Her mind remained clear, her memories intact as life, and hope, flowed into her veins.

"Thank you, Duna." She looked into the light, and began to weep. And then she prayed, for the first time in her life. "Please...help me."

CHAPTER TWENTY-SEVEN
ORACLE

Damian lay awake in his bed. He had tossed and turned all night, rehashing in his mind all that had transpired since his odd encounter at Lake Thyra. The lady in the mist, the Moonbow through the window, Ethan's story about his father, the suitcase filled with magical jars... None of it made sense, and yet he couldn't bring himself to report a word of it. He felt paralyzed, stuck inside a deep, troubled sleep he couldn't snap out of.

He had to choose a side. It had never been his nature to stay neutral on anything, and for the first time in his life he felt himself siding with his heart instead of his head. No matter how hard he tried, he couldn't dismiss the claims of Katsaros, Ethan or Lydia as conspiracy. They resonated with him. They stirred something inside him, opening a compartment of his brain—or his soul perhaps, if there was such a thing—that demanded attention.

He shouldn't have left Ethan's house. He should have reined in his temper and given himself time to process the barrage of information instead of rejecting it altogether. But he'd never been one for temperance.

A bird pecked at the window. He turned to face it and was relieved to see that morning was still a good ways off. It'd been the longest night off his life; one he wished would never end. In just a few hours, Chloe's absence would be noticed at school, and that, he was sure, would mark the beginning of a very long, very thorough, very ugly investigation.

Nervous energy coursed through Damian's body. He made a clicking noise with his tongue as his hands drummed along the side of the bed. He lifted his head and repeatedly dropped it against the pillow.

When his pulse picked up, he kicked off the covers and rocked onto the floor, feeling the sudden urge to run or to wrestle, anything to burn off this anxiety. He didn't have a key to the gym, but he could hit the track early. With the meet coming up, no one would think a thing if they saw him running sprints at five in the morning. That's what he would do: run until his brain and body were too exhausted to bother him with useless whys and what-ifs.

☽

Damian had planned to grab a pair of running shorts out of the laundry room. But instead, he found himself standing in his sister's room looking for her dumb diary. He didn't know why, other than that his subconscious probably figured she might have left some sort of clue as to what was going on with the weirdo at the lake, not to mention the whole Hades hypothesis.

Although it'd been years since he'd stopped stealing it from her, he knew exactly where she kept it: on her desk between a set of bookends crammed with all her reference books. But it was gone. Above its place, an unshelled walnut sat wedged in the gap.

"Well, that's new," he said.

He sat in her chair and examined the desk for any other random objects. He quickly spotted a steak knife popping out of either end of a spiral notebook like a bookmark. "What in the world, Chloe..."

He shook his head as he slid the knife out and stared at the walnut. He'd never cracked open a walnut before. He pierced the seam at the end of the nut and twisted the knife like a key inside a lock. He set down the knife and easily dislodged the walnut meat with his fingers and popped a piece into his mouth. Then he got up, and started toward the door.

"Damian," a voice whispered.

Damian spun around to see a girl standing beside Chloe's armoire, her white robe glowing as if bathed in sunlight although the blinds were closed, concealing any hint of dawn. She wore a diamond-encrusted coronet in her auburn, waist-long, hair, and pearlescent sandals on her feet. The hem of her garment fluttered, though the closed window forbade any breeze. She was a goddess from the mythology books come to life.

Damian opened his mouth to speak, but his tongue refused to move. He'd never seen anything so beautiful. Her sparkling blue eyes smiled at him as she placed a delicate hand to her heart.

> "It is with joy that I deliver the news
> of your sister's prayer,
> I come in peace to tell you she's
> cried out from Hades' lair.
> The truth has been revealed to you;
> there isn't need to doubt or fear,
> The time has come at last; a new
> beginning begins here."

She took a small step forward.

Damian followed her gaze to the walnut halves and the pried-apart shell on the desk. "Uhhhh...was I not supposed to do that?"

Thankfully, she didn't appear angry. He had a hunch that offending a goddess wouldn't be pretty, especially if she was anything like the ones that populated the myths of Olympus.

A soft smile parted her lips, and she began to speak again.

"I gave a walnut to your sister, as
    well as the choice to eat,
In faith she took, and with her eyes she
    saw a glimpse of past defeat.
Her heart has been awakened to
    gifts forgotten yet not lost;
Powers used against your people and
    kept secret at great cost.
Now the choice is yours: take one
    more bite, or turn away,
Duna be with you, Damian; I've
    said all I can say."

"No, wait. I..." But before he could bat an eye, she'd disappeared, leaving the sweet scent of lavender lingering in the air, the only proof he had that she'd been real.

He braced both hands behind his head and let out a breath, her rhymes ricocheting inside his skull; entwining themselves within the mélange of information already entangled there.

This was it. This was when he chose a side. He didn't have to know all the answers to do that. He just had to trust Chloe.

Before he could talk himself out of it, Damian stormed toward the desk as if it were a trespasser up to no good. He snatched up the walnut and ate it so fast that he nearly choked. He planted his hands on the back of the chair and coughed, then watched in horror as the tips of his fingers became fuzzy, followed by his hands, wrists, and forearms.

He jumped back and sidestepped in front of Chloe's full-length mirror. From head to toe, his whole body appeared as a translucent blur, the colors of which were fading by the second. Already, his arms and shins were invisible.

"What's happening?" he yelled.

Frantic, he ran back to where the girl had been standing and strained to hear her voice. But she didn't answer. He pivoted back to the mirror. With a hand over his mouth to suppress his shout, he dropped to the floor.

His reflection was totally gone. And yet...

He could still feel the carpet underneath him, and still breathe lavender into his lungs. He pressed his invisible hand to his invisible chest and felt the rapid beat of his heart. He stood up and scuffed his feet against the floor, leaving no marks. He went to the window and huffed against it, but it didn't fog up one iota. Then he lifted his hand to the pane and hesitated. Slowly, as if worried the glass might electrocute him, he touched it, hardly feeling anything at all as his fingers slid right through it; it might as well have been water.

"Whoa!" Damian felt a light mist on his arm as he waved it outside the closed window. He pulled it back in, and tried it with his legs next, followed by his head. He was tempted to jump into the shrubs below, but then thought better of it; there had to be limits to this somewhere.

He felt his heart rate climb down as a smile spread across his face. He was still there, still very much alive. But unlike before, he was one hundred percent undetectable.

Ethan was the first out the doors when the school bell rang. It'd been the most nerve-racking day of his entire life, not to mention the most unfocused. Ordinarily, he was the most enthusiastic student in all of his classes, always eager to discuss, debate, and problem solve. But today, all he'd wanted to do was to throw his jacket over his head and find a hole to crawl into.

He felt completely helpless. Helpless to find Chloe. Helpless to stop Damian from reporting him and his family to the Fantásmata. Helpless to stop his imagination from speculating as to what might happen to them if and when they were found out.

Ethan had once asked his father what the Justice Council at Enochos did to people accused of withholding their strange sightings, and could still envision the pallor of his father's face when he'd answered, "I'm not at liberty to say."

More secrets. More fear. Ethan had to admit that the government's methods were effective. They had everybody scared and silent, including those in positions of authority, like his father. How could anything ever change if even the upper echelons were filled with cowards?

Ethan couldn't blame his father. Everyone had good reason to fear. They'd been programmed to fear. With copious amounts of literature outlining crimes and their respective punishments. With field trips to religious and judicial centers where old men in robes spoke in ominous tones about fidelity and order. With occasional glimpses of force and "corrective measures." And with frequent rumors of brutality when someone's behavior deviated from "unity and obedience."

At eight years old, Ethan had watched a wolf attack and kill a man, and then witnessed that man come back to life and heal himself, too. He could only imagine what his father, a Religious Council staff member, had been privy to in his twenty years of service.

Even if a single Petrodian were to try and reform things, such as the impermeable mystery surrounding strange sightings, they would never be able to recruit enough people willing to stick their necks out. Everyone—unless otherwise assigned by the powers that be—had a family to think of and protect, another subtle weapon with which to control the sheep-like masses.

Though he wanted to sprint, Ethan walked as normally as possible to his truck. His cheek twitched when he reflexively glanced at the windshield, where Chloe had left her note the day before. He slung his backpack into the passenger seat and climbed into the cab as his phone began to vibrate in his pocket. He clicked in his seatbelt and pulled it out. The text was from his mother: *Meet me at the museum after school.*

His mom's messages were never that bland. Always she would insert cheerful hearts and emoticons, and a *Love, Mom* at the end. Something was wrong. Either she hadn't sent the text, or she was under duress.

Ethan threw the truck into reverse and sped away, not caring who might see.

☾

Ethan stood still to let the camouflaged door lock scan his iris. He squeezed through the door as it opened.

"Mom?" His voice echoed back to him.

A ceiling speaker crackled above his head, followed by an unctuous voice speaking through it. "Ethan, nice to have you here. Come join us in the gallery downstairs."

Ethan clenched his jaw and stared out at his truck in the parking lot. He regretted not bringing a knife, a stick, anything to fight with if he had to. He'd been too flustered by his mom's message to even consider the possibility of having to use force against whomever was waiting for him. His bare hands wouldn't get him far, but it was too late now.

He rolled back his shoulders, strode to the far corner of the room, and followed the staircase down to the gallery.

"Your cellphone, please," came a voice from behind him.

Ethan turned to meet an ancient face he hadn't seen in ten years. It belonged to the chief councilman, the man he and his peers had heard speak the day they learned about the Coronation, the final stage of life when people graduated "from average citizen to ruling sovereign."

Once again, the councilman was dressed in a dark purple chasuble, with a golden rope tied around his waist. His eyes were small, the black pupils of which swallowed up nearly every speck of white. The thin, sallow skin of his cheeks clung tightly, like a plastic film, to the recesses and protuberances of his skull. He was well over seventy-five, the age at which every Petrodian had their Coronation. Ethan wondered why his had been delayed.

"Where's my mom?" Ethan withheld his phone, convinced he could take this guy in a fight if he didn't cooperate.

The councilman placed a light hand on Ethan's back and turned him to face the rest of the room. Five other council members, all as old as their leader, lay on their backs, forming a circle in the middle of the floor. Their eyes closed and mouths muttering, they paid Ethan no attention. Terracotta oil lamps and mounted cressets lined the walls, and somewhere, spicy incense was burning.

"She and your father are busy elsewhere," the councilman answered, his black eyes flickering in the lamplight. "I wanted your full attention without her here, just for a few moments. Will you indulge me?"

He lifted up his hand, and Ethan watched in stupefied silence as his phone flew out of his pocket and slapped against the councilman's palm like a magnet to metal.

"Do you see that compartment there?" The man pointed to a small niche that had been carved out of the farthest wall, beside the fossil of the gryphon's rear foot.

Ethan nodded, trying hard to avert his eyes from the councilmen suddenly convulsing at his feet. "I've never noticed it before."

"Only we know of it. It's been here for thousands of years. It's why we built the museum." He began walking toward the wall and motioned for Ethan to follow. "But since it has come to our attention that you and your mother know more than we ever wished you to, it's time you learned about it, too." The councilman braced himself against the wall and lowered himself onto both knees. He reached inside the niche.

Ethan's head began to swim with the strong scent of whatever resin or bark was circulating through the air. With each breath he took, he felt himself growing unusually calm, sedate almost. He blinked his eyes hard and shook his head, trying to snap himself out of the hypnotic cloud enveloping his mind, and likely the minds of the men around him.

The councilman pushed an amber tablet out of the hole. "Take it."

Ethan picked it up and stared through the translucent block at the parchment encased within it. "What is this?"

"An oracle." The councilman grunted as he got to his feet. He panted for a few seconds, then pulled a syringe from a pocket inside his robe and injected it into a bruised circle on his forearm. He took a deep, even breath, and with a smile lifted the tablet from Ethan's arms. "The Vessel is foretold of in this scroll. The Vessel you've been good enough to track down for us."

"I don't know what you're talking about." The cloying smell of the incense stung the back of Ethan's throat.

"You're an intelligent young man, Ethan. You must know it will do no good to lie. Especially after the notice delivered to you eight years ago, concerning Mr. Zacharias."

He smacked his lips, and gestured toward the men still mumbling and jerking on the floor, their eyes rolled back in their heads. "For days they've been receiving intel regarding your goings-on. I was hoping you'd come to us instead of the other way around."

"Intel from whom?"

The councilman kissed his finger, then pressed it to the scroll. "From Apollo, god of Petros. He wishes to reward your assistance in locating the Vessel with an unprecedented honor."

"We don't want any rewards." Nausea swelled in Ethan's stomach. His eyelids grew heavy. Then he thought of Chloe, trapped somewhere in a room much worse than this, and willed himself to stay lucid. "Just don't hurt Chloe."

"I'm afraid, Mr. Ross, that it makes no difference what you want. The Vessel will be dealt with according to the prophecy, and you and your mother will be justly awarded." The corners of his purple lips turned up in a repulsive smile. "Who would deny an early Coronation?"

CHAPTER TWENTY-EIGHT
PHOBIA

The effects of the walnut had worn off after half an hour, just in time for Damian to shower and get ready for school. Being absent—or worse, somehow being found out as a freak capable of turning invisible—definitely wouldn't help his circumstances.

All day, he'd felt restless, giddy almost, unable to think straight or sit still for more than a few seconds. When a few perceptive friends asked him if he liked a new girl or something, he had to bite his lip to avoid telling them that, yes, there was a girl, but not just any girl—a *goddess*. But he wasn't in love with her; he was overwhelmed by what she'd ushered into his life, and he was champing at the bit to explore it.

He felt like an eagle stuck in a cage, surrounded by domesticated birds with clipped wings that had never known what it felt like to fly. His secret thrilled him. He was proof that the old myths were true—or at least some of them. Granted, he had to keep it to himself for now, but one day...one day his name would be known throughout Petros. He'd go down in history books as the first modern Petrodian to ever be visited by the gods.

Just before curfew, when there was still enough sunlight left for him to wander around, he reached for the walnut. But before he could take it, his entire hand vanished in a split second. He stepped into the mirror as the rest of him disappeared, not gradually like last time, but fast and all at once.

"I don't need the nut anymore?" he asked, then waited in vain for a reply. "I'll take that as a yes."

His first instinct was to find Ethan and Katsaros. Already he'd forgotten that he was no more than a disembodied spirit, a breeze with a brain floating around Eirene. He didn't care, though. He felt invincible, invigorated, and ready to see with his own two eyes what really lay beneath Petros's crust.

He didn't know how long his visibility would last, and that concerned him. Whichever deity Chloe was praying to, he could only hope it was a logical one. He'd need at least until midnight to bring her back from hell—or so he guessed.

He ran out of the house and maintained a steady jog all the way to Lake Thyra, stopping only a few times for water and to tease the dogs in the park, catching their Frisbees and kicking their balls a little farther away before they could fetch them.

The opportunities for wreaking havoc were endless. Why had the goddess in Chloe's room trusted him with this power? He didn't trust himself. If it weren't for the fact that his sister was being held prisoner somewhere below his feet, he would sneak around every council building in Petros and find out how the machine was run, and who pulled the levers.

Damian tore through the old vineyards, and bounded down the hill overlooking the lake in a few agile leaps. He stopped on the beach when he saw a man sitting at the tip of the sandbar, his identity masked by the glare of the setting sun.

"Well, hello there. I've been waiting for you."

"Katsaros?" Damian looked down at his hands. He was still invisible, even to himself. "You can see me?"

"You're not the only one with secrets, you know." Katsaros stood up and dusted the sand from his corduroy pants.

"You've got plenty. You told me all about them yesterday, remember?" Damian picked up a stone and skipped it across the water. So much for having a power no one knew about.

Katsaros smiled. "So Carya paid you a visit, did she?"

Damian could feel himself growing impatient. He had until morning to get his sister out of Hades and somehow hatch a plan to keep the Fantásmata from knowing about their family. He didn't have time for another Q&A session with this guy.

"I'm sorry, but I can't talk." Damian walked past Katsaros and skimmed the water with the midsole of his sneaker, then smiled when no ripples formed.

"I'm sorry to inconvenience you, but the portal cannot be unlocked by mortal hands." Katsaros pulled a white handkerchief from his pocket and dabbed his forehead.

"Then how in Zeus' name am I supposed to get Chloe?"

Katsaros folded his arms and began stroking his goatee. "Tell me, what do you plan to do once you've obtained her, Damian?"

"I plan on figuring that out once she's back. That's the priority, don't you agree?" Damian took off his hoodie and rolled up his sleeves, his temperature rising with every idle second that ticked by.

"Emerging from the darkness is just the first step." Katsaros's gaze drifted out over the old olive tree to the limestone mountains beyond. "One act of faith must lead to another, if you're to have victory in this life."

Damian's fuse was growing short. He alternated clenching his fists and relaxing them, trying to buy some time before he exploded the way he had in Ethan's kitchen. "What do you know about victory?" he said, not trying to hide the incredulity in his tone. He looked Katsaros up and down, silently mocking his disheveled clothes, pockmarked cheeks, and potbelly.

Before Damian could say another word, Katsaros's suspenders snapped off his waistband and fell to the sand, and his button-up shirt split open, revealing chestnut clumps of chest hair. Damian heard a loud ripping sound and watched in bewilderment as a horse's sorrel hindquarters appeared on Katsaros's back end. A rust-colored hoof kicked the corduroy pants into the lake.

"What the..." Damian backed up to the edge of the water, half tempted to turn and sprint back up the hill.

A guttural neighing noise vibrated in Katsaros's throat as he tossed his head, his copper hair shedding to the ground until he was completely bald, save for a black curved line bisecting his scalp. Damian realized it was a snake tattoo, its forked tongue trailing down the length of his nose. It looked just like the golden pin his father had worn on the lapel of his uniform; the Fantásmata insignia.

"Wait..." A shiver shot up Damian's back. "You work for the Fantásmata? And..." He shook his head as Katsaros's bare arms doubled in size, peaked biceps and rounded deltoids bulging where blubber had been. "You're half horse?"

"I am a centaur." Katsaros ran a hand along his smooth head, then dragged it back until it covered the spade-shaped serpent's head on his brow. "And I once worked for the primitive form of the Fantásmata. The Pythonians." He drew a breath and followed a white-tailed eagle with his eyes as it soared overhead. "A very long time ago."

"How long?" Damian reached for his hoodie and pulled it on. Though it was barely the month of Pyanepsion, the bite of winter hung in the air.

"Two thousand years."

Two days ago, Damian would have laughed at something so ludicrous. But how could he argue with his own two eyes? He'd had more than enough strange sightings to last a lifetime; more than enough blots on his record to get him exiled or executed—probably both. That someone could time travel and shape shift wasn't so farfetched anymore.

"How is that possible?" he said. "How are you still alive?"

Katsaros stepped closer. "I told you that heaven existed."

He smiled up at the pink parade of clouds passing over. Then a shadow eclipsed the sun, erasing his smile. Throwing back his shoulders, Katsaros scanned the still water, his head moving from side to side, up and down, as if following another bird. But the air was empty. He whinnied quietly and extended his arms to either side, tucking his chin under as he drew a deep breath through his nostrils.

"Deimos! Phobos!" he bellowed. "I command you in the name of Phos, son of the All-Powerful, be gone from here!"

A howl ripped through a sudden gust of freezing wind, leaving a cold coat of moisture on Damian's skin. "What was that?" He wiped away the wetness with his sleeve.

"Dark spirits...always spying." Katsaros surveyed the area, his black tail swatting the air. "Be grateful you can only feel their presence. They're uglier and stink more terribly than I ever did." He chuckled. "And I assure you, I was a foul sight before I met Iris."

"Iris my ancestor?"

Katsaros nodded.

"She's in heaven now?"

Another nod.

"And I take it that's where you're from."

"I'm no longer mortal. When I died, my spirit was escorted to paradise by one of Carya's kind."

"But in the myths, the centaurs were lower than dirt." Damian dropped his head and lifted his palms to Katsaros as compunction knotted in his stomach. "No offense."

"That brings us back to victory, doesn't it?" Katsaros smiled. "I'm living proof that faith can save the soul of any wretch, even a murdering, thieving, lying, cheating, centaur such as I was."

Damian lifted his shoulders in a heavy sigh. "I want to talk, I really do, but even you said time was short."

"Time is irrelevant when you don't have a plan."

Katsaros turned and walked to the white shirt lying crumpled on the sand. He squatted onto his haunches and pulled something from the front pocket and brought it to Damian. "You've seen that there's much more to your existence than meets the eye." He held his fist closed and took Damian's hand, then released the jasper stone into it. "Now you must learn to walk by faith, and not by what you can see."

Damian unfastened the chain and clasped it around his neck. He held the rock between his fingers. "Did my father believe all this? Did he see what I've seen?"

"Your father received his doma at eighteen, following the pattern set by the very first Asher in ages past." Katsaros frowned and scratched his ear as a heron warbled in the distance. "He suppressed his power, as was your family's custom for hundreds of years. Their fear closed the door to Duna."

Damian's heart sank as a thousand questions shot off like fireworks inside his brain. What had their powers been? What might have happened if they had rallied together, or if just one of them had been brave enough to see what their doma could do? Had anyone ever even tried? Is that why his father had died?

"But in the end," Katsaros continued, "his heart softened. He *prayed*."

"To Duna. The god that the goddess person at my house talked about." Damian said it flatly, as though it all made perfect sense. In reality, it was like a million jigsaw puzzle pieces had been scattered in front of him.

Katsaros knitted his brow. "Her name is Carya. She's his messenger." He closed his eyes, and in a few seconds he was transformed back into the avuncular man Damian knew him as, replete with a new wrinkled shirt and pair of plain suspenders.

"There is just one god, Damian," Katsaros said. "He's the one who created all things, even those things which have forsaken him."

Damian felt his chest rise and fall against the cool red stone as he breathed. He'd never been fearful. Only on those occasions when he could sense his sister's distress was he ever the least bit afraid. Not even the prospect of venturing into hell daunted him. But suddenly, his fight-or-flight response was reversing; willing him to flee rather than confront whatever unknowns loomed before him.

"You feel frightened," Katsaros whispered.

Damian looked closely at Katsaros. He could detect the faint form of the snake tracing the ridge of the man's nose like two parallel scars. He hesitated. He didn't want to admit that he wanted to hide like his family had always done.

"It's all right to admit you have fear, Damian. It's an attack on your psyche, direct from Duna's enemies. They sense boldness like blood in the water and will devour it if you let them. I'm here to tell you that you don't have to succumb. You don't."

"How? And how could we ever stand a chance against the Fantásmata?"

Katsaros shook his head, then looked toward the sky as if invoking its sympathy. "I feel as though I'm conversing with my former headstrong self. Your ears are just as deaf as mine were."

"Using my head and being headstrong are two different things, Katsaros, or whatever your name really is. My family had every reason to keep their domas under the radar. What possible difference can I or my sister make?"

Damian's throat tightened as tears threatened to spill over his eyelids, guilt and remorse stilling his mind, ridding it of every thought but Chloe. He'd kept her at a distance for so many years because she embarrassed him, because she was different, because they had nothing in common—or so he'd thought. Now everything had changed; they shared more than DNA. They were Ashers. And she'd had the courage, or perhaps the idiocy, to explore what that meant, while he, the athlete who knew no fear, wanted nothing more than to retreat and forget the day he'd watched her walk into that mist.

"I'm sorry, Chloe," Damian whispered. He could feel his boldness shriveling inside him like a flower parched by the sun, and he was helpless to revive it. "I can't do this."

Hot energy buzzed through his body as bones, sinews, muscles, and skin materialized in rapid flashes over his hands. His hoodie appeared on his arms, followed by his jeans and shoes.

Katsaros's face hung long with sorrow as Damian removed the necklace and cupped it in his hand. "This should have been for Chloe, like Ethan said." Then he gave it to Katsaros and tramped back up the hill.

"And what of your sister?" Katsaros shouted after him. "You're choosing to leave her? I came here to open the portal...for *you*."

Damian stared ahead, the evening breeze soughing through the brambles. He made a quarter turn and forced the words off his tongue: "If Duna is so powerful, he doesn't need me to help her."

CHAPTER TWENTY-NINE
LETHE

Chloe's eyes flew open as she felt cold hands seize her ankles and drag her down the bed. She clawed the sheets as she looked down at Deimos's hooves; a rope hung from one of his talons.

"What are you doing?" she yelled, kicking uselessly as Phobos squeezed his thumb into a pressure point near her shoulder blade. She screamed in pain and let him pull her onto the floor.

Gazing around the room, she saw no shaft of light, nor did she feel that peaceful presence that had relieved her earlier. The gold cup she'd drunk from was in pieces near the wall, and the sense of calm she'd felt was just as shattered. Had her prayers not been heard at all? Had the brilliance that had filled the room, and the water that had quenched her thirst, been just another stunt of magic?

"Bind her hands," ordered Deimos as he tossed Phobos the rope. "It's your lucky day," he said to Chloe, his many voices creating a bone-splitting sound that whooshed around the room in a flurry of haunting echoes.

"Don't tease the poor waif." Phobos wrenched Chloe's wrists as he joined them behind her back. "Her brother has just abandoned her. She's neither loved nor lucky."

Chloe opened her mouth, but then restrained herself from taking the bait. She lifted her chin and stood perfectly still.

"Oh, you must want to know the reason why." Phobos stepped in front of her, his coarse mane abrading the side of her cheek.

"Do what you came here to do," Chloe said, her heart already frozen inside her chest.

She wished that she found what Phobos had said hard to believe, but she didn't. She had never been more than a nuisance to Damian, a thorn he'd had to tolerate for their parents' sake. He probably thought that she deserved this, and maybe she did. Her disillusionment, paired with her intractable curiosity, had led her too far afield from Petrodian mores. And now she was paying for it.

Phobos inched closer, sniffing her with his large, brown-speckled snout. "You can try to act brave all you want, but I smell your fear. My name isn't Phobos for nothing." He hissed as he sucked in a humid stream of air through his fangs. As he turned away, his ear twitched, and he gave an arch grin, twirling a whisker around his sooty finger. "And that..." He sniffed again. "It's your sadness, so strong, stronger than anything else."

Chloe pushed her tongue against the roof of her mouth and closed her eyes.

The first thing she saw was her treehouse, the getaway her father had built for her when she was four years old after Damian had made her cry—over what, she couldn't remember. "Every little girl needs a hideout," her father had said. Then he went to work and completed it over a weekend. It was as if he knew she'd need it, as if he knew it would be the only place in which she would find solitude and escape into her imagination after he was gone.

What she wouldn't give right now to sit in the tire swing and have him push her in it one more time, or to go down the slide into her mother's arms, then host a tea party inside for them both.

Where were her parents now? The thought of them wandering through the Fields with Anastasia and Calix, mindlessly picking flowers without knowing one another's names, pierced her heart like a knife.

"She is perhaps the saddest girl I've ever seen," said Deimos. He crossed the room and picked up the pieces of the golden cup. "Her parents are killed, her brother betrays her, the All-Powerful gives her only water to sweeten her hours in hell..." He clucked his tongue and shook his head in mock pity. "And worse yet, you cannot be killed."

"Not entirely," Phobos said. He motioned toward the golden fragments in Deimos's hands, and the pieces hovered into his own. "Fortune has not turned her back on the girl completely."

Chloe felt like she was floating somewhere high above the room, looking down on her body, witnessing her own death from afar. Though her heart still beat, she was just a shell, a corpse cursed to be left unburied. "Let me drink from the Lethe," she heard the corpse say.

"I *knew* she would volunteer." Phobos's green eyes flashed.

The fragments levitated in the air between them, then in a yellow blur, the cup put itself back together.

Phobos spun Chloe around and loosed the rope from her wrists. "I told you the rope was needless, Deimos. Even if she has a doma, she's too pathetic to use it now."

"This is on your head if anything happens," Deimos blustered. "Those were our orders."

Phobos waved him off and pushed the cup to Chloe's chest. "Come, let us watch the Lethe wash away your sadness."

☾

Throngs of sackcloth-covered souls lined the banks of the gully, and Chloe noticed that there wasn't one child among them. The youngest girl and boy she saw couldn't have been younger than twelve. All of them, huddled together like hapless sheep, gripped their baskets tightly, just as Calix had when Chloe found him by the dead olive tree.

"Why do they love those flowers so much?" Chloe couldn't help but ask.

A few strides in front of her, Deimos leaned over and dragged a talon along a long line of flowers, slicing off their glowing, star-shaped heads. "The judges of Tartarus found the task a fitting pursuit. These spirits did nothing exceptional or egregious in life, and so in death they do the same."

Chloe jumped as Phobos, nearly clipping her heels with his untrimmed toenails, erupted with a heart-stopping roar. He came alongside her, pointing and snickering at the screaming swarms of people who didn't even know what a lion was.

"The weak and cowardly come to Asphodel," he whispered, disdain dripping off his tongue. "They never stood for anything, always strove to blend in. Cowards, the lot of them." He spat on the ground. "Sniveling little worms. That's all your world is full of now."

Chloe's vision blurred. Blue waves rippled at both tear ducts, then flowed onto the corneas, filling her eyes with the sight of an ocean she knew wasn't there. The image was fuzzy, as if she were looking at it through fogged glass, but there was no doubt it was the Great Sea; water that blue didn't exist anywhere else.

"Settle down!" Deimos shouted toward the souls. "Pick up your cursed flowers before they get swept into the current."

Chloe squeezed her eyes shut until every speck of blue had disappeared.

"Your salvation approaches, Asher," Phobos whispered to her, then he pounced on all fours and took off into the gully.

Chloe held her breath as Phobos stood and stretched out his arms, then swiftly dropped them, all ten fingers flexed toward the dry riverbed. She watched as the ground beneath him started shaking, and all the waiting souls shouted with hoarse voices and clapped their hands against the wicker baskets.

"Lethe, flow!" Phobos commanded.

In moments the water had risen to Phobos's shins. He turned and slogged his way back to the bank and joined Deimos. The pair watched the throng stampede into the river like a pack of rabid dogs.

Deimos reached back and pinched Chloe's arm. "What are you waiting for? No one is coming to save you, Asher. You're alone down here, and the only person who knows where you are has already moved on with his rotten life."

Chloe skimmed the sea of faces, searching for her parents. She knew they were out there. If she just searched hard enough, she could find them, and know them, even if they couldn't know her. She couldn't let herself give up. Not yet.

Lowering her head, she stepped forward toward the river.

"Good girl," Deimos cooed. "Empty your mind, and be free at last."

Head down and strides long, Chloe made a beeline for the river, surreptitiously scouting for an empty area where a careless splash of water couldn't make its way down her throat. She waded in, her body going rigid as the cold waves nipped at her hot-blooded legs and hips. Her toes plunged into the gritty sand and pushed across the pebbles.

She had never before stood in a body of water that wasn't a pool, as there was a law against "trespassing" into the myriad tributaries and rivers that snaked through Petros and the Great Sea into which they flowed. The only sea that men could touch was the Sea of Enochos, where the Justice Council erected floating pyres and burned alive the worst criminals, but even these never touched the sea; by the time they hit the water, they were already dead, reduced to ash and bone.

"It's the sweetest drink you've ever tasted," shouted Phobos. "The nectar of the gods."

Chloe dipped in her fingers and dragged them across the crystal water, struggling to control the adrenaline pumping through her veins. Her heart thumped quick and loud in her ears, like the frenetic drumbeat of the Lycaea festival. She felt as though the water was penetrating her pores, stinging as it mingled with her undead blood. Her vision tunneled and blurred at the edges once again, this time zooming in on her hands as she cupped them together in the water and lifted them to her lips. She would have to make this convincing...

Splash!

The hair on Chloe's neck bristled. She turned to see Deimos charging through the river, ripping through the water with his talons, his fangs slick with saliva as he shouted at her.

"The river won't be here all day, Asher. Drink from it or I'll drown you."

Chloe tilted back her head and threw the water against her mouth, the excess flowing onto her neck.

"Look at me, Asher!"

Chloe obeyed and locked eyes with the bloodthirsty hybrid stalking toward her. Instantly, she recognized her mistake.

"Unafraid, are you?" Deimos turned to look at Phobos, who was crouched on the bank, his ears retracting as his tail began to twitch.

"It looks to me like the Vessel is having second thoughts," Phobos yelled. He dug his hand into the dirt and growled deep in his belly.

"Then I'll see to it that she has *no* thoughts." Deimos whipped back to face Chloe, reaching out his claw to hook her like a fish.

"Help me," Chloe whispered.

"Who are you talking to, you fool?" said Deimos. "He doesn't hear you. You're as good as dead." He pulled back his arm and thrust the tip of a talon into her forearm, grinning as a circle of blood pooled on her flesh.

Chloe hissed as she watched her blood spill into the clear water, staining it crimson like paint splashed on a windowpane.

"There is a way, there always is, to escape the enemy's snare," she murmured, replaying Carya's last message in her head. She looked around one last time for any sign of Carya or a symbol of hope, but only empty faces and meaningless flowers met her gaze. "But what way?" she whispered. "There's isn't a way."

His patience expired, Deimos grabbed the back of Chloe's neck and forced her head down to the water. "Your mind's left you already. Now *drink*." His dagger-like finger was pressed dangerously close to her jugular vein.

Chloe folded her lips together, shaking her head, resisting Deimos's grip, but to no avail. He closed his free fist around her nose, and she had no choice but to open her mouth and let the Lethe fill it.

"Let me see it go down." Deimos bent beside her, hot breath panting against her neck.

Chloe squeezed her eyes shut, tears sliding through them as she willed herself to loosen her tongue and swallow.

Her parents' faces filled her mind as she silently recited their names over and over and over again, as the water moved smoothly down her throat...

"There," said Deimos. He released his hand from her neck and shoved her forward.

Chloe fell headlong into the water. Her arms and legs flailed as she hurried to right herself. She screamed at the sight of the beast with an animal-like body and ugly human head, his brown eyes blinking fast as he looked her over with a wicked smile. He raised a bloody talon to his lips and licked it clean.

"Farewell, Chloe the Asher."

Then he turned and swam to the shore, heavy hooves pounding against the water. He joined another monster, and together they took off toward the cloud of fog that was settling over the sickly green hills.

"My name is Chloe," she whispered. And that was all she knew.

CHAPTER THIRTY
NICHOLAS

S lowly, the river peeled away from Chloe's sides, receding back to the banks and sinking into the sediment. The only one still standing in its midst, she plodded toward a gently sloping knoll on which three people stood watching her.

An old man and woman with deep wrinkles and tattered tunics reached out their arms, beckoning her with slow, tired waves. A younger man beside them held his elbow with one hand and covered his mouth with the other. Beneath them sat a row of wicker baskets, each one filled to the edge with white flowers.

"Chloe, come here, child," shouted the woman, her shaky voice cracking as loose skin quavered on her thin, leathery arms.

Chloe blinked up at the pale expanse of motionless sky above her. A dull ache throbbed in the back of her head. Her limbs felt leaden, the deadness of the air settling into them, stiffening her bones, clotting her blood. Her stomach rocked with nausea as unbearable pressure tightened around her skull, disorienting her as she stumbled to stay balanced. She forced one foot in front of the other, for no other reason than to be free of the river before it rushed back and consumed her.

The younger man rushed down the hill, his face taut with a strange mixture of anguish and joy as he ran toward her, calling her name.

Chloe doubled over and vomited onto the rocks and mud, flushing out her headache with every heave. She rose and took a deep breath, filling her head with musty air that stuck to her throat and sharpened the acrid taste of bile.

The man froze a few feet away from her and crashed to his knees. His sandy-blond hair fell across his eyes, almost hiding the tears streaming out of them.

"Who are you?" Chloe took a step back. She'd never seen this man before in her life. What could she possibly have done to upset him?

The man put his head down and cried into his hands. Behind him, the old woman stepped closer to the man next to her and whispered into his ear.

"What's the matter?" Chloe asked. When the young man didn't respond, she walked forward and shook his shoulder. "Please talk to me." She winced at a shooting pain in her left arm and gasped when she saw globules of blood falling from it, staining the flower petals red.

After a long minute passed, the man lifted his head and sat back on his heels, a bleary smile resting in his eyes. "I'll show you." He stood up and started toward the riverbank. "Follow me." He turned back to her, wiping the tears from his cheeks and staring at her intently, curiously, as though to be sure she was real.

Chloe thought he had a kind face, with warm green eyes much brighter than the grass in this stagnant haze of country. From the laugh lines around his eyes and the gray stubble along his jaw, she guessed him to be middle-aged. Then she wondered how old *she* was.

She ambled behind him as the other two hobbled over to meet them.

The old woman took Chloe's hands in hers and kissed them with cold lips until she was out of breath and blubbering. "Poor thing," she said softly. "Poor thing." She removed her cloak and wiped away the blood on Chloe's arm. Then she wrapped it tightly around Chloe's elbow like a bandage.

The old man's bushy eyebrows furrowed as he looked down at his dirt-caked feet. He scratched a sore spot on his head and rubbed the woman's back as she cried.

What was wrong with these people?

The blond man lowered himself onto a dry patch of grass and patted the ground beside him for Chloe to join him. He spoke to the others in a language she didn't understand. They all knelt where they were, closed their eyes, and bowed their heads.

"What's going on?" Chloe asked. She peered over her shoulder at the wicker baskets and pointed at them. She started to rise. "Shouldn't we get back to work picking the flowers, or at least go get the baskets before someone steals them?"

A reluctant smile pulled at the younger man's cheek. He rotated his torso toward her and studied his palms. "Duna," he whispered, closing his eyes. "Work through these hands." Then he stretched out his hands and placed them on either side of Chloe's head. "This may hurt."

Without further warning, he pressed the heels of his icy hands against her temple and buried his fingertips into the base of her skull.

Chloe yelped as searing pain blazed across her brain. Her heart raced, thumping wildly as though it might explode from her chest at any moment. Sweat poured from her forehead. She seized the man's wrists and tried to pry his hands away. But he persisted, shushing her calmly as the pressure intensified.

She tilted her chin back slightly toward the old couple. "Make him stop, *please*!"

Her ear canals buzzed as whirring heat rushed through them. She lost focus on the man's face, the color of his hair, his eyes, his skin; fading to blobs of black and gray...and then, nothing.

A gentle breeze blew across her face. She felt her muscles relax and her jaw stop clenching. The man slowly slid his hands off her head and onto her wounded arm.

She opened her eyes. "Daddy..."

The man's nose twitched as tears trembled in his clear green eyes. He nodded his head and smiled, twin tears streaking down either cheek. "It's me."

He held her forearm firmly with both hands as the old couple that she now recognized as Anastasia and Calix circled around them. A few seconds later, the pain in her arm was totally gone, replaced by the subtle sensation of heat filling the space where the gouge had been.

Chloe fell into her father's arms, and not knowing whether to laugh or cry, she did both for a good long while. She let her mind be emptied once again, though now it rid itself only of the shadows and sadness that had invaded on the day her parents died. In their place surfaced foreign tremors of happiness that vibrated from the deepest sanctum of her being, bubbling up into her heart and head and kindling every cell.

She could have stayed here forever, absorbed in this sublimity, with her father's chin on her head, her ear to his chest...

She pulled away, her elation draining into the grass beneath her as an eerie uneasiness trickled in. She pressed two fingers into his icy wrist. "You don't have a heartbeat."

Nicholas brushed her fingers with his as he gazed out over the desolate gully. "I'm dead, Chloe. As dead as they are." He gestured to Anastasia and Calix, who sat making wreaths with the stems of asphodels. "But you..." He touched her chin and gave her that same warm, understated smile she always envisioned on his face. "You've kept my hope alive all these years. Not even death could kill that."

"How..." Now that the shock of seeing him again was starting to wear off, Chloe didn't know which question to ask first. "How did you know I was here?"

Nicholas sighed and scratched the back of his head. "Would you believe me if I told you a messenger named Carya appeared to me after I died and told me to find an old curmudgeon named Calix?"

Chloe laughed. "I think I can believe anything now. Where's Mom?" she asked.

"She's here," he said quietly, "and she's like you." He tapped his forehead. "Her memories are all intact. We stay separated so we won't draw attention. I couldn't bring her to meet you. Not yet."

"I understand." Chloe removed Anastasia's cloak from her arm. There wasn't so much as a scratch left to indicate she'd ever been injured. "So you healed us with your..."

"Doma. Yes." Her father stood up and held out his arms. She latched onto them, letting him pull her to her feet. He closed the distance between them and whispered in her ear, "Your doma is imminent, Chloe. Don't be afraid." He hugged her to his side and kissed her hair.

Calix grunted something, and Nicholas said to Chloe, "Calix is right, I should leave you now before Deimos and Phobos make their rounds."

"You understand Próta?"

Nicholas lifted his head and chuckled. "I suppose that's a perk of having lived in the Underworld for nearly a decade."

Chloe laughed as more joyful tears welled and slipped from her eyes. "Daddy, you don't know how much I've missed you." She wrapped her arms around him, trying not to shiver at his cold hands on her tunic.

If only this could be the end. She would settle for this—picking worthless flowers in Asphodel and dying naturally when the time came. As long as she was with her parents, she didn't need any doma to deliver her.

"I don't want you to go." She pressed her wet cheek into her father's chest as her eyes met Anastasia's.

"Child, you must be brave," said Anastasia, her hands joined at her heart. "Remember what the messenger told you. All of us can be restored if you'll trust Duna, the god who answered us when we didn't even know his name."

Anastasia looked up into the pseudo sky, tears of thanks glistening in the mud-colored pools of her eyes. She shook her clasped hands, beseeching Chloe one last time. Then she linked her arm with Calix's and together they trudged back to their baskets.

Chloe's shoulders slouched as a heavy weight settled in her stomach. Was she really going to forget what Carya had said and done for her? Was she really ready to abandon Calix, Anastasia, and the others while they stood a chance of becoming themselves again and getting out of this place?

She'd come all this way, learned so much, seen and heard far more than she'd bargained for. Stopping now would be the most selfish thing she could possibly do. She knew that if she listened to herself, to her exhausted body and muddled mind, she'd curl up right there by the Lethe and live off of glimpses of her mom and dad whenever they passed by. She needed her father's strength if she was going to take even one more step.

"Daddy, what do I do?"

He held her shoulders gently and rocked her back so he could see her face. "You do nothing, sweetheart. You only have to wait."

She'd never seen him so serene, yet instead of feeling comforted, she sensed her nerves unraveling. "How do you have that much faith in a gift I haven't even been given yet?" She spread her arms and pivoted side to side, displaying her empty palms, scraped knees, and shins bruised by her tormentors. "Look at me, I'm nothing special."

She folded her arms and smashed her heel into a flower. "It should have been Damian," she said under her breath. "He's better at everything anyway."

Nicholas sighed and shut his eyes for a moment, as if searching for the right thing to say. He had to agree with her. Even as a kid, Damian had outshined Chloe in every sport, and just about every subject in school. He was popular, charismatic, and lauded by his teachers and friends as someone with the makings of a future chief councilman in any one of the four colonies.

"Those are lies, Chloe," he said. "I don't claim to know everything about Duna, but I'm certain of this: he doesn't make mistakes." He paused, and she raised her eyes to his. "Your being here is part of his plan."

"Did you know Damian knows I'm here?" she said, her anger rising. "Phobos told me. Damian knows I'm in hell, and he betrayed me."

Nicholas's expression didn't waver. Only a faint twitch of his cheek hinted at his displeasure. "You shouldn't have listened to a word that monster said." He took one of her hands in his. "Even if that is true, it'll do no good to dwell on it. The Fantásmata haven't made it easy to act bravely or take chances. Damian might have more of his old man in him than I realized." He forced a quick smile as his eyes fell to his fingers.

"What do you mean?" She willed herself not to retract her hand from the ice of her father's cold, cutting grip.

He squeezed her hand and let it go. He canted his head to one side, apprehension flickering across his countenance. His forehead crinkled as he swallowed hard. "I was a coward, Chloe. My family needed to know what I was, but I was too afraid, just like every Asher before me."

The squawk of a seagull sounded overhead. Chloe jerked her chin to the sky. "Did you hear that?"

Nicholas looked around. "No, hear what?"

The blue of the Great Sea slid across her eyes like a sheet of cellophane. The pungent smell of salt and seaweed clogged her nostrils. "Daddy..." She reached out for him, clutching his hand like a lifeline.

"It's okay, sweetheart. It's okay..."

She strained to hear his voice above the din of seagulls squawking in her ears. She rubbed her eyes with her free hand, but the motion only sharpened the image taking shape before her: the back of a woman with auburn hair, and bright orange flames shrinking over her palms.

CHAPTER THIRTY-ONE
PUNISHMENT

Tiny hailstones pelted Damian's head and shoulders as he stormed up the walk to Ethan's door. It was well after curfew, but he didn't care. He had to warn him—or perhaps threaten him, if it came to that—to keep his mouth shut before they both ended up on the Fantásmata's hit list.

Damian wiped his feet on the welcome mat and punched the doorbell. He waited for a few seconds, then rang it again as he knocked. He peeped through the beveled glass and saw a man, Mr. Ross he guessed, get up from a chair in the living room and creep slowly toward the door. Damian stepped back and cleared his throat, thinking up a lie that would let him in, no questions asked.

The door clicked as the man unlocked it. He cracked it open, just wide enough for one hooded eye to get a look at Damian.

"Are you Mr. Ross? I'm one of Ethan's friends."

The man's eye squinted at him. "The Rosses were evicted this afternoon."

Damian lifted his chin and stared the man down for a moment. "Oh, really. And what are you doing here?"

"Protecting the place from squatters," the man grunted, then slammed the door in Damian's face and turned the lock.

"Right," Damian muttered. "And I'm here to work on a physics project with Ethan."

He readjusted his hood and stomped back into the rain toward home. There was nothing more he could do.

Like his sister, Ethan and his family had stuck their noses where they shouldn't have. Damian couldn't blame them, really. Who didn't want to step behind the well-staged scenes of the Fantásmata, uncover their history, and learn their secrets? Everyone loved a good mystery. The prospect of solving it was nearly impossible to resist, but not quite. Damian had proved it was possible by leaving Katsaros's offer at the lake.

If anyone could infiltrate the government unnoticed, it was Damian. But he wasn't a fool. He knew better than to play with fire when he'd seen it devour his own flesh and blood.

The Ashers had had their chance to act. Besides, he was just one person. Dabbling with this magic gift of his, whether he went after Chloe in Hades or sneaked around the council premises, would be suicide. He would be caught eventually, and killed soon after that.

The wind howled past Damian's ears as he turned west toward the orange half-circle of sunlight bobbing on the horizon where the sky was clear—clear except for the Moonbow, its seven bands barely visible through a distant sheet of rain.

The Moonbow is the warning and the Way.

The words spiraled in his mind like autumn leaves caught in a whirlwind, never hitting the ground, impossible to rake up and throw away.

He cursed and tore his gaze from the Moonbow. He'd been warned enough. He didn't need the Moonbow and its so-called "Way." Whatever the Way was, he needed more than a pretty poem and a centaur to convince him it was worth risking his life for.

Leaves crunched behind him, followed by the sound of pattering footsteps on the sidewalk. He turned to see the man from the house jogging toward him, a hard scowl compressing his square, thick-skinned face.

"I'm leaving!" called Damian through the whipping wind.

"There's been a change of plans, *Mr. Zacharias*," the man growled. He reached under his overcoat, crossing a hand to his holster. "I don't expect to outrun the track star..."

Damian's blood ran hot as he glimpsed the black grip of either a gun or a Taser. Faster than he could think, an electrifying tingle raced up and down his body. His shoes and hands disappeared, and he took off running, soundlessly and safe, straight past the would-be assailant and into the Rosses' house.

He barreled through the brick wall and skidded through the kitchen, finally stopping when he stumbled into the dog dish, spilling kibble onto the floor. He heard jingling, then a yippy bark as an overweight dachshund rounded the corner. It stared directly at him as it bristled and bared its teeth.

"You can see me?" said Damian. He held out an invisible palm for the dog to sniff, but the animal growled and bit two fingers, though not hard enough to draw any blood. "Son of a..." Damian shook the pain from his hand. "I guess that was your warning, huh?"

The dachshund's hackles lowered as it sniffed around Damian's shoes and licked his shoelaces.

The front door swung open. The man swore and slammed it behind him, causing the dining room chandelier to shake. Not feeling so confident in his invisibility now, Damian ducked behind the island and scooted around to the edge farthest from the living room. The dog lapped up its water, then waddled back to the dark room it had come from.

Damian started to crawl for the wall, but stopped himself. Why was he back in this house anyway? What had his subconscious been thinking? Everything had happened so fast outside when he saw the man reach for his weapon, from his doma manifesting again to deciding in a split second in which direction to run.

"It worked like a charm," said the man, presumably into a phone. Damian heard him kick back into a recliner. "I scared him, and the doma took over."

Seeing a mirror opposite the dining room table, Damian stood in front of it. He was still invisible, but for how long? Only until his fear wore off?

"Invisibility," the man said, drawing out the word as though he were particularly impressed. "Can you believe that? Never seen anything like it. Makes you wonder what the girl can do."

Damian tiptoed across the entryway into the study where a briefcase sat open atop the executive desk. He carefully flipped through its contents, but it was too dark to see anything clearly. He toyed with a nearby lamp switch, but turning it on would be too risky. He'd have to take the briefcase with him.

"Oh." The man's recliner snapped closed. "I'm sorry, sir. I didn't think about that." Even from yards away, Damian could hear an angry voice yelling on the other end of the line. "I'll see to it, sir."

The man kicked something, and then his footsteps approached the study. Damian shut the briefcase as quietly as he could just as the man turned the corner and saw it disappear.

"Damian!" the man yelled. He charged the desk, his arms outstretched as he jumped and turned like a bull that had been bitten by a horsefly.

"Don't worry," Damian said from the fireplace. "I'm not squatting. I'm *stealing*." Then he walked into the mantle, through the chimney, and stepped out of the house with not a clue what to do next.

(

"Ethan? Ethan, please...please wake up, honey."

Ethan groaned as he opened his eyes, a massive headache pulsing behind them. The bright fluorescent lights over his head were nearly blinding. He was thirsty and nauseated. What he wouldn't give for some fresh air...

He tried to push himself up from the bed he was lying on, but he couldn't move—and not because he was paralyzed. He was strapped in. He kicked with his feet, but to no avail. They, too, were confined to the bed by what might as well have been concrete slabs crossing his body.

"Ethan, can you hear me?"

He sucked in air through his teeth, making a hissing sound as his mother's voice reverberated like a brass gong in his ears. He could hear her, all right. He turned his head toward her, blinking away the black globs and flashing lights that smeared his vision. The only thing he could think of to account for

329

how awful he felt was whatever incense had been burning in the gallery. He couldn't remember ever leaving that place, or what he'd said to the councilman after learning he was being "rewarded" with a premature Coronation.

His eyesight finally returning, he saw that he was sitting up on a gurney, and that a network of neon yellow belts secured his chest, arms, knees, wrists, and ankles. He looked at his mom, words catching in his throat as he saw that she was in a gurney beside him, wearing an olive-green hospital gown and the saddest expression he'd ever seen.

"Are you hurt?" he asked her.

Black mascara trailed to her cheekbones. White lines streaking her makeup gave further proof that she'd been crying. She didn't appear to be in any physical pain, like he was, but her eyes were filled with a heart-rending fear that he could hardly look upon.

Lydia shook her head and smiled weakly. "You've been asleep for hours. I was worried about you."

Ethan looked around the room. It was white and windowless, empty except for the two gurneys, a large mirror on the wall, and a clock above the sliding glass door, ticking away the seconds. "Where are we?"

His mother dropped her gaze to the harsh glare of the epoxy floor. "The third floor of the Religious Council building." Her mouth quivered. "Where your father works."

"Dad works here?"

Ethan knew his father worked for the council, but he hadn't imagined his workplace looked like this. He'd assumed that his dad worked with classified ancient texts and religious relics, or with festival planning, or the treasury. Not with ordinary citizens constrained on stretchers.

A sequence of beeps blared from the glass door. Silently, the door glided open and a tall, aluminum platform rolled into the room. A familiar pair of brown Oxford shoes followed it.

"Dad?"

Mr. Ross slowly lifted his head from behind the platform. "Son." His red face was struggling to keep his emotions in check. He slipped off his glasses and put them in the breast pocket of his lab coat. "I'm so sorry," he said, losing his grip on the platform. It rolled away from him, and a tray of syringes clattered onto the floor.

"Moris, don't say that," said Lydia, her broken voice barely above a whisper. "This isn't your fault." She fidgeted with the edges of the restraint belt at her knees. "They shouldn't make you do this. You knew nothing about the artifacts."

"Do what?" Ethan looked back and forth between their faces, but neither one wanted to answer.

"They're punishing me because I told you about this." Moris's shoulders drooped, his shame-filled eyes glazing over as he stared at the opposite wall. "They found your journals, Lydia. They read everything."

He went to her side and did his best to hold her without crying. When he locked eyes with Ethan, the tears poured out.

"Dad, what are you talking about? The chief councilman said we're having our Coronation."

But no matter how hard Ethan's coping mechanism tried to persuade him that Coronations were benign, honorary, even fantastic affairs, he wasn't fooling himself. It didn't take a genius to realize that the chief councilman had no intention of sending him and his mother off to their respective Elysiums. What he hadn't been so sure of was whether Coronations were this way for every Petrodian when they reached seventy-five, or if the irony was unique to these circumstances.

But now his father's face was telling all.

"A Coronation is a..." Ethan's heart leapt as he glanced down at the syringes and the stainless-steel needles sticking out of them. "You're going to kill us?" He hadn't meant to sound so accusatory. Of course his father was innocent. None had a say in their vocation. They were urged to "obey and comply," or bear the consequences.

His father sat up straighter and sniffed back his tears, trying to collect himself. "They tell us it's only the body that dies. That our souls go to paradise, or whatever place the serum determines we're to dwell in and rule as sovereigns."

"You believe that?" Ethan asked. Surely his father wouldn't lie to him now.

As if feeling the eyes of his overlords behind him, Moris tightened his jaw and subtly turned his head—a discreet headshake.

"You can't do this!" Ethan shouted. Then he looked into the mirror, certain someone was looking back at him from the other side, and said, "Don't make him do this." He wasn't saying it for his sake, but his father's. What man could live with himself after dealing death to his own wife and only child?

"Ethan..." Lydia's voice was soft as she laid her head on Moris's shoulder and interlaced her fingers with his. "Let's enjoy these moments. Please." She looked up at Ethan, her eyes imploring him not to...not to what? Not to try to protect his father from murdering his family against his will?

If he only had minutes to live, Ethan wasn't about to waste one of them playing by the Fantásmata's rules. There had to be *something* he could do.

"They're being merciful, son." Moris almost sounded sincere. "Believe me when I say your death at Enochos would be much, much worse."

That, on the other hand, was unquestionably sincere.

Ethan took a deep breath and closed his eyes. The first thing he pictured was Chloe's face. Desperation gripped him, singeing his skin from the inside out. She didn't deserve to be in Hades any more than his father deserved this diabolical form of punishment.

"You will commence the Coronation now, Mr. Ross."

The voice came from a round, gray in-ceiling speaker in the corner.

"You should be the one doing this, you coward!" Ethan yelled at the councilman. "Not my dad."

Moris kissed his wife's hair. She grabbed his neck, pulled him to her and kissed his mouth. "I love you so much," she said, loud enough for the councilman to hear. "I always will."

"I love you, too," Moris said, then turned and glared at the mirror.

"Come now, Mr. Ross. Inject the serum so that their final destinations may be determined."

Moris's hand shook as he bent down and retrieved the tray. He wheeled the platform over to Ethan's bed and removed a pair of latex gloves from the top drawer.

"No, Moris, let me go first," Lydia said.

Ethan felt his heart constrict as all the blood in his body rushed down to his feet. His breaths became labored and shallow. His tongue and fingers were numb. Shock dizzied his mind and made the room spin in circles. It was as if he was succumbing to death already, a death beginning in the seat of his soul, where acute, inextricable emotions now boiled and churned. He was living the darkest nightmare, one he never could have thought up on his own, not in a million years.

Forcing his tongue to loosen and his lips to part, he focused long enough to tell his dad he loved him.

CHAPTER THIRTY-TWO
TRAVELLER

Ethan laid his head back and closed his eyes. Though he was stationary, he felt like he was hurdling through space, seconds away from being sucked into a black hole. He was sweating and shivering at the same time. He heard his father pull on the gloves.

Duna, if you can hear me, please do something.

Katsaros had told Ethan he was one of Duna's messengers. And so far everything he'd said had been true, corroborated by his mother's own research. If Katsaros had been right about the portal in Lake Thyra, right about Iris, the domas, and the Moonbow, why wouldn't he also be right about the god above it all?

Katsaros had also said that part of his mission was to restore faith to Petros, beginning with Ethan. But what could faith possibly do for a man on his deathbed? Regardless of his doubts, Ethan prayed as terrible silence roared through the room.

"Shhhh," a voice whispered in Ethan's ear. His eyes flashed open as he jerked his chin toward the sound. "Shhhh," it repeated. "It's me. It's Damian."

Ethan could feel the pulse in his neck thudding against the pillow. With no time to process whether what he heard was a hallucination or wishful thinking, he gave a slight nod and with a long exhale, mouthed the word, *Hurry*.

"I'm gonna get you out of this thing," said Damian. "Stay here until you can't see your parents."

Ethan fought to keep his face from moving.

"I'll hold their hands, and then I'm going to touch you. You can't let go of me. Blink twice if you understand."

Ethan did.

"Grab my shoulder. Then we'll take the escape route out."

"The door," whispered Ethan. "It's locked."

"I can go through it."

Even though Damian was invisible, Ethan could still imagine the proud smirk on his face.

Ethan glanced over at his father, who held his mother's elbow with shaking hands, the needle poised and ready to inject.

"Now," Ethan urged Damian.

But he hadn't had to give the command; he felt the straps immediately slackening. He froze, resisting the impulse to jump off the gurney now and rip the syringe from his father's hand. He held his breath and tensed his muscles. *Stay calm. Just stay calm.*

In his peripheral vision, he saw his father take a step back. He knew he was listening to Damian.

"*Proceed*, Mr. Ross," came the chief councilman's voice.

Let this work, Ethan prayed, his fingers twitching. Then he watched in awe as his parents disappeared and his mother's restraints snapped apart, one by one.

"Secure the cell!" the councilman barked.

Ethan sprang from the gurney and pushed it into the doorway as two humongous guards with guns waited impatiently for the door to open. Then he stood still as his father faded into view for a moment; long enough for Damian to reach out, touch Ethan's hand, and guide it to Damian's shoulder. Ethan grabbed hold with both hands and tried not to flinch as Damian led them straight through the steel walls.

"Don't look back, just run," Damian said, as they sped down the hall, heading toward the exit sign.

"They'll know we're going that way," said Ethan.

"He's right," his mother said, panting. "We need to take another way out."

"You know another way?" Damian slowed and turned to each of them. "It helps that I can see you. I wasn't sure I'd be able to. Still figuring this out."

Ethan tightened his grip on Damian's back. "Thank you for coming."

Damian turned his profile to him. "We're not out of the woods yet."

"Doesn't matter."

Damian gave a curt nod. "You're welcome."

Adrenaline surged through Ethan's veins. His mind raced a million miles per hour as every neuron activated and fired, desperate to devise a way out. After what seemed like an eternity had passed, he had formulated a crude plan. There were no guarantees it would work, but it was their best shot.

The councilman had likely already filled the stairwell with police, one touch from whom would make them visible and break them apart. But he'd have to keep his idea to himself.

Ethan stuck his head inside a janitor's storeroom, switched on the light with his free hand, and looked around.

"Ethan!" Damian rasped, tugging him forward.

Ethan resisted and stepped into the closet, pulling the other three with him.

"We can't hide in here," Damian said. "They'll be here any second."

"Son, what are you doing?" his father said, as he accidentally stepped on Ethan's toe.

Ethan looked at his father's flushed face; he looked like he'd just run a marathon.

Ethan let go of Damian and grabbed a stepladder from a lower shelf. He stood on it and rifled through the assortment of bleach, trash-can liners, and microfiber cloths.

"Looking for a rope," he finally replied.

"Down the hall, last room on the left," Moris whispered. "Why?"

"Come on," Ethan said. He placed his parents' hands in Damian's and grabbed onto Damian's arm, knocking over a mop as he turned off the light and pulled them back into the hall.

The two guards were in the middle of the corridor, their thick arms jutting out to either side as they stalked in small circles, waiting. A door slammed inside the stairwell just a few feet away, followed by the echoing voices of the councilman's goons. They were trapped.

Ethan halted abruptly, and pointed over Damian's shoulder toward a room on the left. The room seemed a hundred light years away, but what other choice was there?

"Dad, switch places with me."

Without hesitation, Moris turned and placed his hand on the back of Damian's neck. Ethan latched onto Damian's forearm, lifted one hand from his shoulder, and ducked under the web of limbs as his arm slid its way to Damian's hand. Then he stepped forward, positioning himself ahead of the others.

"Follow me," Ethan whispered.

Damian pursed his lips as a muscle jerked in his jaw. But he kept his mouth shut. He didn't have an alternative plan, so Ethan's would have to do.

Ethan led them within just a few feet of the guards. He stopped dead in his tracks at the sight of the cameras mounted on the right side of their helmets. He was almost positive they were thermal-imaging devices. A momentary panic flooded his system, but it was soon replaced with relative calm as logic kicked in: if they could be detected, they definitely would've been caught already.

Ethan breathed out slowly as a prayer of protection went up from his heart. Ahead of him, the guards continued to spin and haphazardly wave their arms, the black holsters across their chests daring him to come closer.

"What if they ran through the wall up here and took off flying?" one guard asked.

"The Asher just has one doma," grunted the other.

"We were also told there's just one Asher per family."

The other guard stopped moving, tempting Ethan to make his move then, but he held back.

"True. Take it to the councilman and see if he wants to dispatch an air squadron."

The first guard nodded. Then he sprinted toward the Coronation wing, leaving half the hallway wide open.

Ethan squeezed Damian's hand. He glanced at his mother on Damian's other side, and his father behind him. Then he signaled with his free hand, and together they slipped past the remaining guard like ghosts in the night.

They stepped through the closed door into the sterile room, which was identical to the Coronation cell. The only difference was that instead of gurneys there was nothing but a tall, steel pole in the center, with a stepped platform beside it. Seeing a noose dangling off its edge, Ethan felt a freezing chill shoot up his spine.

He didn't have time to entertain the emotions of horror, fear, hate, and sadness coalescing like storm clouds in his psyche. Terror had paralyzed Petros long enough. He had to keep going, to keep swimming with the current of adrenaline flowing through him.

"I hope no one has a fear of heights," said Damian. Apparently, he'd caught on to Ethan's plan.

"We'll get over it," Lydia replied.

Ethan led them to the platform and snatched the rope.

"I saw that." It was the councilman's voice. "I knew you'd give yourselves away eventually."

Ethan looked up into the corner of the room. He could almost see the councilman's lightless black eye winking through the camera.

It hadn't taken long for Chloe to be noticed on board the ship, the same ship she'd dreamed of—or at least she thought she'd been dreaming—in the treehouse during her birthday party.

Last time, with a grotesque sea monster named Scylla terrorizing the boat and its crew, no one had noticed Chloe clinging to a rope behind the mast. But now the seas were calm. Scylla was gone, and all the sailors were behaving normally—or as normally as could be expected considering they'd just witnessed a strangely dressed teenaged girl appear out of nowhere.

They had all gathered around her, pointing and shouting in Próta. Not knowing a single word of their language, she'd finally stopped repeating her own name and said the name of the only other woman on the boat: Iris. That shut them up, and immediately two oarsmen had taken her by the arms and escorted her to the stern.

There, gazing out over the cobalt-colored sea, stood Iris, her flame-red hair blowing in the breeze as she hummed quietly to the young girl asleep on her shoulder. A few feet away, two men were kneeling on the deck, their heads bowed and their eyes closed. Though Chloe couldn't understand them, she knew their moving lips were speaking something sacred.

The oarsman on her right, a squat man with a thick blond beard that appeared incongruous on his boyish face, spoke softly, respectfully, to Iris, never once making eye contact with her. She stopped humming and turned to them, her long hair now whipping across her face, covering all but her eyes, the blue in them like the indigo tip of a torch.

"*Aspádzomai*, Chloe," welcomed Iris.

She was younger than Chloe remembered, probably not much older than twenty. Chloe looked down at the sleeping fair-haired toddler. Was this Iris's daughter, the girl from her visions who had the power to vanish?

Chloe repeated the foreign greeting as best she could and then looked at the little girl. "Charis?"

Iris nodded, half smiling, and half frowning in puzzlement. Then she said something to the two oarsmen, dismissing them.

Chloe touched her chest. "Asher. I am an Asher."

A flock of seagulls, the ones Chloe had heard calling to her down in hell, circled overhead. Why had she heard them? Why was she here, even farther from her family than before? Her family didn't even exist yet.

And then it hit her. Her doma. She'd had it all along, ever since her birthday when she'd first been on this boat. It had never been a hallucination or a dream. It had been real, as this was real.

I can travel in time?

Iris turned to the two men kneeling nearby. Her lips parted to say something to them, but seeing they were still praying, she closed them and impatiently rubbed them together. She held her forefinger up to Chloe as if to say, *Just a second*. Then she gently settled Charis on a woolen blanket.

Iris approached the men and bent down to whisper in the younger one's ear. He glanced up at Chloe, a flash of a smile in his warm brown eyes, and immediately she recognized him as the man from the fire tunnel. Well, the only whole man, anyway. The other had been a centaur, just like those on Circe's crazed island of Aeaea.

Before Iris could take a single step toward Chloe, a shaft of white, crystallized mist materialized between them. The scent of lemon and lavender wafted out of it, followed by the mellifluous sound of a girl's sweet humming.

"Carya?"

Iris and Carya locked eyes through the mist; they'd spoken the name in unison.

Chloe could see Carya's radiant body encased within the thick haze, the royal purple of her robes and the violet of her hair creating a watercolor cloud come to life.

Carya lifted her arms and punched her white fists through the opalescent canopy above her. A loud whooshing sound accompanied the broken mist as it drifted out and dissipated over the whole ship, blanketing the deck with a wintry shimmer. Then, as quickly as she'd appeared, Carya dissolved into the halo of light still surrounding her, still humming that heavenly tune.

344

A shrill chiming noise sounded in Chloe's ear as she watched the flabbergasted crew stare at one another. Some of them reached down to touch the snow-like substance on the deck, but they couldn't get it to budge. Chloe tried to kick it, but she stubbed her toe as though it were solid rock. Evidently, Carya was much stronger than she looked. Or maybe it was that mortals were just pathetically weak.

Chloe crossed the boat to where Iris and the men who had been praying now stood. "What was that about?"

"I'm not sure," answered Iris. "Is she ever straightforward with you?"

Chloe shook her head. "Definitely not."

"Back to work!" barked the older man to the sailors. He lowered his voice as he turned to Chloe. "Excuse me. These men act as though they've never seen anything out of the ordinary." Then he brushed passed her, calling out orders left and right, the heels of his boots clapping along the hard, ethereal substance.

Chloe laughed as the ringing sound finally faded from her head. "I can understand you! *That's* what Carya did."

Iris's eyes went wide. "Well, then..." She steadied herself on the edge of the stern and took the hand of the man beside her. "We have some catching up to do."

CHAPTER THIRTY-THREE
SACRIFICE

The past hour had felt like an out-of-body experience to Damian. Just that afternoon, he'd resigned himself to following in the footsteps of the Ashers before him and forgetting all about his gift. He'd returned the jasper stone to Katsaros, and he'd turned his back on his sister. He wasn't about to risk his life over some long-dead religious sect or mystical poem about the Moonbow. The Fantásmata were too powerful. They'd tolerate a revolt just long enough to make a gory example of every one of its conspirators.

But a switch had been flipped back at the Rosses' house when the guard started chasing after him. He realized then that even if he cooperated, even if he swore never to speak of his strange sightings and did his best to blend in and let his power lie, they'd still come after him, just as they'd gone after his father. And if he was going to die, he might as well die doing something right.

He would never get the chance to apologize to Chloe for being a coward, but at least he could help someone who was brave, someone who would have tried to save her if he'd been the one with the doma. If Ethan and his family could survive, maybe they could make a difference somehow.

Damian pressed his face through the wall. In just a few seconds, the councilman's men would be in the room, and his invisibility wouldn't last forever. Rappelling down the wall with the rope Ethan had taken was their only feasible option.

"It's clear," said Damian. "But we've gotta be quick."

"I'll go first," Mr. Ross said, taking the rope from his son.

Damian glanced toward the door. His heartbeat mimicked the guards' heavy footsteps racing down the hall. "I'll anchor the rope with Ethan so they can't see us. Mrs. Ross, you go after your husband."

Lydia nodded and squeezed his hand.

Back to back with Damian, Moris straddled the rope, wrapped it around himself, and secured it between his legs.

Then, with just one foot pressed against Damian's heel, he leaned back and slipped silently outside.

A barrage of gunfire peppered the acrylic door, shattering it in a matter of seconds. Three guards in tactical gear rushed in, dividing the cell into thirds like a pack of bloodhounds hot on a scent. They took lumbering steps, zigzagging up and down the floor, slicing the air with their arms, swiping their weapons over the bone-colored countertops lining the room.

One guard jumped up onto the platform, crouched down, and became unnervingly still. "They're not in here." He ripped off his gloves and cracked his knuckles. "They're using the rope to lower themselves down. We're wasting time." He clicked on the radio on his shoulder. "Surround the outside perimeter." Then he turned to the other two guards now standing at attention, awaiting instruction. "Go. I'll stay in here."

The men nodded and hurried out of the room. Mr. Ross was already three-quarters of the way down the building.

Ready? Ethan mouthed to his mother.

She leaned across Damian and kissed Ethan's cheek.

With Ethan and Lydia holding onto his waist, Damian pushed his head through the wall to check on Moris one more time. As soon as Moris's feet hit the ground, Damian pulled up the rope as fast as he could and tied it around Lydia. She closed her eyes and swiveled around Damian until her back faced the wall. He slowly backed up, holding his breath as he felt her weight tugging on the rope.

Though he was invisible to her now, Lydia gave a thumbs-up in Damian's direction, grimacing as the rope rubbed against her back and tightened around her pink forearm.

She was moving at a snail's pace. Damian wanted to yell at her to move faster, but even a whisper would be suicide. The guards would be on them any second, ready to deliver them to their master and watch them bleed.

"Are you in here, freak?" the guard called out, his deep voice muffled behind his helmet.

With half of his face peeking through the wall, Damian remained still, watching Lydia's every move, preparing to rip up the rope and fasten it to her son.

"What will it take for that little power of yours to wear off and let me see you?" the guard said.

Damian heard the guard pace around the room, then stop with a frustrated sigh before sending a hail of bullets into the cabinetry. When he was done showing off, he grunted and jumped on the platform. *Let him keep talking and making noise*, Damian thought. The more he entertained himself, the less attention he was paying to them.

Lydia was almost down now.

"We're going to need that rope back so we can hang you with it," the guard announced, flicking the pole with his fingernail. "However, I have a feeling the councilman has a more creative method of dealing with Ashers."

Moris untangled his wife and kissed her quickly. Then they dashed into the hedges as Damian pulled up the rope.

"I'll never forget this," whispered Ethan. Then, before Damian could register what was happening, Ethan had grabbed him by the shoulders and spun him away from the wall. "It's your turn now."

Damian shook his head and pointed angrily at the rope, then stabbed a finger in Ethan's chest, trying soundlessly to convey that this wasn't part of the plan, at least not part of *his* plan. Didn't Ethan know that the instant he stopped touching him he'd be seen and probably shot by the guard? If he was lucky, Damian could help Ethan down and then find another way out; but he had a feeling Ethan wasn't satisfied relying on luck. Moris and Lydia needed Damian if they were ever going to escape, and they needed him soon.

Ethan removed a hand from Damian's shoulder. Both of them turned to the guard sitting on the platform, his legs dangling over the edge as he sharpened a curved dagger on a short steel rod. Ethan's temple pounded as he clenched his jaw.

Damian didn't know how far Ethan's plan went, but he was almost positive it didn't move past the guy with all the weapons. If things were different and it was *his* mom and dad down there waiting, Damian liked to think he'd do the same and be the hero who stayed behind. But he'd already proved he wasn't a hero. Chloe's only chance of escaping hell had been squelched the second he'd handed Katsaros the jasper stone and gone his way. He was spineless, gutless, a scared kitten masquerading as a lion. What made him think he'd act any differently for his parents?

Heat surged through Damian's veins. He gave Ethan a stern nod and began situating the rope around his own back. Ethan squeezed Damian's shoulders and then, once Damian was secured, released his grip and took hold of the rope with both hands.

A twinge of doubt burned at the edges of Damian's mind. What if the guard got to Ethan before Damian reached the bottom of the building? He'd fall, break his legs or his back, and be no good to anyone. But it was too late to backtrack or sort out what-if scenarios. Ethan was leaning back, and Damian was moving downward as a lump the size of an apple swelled within his throat.

When Damian was two-thirds of the way down, Ethan waved at him to move faster. Damian had a better idea. He pulled from his pocket the sharp pair of scissors he'd used to cut Ethan out of the gurney, and snipped himself free of the makeshift harness. He didn't even feel himself hit the ground.

His power was that strong after all. They could have bypassed the rappelling altogether and simply jumped through the wall. Damian wanted to scream at himself, but there wasn't a second to waste stewing over his own ignorance.

He couldn't help what he didn't know, and jumping three stories without knowing it was possible to land in one piece would've been too big of a risk.

Land on me. The thought seemed absurd as it blasted through his doubt, but if he could drop fifteen feet without gaining so much as a scratch, it stood to reason that he could absorb someone's weight falling onto him.

"Jump!" Damian shouted. He didn't care who heard. "Jump on me, Ethan, I'm right here." And then he remembered they'd passed through a solid wall. There were no windows in the room.

"Where's Ethan?"

Damian heard the confusion in Lydia's voice, followed closely by the escalating sound of the guards' shouts as they rounded the building.

"This way!" one yelled. "They just escaped through the wall on the northwest side."

Damian jumped into the shrubs and grabbed the Rosses by the arm. "We have to go *now*."

As soon as they were fully invisible, they took off running for the woods. Around them a gentle rain started to fall, which they couldn't feel. Above them flashed jagged lightning that couldn't strike them. And hanging low in the last clear patch of sunset sky shone the brilliant bands of the Moonbow. Staring at it, Damian had the haunting suspicion that, despite his power, it was staring back.

Hours had passed since the ship had docked in Limén, a city that, even in Iris's time, was teeming with hardworking laborers skilled in all manner of trades.

In modern Petros, Limén was the place of residence for Petrodians whose occupations ranged from aerospace engineer and physician to automotive mechanic and farmer. Ancient Limén, according to Iris, attracted textile workers, artisans, farmers, and fishermen, not because they had been preordained by the government to be such but because that's what they and their families had carved out *for themselves*.

Here, in this new now, people had the freedom to do what they pleased. But it hadn't always been that way.

Chloe sat in the small kitchen of an elderly couple, both of whom were snoring loudly in the adjacent room. Her belly was full of bread and lentils, and though her eyelids drooped and her head felt heavy, the last thing she wanted to do was sleep.

Across from her sat Iris and her husband Tycho, the man she'd recognized on the ship. Since Carya had made it possible for them to communicate, Iris hadn't stopped talking. It was almost as if she'd been expecting Chloe to show up, as if seeing a teenager from the future pop up on her boat and introduce herself as a relative was a semi-regular occurrence.

But from what Chloe had heard thus far, her arrival had been far from an unusual. The gryphon fossils from the museum, the centaurs she'd seen on Circe's island, Circe herself...none of it came as news to them. All of it was familiar.

Just as the early birds began to chirp, and soft yellow sunlight flooded beneath the door, it finally came time for them to learn what they *didn't* know. And so Chloe told them about Orpheus, Hades, the walnut, and her dreams—or rather her time travels—in which she'd seen their grown-up daughter disappear with a scroll, and then the three of them, along with a centaur, running between walls of fire.

Chloe hadn't been sure anything would astound these two, but apparently she was wrong. Carya they understood. Orpheus's ruse made sense, somewhat. The premonitions they recognized as warnings from Duna. But what they could not readily discern was the next step.

It was obvious, given Chloe's doma, why the Fantásmata had done everything they could to disable her, first by trying to turn her into an animal on Aeaea, and then by imprisoning her in Hades and forcing her to drink from the Lethe. She was the only person alive who could turn back the clock and change history. Whatever had been chasing Iris and her family, Chloe was the only one capable of stopping it.

"Charis was my age when I saw her in the fire tunnel, and inside your house," said Chloe. "Why did I come back to this point in time?"

Charis rubbed the sleep from her eyes as she climbed onto Tycho's lap. Tycho directed her small hand to a cup of milk, and she gulped it down.

"You said you traveled back here on your birthday," Iris said. "You saw Scylla?"

Chloe nodded, the hair on the back of her neck standing on end as she envisioned the monster with its six hideous heads and the barking dogs bulging from its waist.

"Did you see the boy?"

Confused, Chloe shook her head, and then stopped herself as a short snippet of memory darted back into her mind's eye. "I saw you," she said. "But there was a smaller man next to you. I watched him crawl to the edge of the boat while no one was looking."

Iris covered her mouth with her hand and turned her face to the sunshine cracking through the shutters on the window.

"I saw the fire come out of your hands and float toward the monster," continued Chloe, "but then I woke up, or came back, I mean." Tears burned in her throat as she recalled the reason why. "My brother had been looking for me."

"Does he know about your gift?" asked Iris.

Charis wedged herself between her parents and stuffed her hands into a bowl of purple grapes, giggling as she felt them squish.

"I don't know." Chloe's fingernails dug into the sides of her chair. "I never told him. He would've thought I'd lost my mind."

Tycho leaned forward onto his elbows. "But you think perhaps someone told him?"

Chloe shrugged. "I'm not sure. One of my charming captors down in hell implied Damian knew I was there and that he just decided to leave me." She sniffed back her tears. It would do no good to dwell on it, just like her father had said. "So what happened to the boy I saw?"

Iris whispered something into Charis's ear that sent her scurrying off to a pile of toys near the stove.

Tycho sighed. "He saved our daughter by taking her place. Scylla had made a bargain with Apollo, which is what I imagine Orpheus did as well. If they brought Apollo what he wanted, he'd give them their greatest desire."

"What did Scylla desire?" asked Chloe.

"To be beautiful again. One must always be wary of beautiful women," answered Iris with a wry smile.

"And even though Orpheus succeeded in delivering you to that portal," said Tycho, "the victory is ultimately yours, because you, just like the boy, placed your faith in something far greater than yourself. Not even death can defeat such faith."

A tear slipped from Chloe's cheek, and she wrapped her hands around her cup of chamomile tea.

"Chloe, sometimes Duna shows us things through symbols," said Iris. "With me, every color of the Moonbow held meaning for my life. I don't know why Duna ordained for you to travel back to this part of the past, nor can I tell you why Carya's walnut showed you some future peril. But what I can tell you is that Duna never reveals the whole path to us. Only one sure step, or abstract symbol, at a time."

Chloe took a sip of her tea, which by now was cold and over-steeped. "I think Duna might have overestimated my deciphering skills. I can't make sense of any of this."

"Give it time," said Tycho. "After all, time is your doma, isn't it?" Though he was joking, the inherent wisdom in his words gave Chloe comfort, and a palpable peace she relished.

Iris reached out and took Chloe's hand in hers. "What you've seen and heard will make sense when the time is right, whether that's our time or yours."

CHAPTER THIRTY-FOUR
ESCAPE

*W*here...are...the sacrifices?"

Apollo's yell whipped through Hermes' skin and rattled against his ribs. They stood in the throne room, just inches apart, the black Wall of Sacrifice presiding over them. It was supposed to be flowing red with the blood of the Petrodian traitors, but it produced not a single trickle.

Hades sat on the edge of the cliff, his broad shoulders rolled forward and his horned helmet by his hip. His glaucous bald head, which seemed two sizes too small for his body, rolled from side to side, and he uttered long and ghastly groans.

"I do not know, sire," Hermes said. "I haven't been to the Upperworld today." Hermes' eyes jumped around the room. "Where is Orpheus? Perhaps—"

The bloodless vein in Apollo's neck distended like a bloated worm. He backhanded Hermes' cheek. "Don't change the subject. Orpheus did his duty. He delivered one of the Vessels to Hades, and there she resides as we speak."

Hermes lowered his hand from his cheek. "What do you mean *one* of them? There can only be one, and I deposited her in the Fields myself."

Hades' groans grew louder, their echoes blending into a cacophonous symphony that clawed against Hermes' ears.

Apollo took Hermes by the throat and squeezed as he lifted him off the floor. "*You* are supposed to be our eyes and ears among the mortals. *You* were chosen because you are supposed to be clever." He slammed Hermes to the ground, knocking out his breath and breaking bones that would soon regenerate, only to be broken again.

Hermes' neck cracked as he twisted it into place. He sat still, staring into the orange whorls of mist rising out of the river below, trying to suppress his own ire. Yes, he was clever, but he wasn't omniscient. How could he have known there could be more than one Asher in a family? If he'd taken his focus off of the girl for one millisecond, Apollo would have flayed him himself. But it would prove futile to try and convince him of that or make him see reason. Better to confess his oversight and feign repentance than argue and be sent to Tartarus for his penalty.

"I will find them," Hermes said. "I will go—"

"You have done enough!" bellowed Apollo. He pointed at his brother, who was now rocking back and forth like a maniac, one of his hands curled inside his mouth.

"Then who will you send?" Hermes couldn't help himself. His pride wouldn't let him be usurped so easily. "I am the only one permitted to fly between all the realms, even to go to the Vale, the Fields, or Tartarus itself to fetch whichever soul you wish to recruit." He lifted his chin and got to his feet. He had more power than his brothers ever gave him credit for. Perhaps they simply needed to be reminded.

Apollo lowered his voice, as if to keep Hades from hearing. "I am sending no one."

"And what, you'll continue to speak through your channels and hope *they* will stop the prophecy?"

Hermes was incredulous. Could Apollo really trust the fate of the Underworld to a bunch of powerless, half-witted mortals?

Apollo rushed forward and lifted his hand halfway, his muscles shaking as he decided whether to strike him again. "The Fantásmata have proved themselves immensely less fallible than you. They were the ones who revealed to me the second Asher." He pointed down the endless, smoke-filled aisle to the gate. "Leave us."

Hermes' jaw fell open. His heart thudded like a bird beating against the walls of its cage. Not once in the eons since the War had ended had his power and role as messenger been undermined. For millennia, he had served his brothers faithfully, doing his part for the dark trinity they had established, lying, scheming, tempting, seducing, all so the three of them might increase their authority and win worship for themselves.

Hades thrived off the blood of the Coronations. Apollo acquired strength through the prayers of the mystics who claimed him as their god. And Hermes' delight had been in bending mortals to his will. What would become of him now that he had been supplanted by Apollo's disciples? He would be no better than one of the lovesick wraiths moaning in the shadows of the Vale.

Apollo drew his sword and pressed its tip into the hollow of Hermes' throat. "Leave us, I said, before my mercy fails me, brother."

Hermes lifted himself with his winged sandals and floated past the flickering tripods, sure there was no greater torture than to have a hubris matched only by two other spirits in the universe, and no purpose or outlet with which to gratify it.

(

The warm blood began to harden into sticky specks and blackened clumps on Ethan's hand. He couldn't keep his other hand from trembling as he tried to pick it off. Not once in his life had he made another man bleed. And never had he imagined he'd be capable of killing someone. But there had been no other choice.

Ethan sat slumped in the corner of the room, staring at the wall Damian and his parents had escaped through. Five bullet holes surrounded the space where he'd been standing, and yet, by some miracle, he hadn't been shot. He'd evaded them all, then somehow managed to wrestle the gun away from the guard, shoot the security camera without aiming, then twist the arm that held the knife and drive it into the guard's neck.

It had all happened so fast. He hadn't even expected himself to put up a fight, but rather had hoped the guard would spare him the noose or the needle, and dispatch him with a single bullet. But his survival instincts had been stronger than he'd anticipated, overpowering almost, and he wrestled better and more aggressively than he ever had in school. Even the last expression on the guard's face was one of utter surprise.

Now, the guard's lifeless corpse was hidden under the cabinets across the room, covered up by Ethan's clothes.

Ethan had put on the guard's uniform and was dressed head to toe in tactical gear, the chest and shoulder panels of which fit a bit too loosely. He'd had to pull up the shin and elbow guards well past his joints to keep them from sliding.

With no faucet in the room to wash off the blood, he slipped on the gloves and took a deep breath, the sour air in the room burning his lungs. The adrenaline had dissipated, leaving him exhausted, guilt-ridden, and above all, mystified that he was still alive. But he *was* alive, and he had to believe it was for a reason.

Taking what confidence he could from that thought, he got up, holstered the gun, and stepped through the shattered door.

The hallway was empty and eerily silent. He jogged to the window at the far end and looked out, only to see a few guards standing around on the lawn. One of them was pointing off into the distance while another searched the horizon through a pair of binoculars.

They got away. Relief washed through Ethan's body, tingling his hot skin beneath the suit. He thanked Duna in his thoughts, and then asked for his help once more.

"I'm following your lead here," he said aloud.

Then he turned back and stared in the direction of the Coronation cell. What if the chief councilman was still in there? If he were, wouldn't he have gone into the room after he'd noticed the commotion in the surveillance camera and then seen the camera go black with the gunshot? Ethan could wait for him to come back, perhaps, and then kill him easily, with his bare hands if he had to. The man had tried to murder him, after all, and he would try again if he got the chance.

Ethan took a step forward, then paused as reason overrode his impulse. He glanced up at the corner of the ceiling. A gray dome camera, barely noticeable and likely impervious to bullets, was waiting to catch him screwing up. Maybe he'd been lucky, and the councilman hadn't seen the confrontation with the guard. Maybe the councilman had been outside giving orders, or back at the museum consulting the drugged-out weirdos.

Ethan made the decision not to defy the odds again. He'd save his vengeance for another day.

Anxious to slip passed the heavily armed personnel below, he pivoted on his heel and was almost to the stairwell when he heard a soft panting noise, paired with a low, monotone hum, drifting up to him from the doorway. His adrenaline surged once again, and he ripped the gun from its holster. He leaned into the door, and with the pistol raised pushed it open.

His heart raced as he stepped onto the landing. The lights were off, and a row of small octagonal windows dotting the center of the wall did little to illuminate the shadows. He clumsily probed the wall for a light switch, but found nothing. He leaned against the door, held the raised gun in his right hand, and fiddled with the side of his helmet.

After a few slow seconds, the thermal-imaging camera flickered to life, and even though it only affected his sight, all of his senses seemed to heighten. He could almost feel the finger grooves in the grip of the gun bristling through his glove. He could smell the sweat, blood, and body odor encrusted within his suit. And he could hear the humming sound fade to shallow breaths.

With the camera's grayscale palette, the stairwell was as dark as before. He didn't have time to try and change the settings. He didn't even know what the different settings did. But no matter the colors, if a person was down there, they would stick out and he could protect himself. He just needed to get closer. He rocked up from the door, steadied his breathing as best he could, and with his back to the wall and his face toward the railing, descended the stairs, crossing one boot over the other.

Ethan was standing at the top of the second landing when he saw the ghostly image of a woman at the end of the stairs, the infrared radiation from her body making her glow like a star in the night sky. Her hands were pressed against the wall, her white chest rising and falling to the rhythm of his own breaths. She was scared, as was he.

"Who are you? What are you doing up here?" he demanded.

If there were cameras in this area, he wasn't about to appear soft. He hurried down the stairs and, making sure he wasn't touching the trigger, swung the gun into her periphery. "Speak!"

The woman turned toward him and wiped her cheek. "I'm Chloe Zacharias."

CHAPTER THIRTY-FIVE
SMOKE

Ethan's hand flew to the side of his helmet and clicked off the camera. He blinked hard and flipped up his visor, then crept closer, logic arguing with his eyes.

This couldn't be Chloe. Chloe was in Hades. He'd seen her walk into the mist at Lake Thyra, and he knew Damian hadn't gone after her. This had to be a trick, a sadistic ploy by the councilman to punish Ethan's emotions before he tortured his body.

The girl's blue eyes stared at the barrel of the gun; her long blond hair, ashy in the darkness, was hanging close around her cheeks and mouth. "Duna, please..." Then she tipped her head forward and closed her eyes, as if waiting for him to squeeze the trigger.

Ethan holstered the pistol and took a step forward. He watched her body stiffen as he leaned toward her to whisper into her ear. "It's me, Chloe. It's Ethan."

Chloe lifted her head and searched his eyes until she was sure. Finally, her tears evaporating as a smile warmed her face, she took his hand and squeezed it. "It's good to see you."

"You, too."

That was the biggest understatement of his life. If circumstances were different, he would have thrown off his helmet right then and there and kissed her as he'd wanted to for so long. He swore to himself that the second circumstances were different he'd take his time telling her exactly how he felt.

"You need to get out of here," he said.

"No, *you* need to get out of here. That's why I came. I mean, I think that's why I came."

"How did you—"

"You won't believe it." She released his hand and shook her head, as if she didn't believe it herself.

"Try me."

The door above them crashed open and banged against the wall. "Yes, Miss Zacharias, try us." The councilman's oily voice dripped like tree sap down the stairwell. "Dazzle us with that spectacular talent of yours."

"Run!" yelled Ethan. He pulled out his gun once again and sped down the stairs after Chloe.

She pushed through the door below the exit sign and raced out into the foyer, a place Ethan hadn't seen since their field trip ten years prior. She held a hand on her hip and bent over halfway, catching her breath.

The elevator behind them dinged. Ethan turned to see the councilman, dressed as a holy man in his gaudy, purple garb, step out, his hands lifted in welcome.

"Quite a fighter you are, Mr. Ross. Not the shuddering little nebbish your father is."

Ethan's finger twitched onto the pistol's hammer. He didn't know much about guns, but he knew enough to put a bullet between a man's eyes. He widened his stance on the marble floor, lifted the gun with both hands, and held his breath as he aimed through the sights.

"Are you sure you want to do that, Mr. Ross?"

A sharp ticking noise, like the second hand of a watch, clicked beside Ethan's left ear. He threw off the helmet and resumed his position.

"I designed those suits with a unique capability," said the councilman, a pompous smile deepening the wrinkles of his pale, sunken cheeks, "to self-combust at the touch of a button, should desperate times call for desperate measures." He held up a small black fob, his thumb poised on its center.

"It seems like any time is a good time for you to kill innocent people," said Ethan, the faint ticking sound quickening its cadence from the floor.

"If you don't tell me where Mr. Zacharias has run off to in the next ten seconds, you will burst into flames." The councilman gathered his robes and walked forward.

Ethan looked over the man's head at the wall of stained glass behind him, the colors of the crescent moon and serpent it depicted dulled by the evening sky beyond it.

The councilman jerked a hand toward Chloe and pointed at her. "And if you move, he dies."

"I don't know where he is," said Ethan. "That's the truth."

The councilman's black eyes squinted at him as he licked his cracked, purplish lips. "I'm to believe that you and your fellow conspirators never discussed a rendezvous point while you were haunting my halls?"

"What's he talking about?" asked Chloe. "Where's Damian?"

"Answer her, Mr. Ross. Where's Damian?"

Resisting the urge to look away from the councilman's interrogating gaze, Ethan stood up straighter and thrust out his chin. "I wasn't planning on surviving."

Chloe gasped.

The councilman whipped his head toward her. "What is it, my dear? What's wrong? There's nothing for you to fear." He went to her and cupped her chin with his hand. "My heart breaks for you and your brother, for what you went through with your parents."

Ethan's eyes fell to the helmet on the floor, his ears burning more with every ticking sound it made. Around him, the suit felt as if it was tightening, gripping his arms and legs like a python's coils, squeezing around his ribcage, tempting him to break free from it. He needed to think fast, but his mind was stuck, his thoughts sabotaged by the countdown as it accelerated until the ticks were almost indistinguishable from one another.

"I may be a man of power, but I'm a man of pity, too," continued the councilman. He leaned forward and pressed his lips to Chloe's forehead.

She grimaced and squeezed her eyes shut. Her limbs went rigid, petrified for Ethan's sake.

"It isn't your fault you were born an Asher. I have no intention of harming you. I just need your friend here, and your brother, wherever he is, to cooperate." The man slid his hand down her neck, laughing softly at her disgust.

Ethan was sweating under the suit. He fought the urge to pull off the gloves and implore Chloe not to believe the man, that everything they'd ever been taught about the Religious Council, and all Petros, for that matter, was a lie. But he had a

371

feeling she knew that already. He could only imagine all she'd seen and heard if she really had been in Hades.

"Is it getting hot in there, Mr. Ross?" The councilman held up the fob again. "Tell me what I need to know and I will relieve you."

"I told you," said Ethan, barely opening his mouth. "I don't know where he is. I didn't plan on getting out of that room."

The councilman sighed and bowed his head. "My patience has run its course, Mr. Ross. We will find the Asher. And as for your parents, I'll see to it personally that they die as slowly as possible."

"No!" Chloe lunged forward and grabbed hold of the councilman's sleeve. He held the fob high in the opposite hand, his weak breath whistling as she leapt for it.

"Chloe, stop!" yelled Ethan.

But Chloe didn't stop. She seized the councilman's wrist and became very still, eerily still, frozen in time. The clock stopped ticking. Ethan closed his eyes, ready for whatever was rigged within his suit to engulf him in flames.

The silence lingered. His breaths persisted. He opened his eyes and saw no trace of Chloe or the councilman.

"Chloe?"

He could hear the guards talking to one another outside, followed by the sound of the foyer's bronze doors creaking open. Ethan snatched his helmet from the floor and put it on. He could only hope that wherever Chloe was, she had possession of the fob. He'd find out soon enough.

It had worked. A few moments ago, Chloe had been focusing on this time and place, concentrating not on an image but a prayer, a yearning that had inexplicably arisen the moment the councilman had made clear his intentions.

Now she was standing in the midst of what she could only guess was the ancient temple in Eirene. Around her were throngs of people and a heap of ruins, huge stones and toppled columns strewn over acres of rubble. Though the area was filled with evidence of destruction, the people there were jubilant, dancing and smiling, laughing and singing, jumping and twirling with a happiness she'd never seen.

Stretched over the remaining columns of a colonnade were two halves of an indigo veil; dozens of worshippers lay prostrate beneath them, the pieces flapping lazily in the breeze. Children danced, and acrobats flipped to the music of pipes, drums, and tambourines. The air was crisp and refreshed Chloe's body as she breathed in the alien atmosphere. She wished everyone from her time could see this.

Not far from where she stood was a rectangular rock-cut pool, about one quarter of the size of her swimming pool back home. She turned to the councilman a few yards away and let him watch as she dropped the fob into the water.

"He'll live a little while longer, then," said the councilman. His gaunt, skinny body looked like a corpse against the colorful backdrop of whatever celebration was being held there. "You have no idea what you're doing, do you?"

It wasn't a question, but an observation. And in truth, Chloe *didn't* know what she was doing. It had been her hope to bring him here so together they could see what had happened to their world. Petros's history had been corrupted long ago, and its rulers brainwashed by a nefarious ideology, the source of which she'd seen with her own eyes.

She couldn't fully blame the councilman for his actions. He'd been indoctrinated since birth, programmed to carry out the plans of his predecessors and their predecessors before them.

"This is Petros before there was a Religious Council," Chloe said. "They're happy because they're free. Free to be what Duna created them to be."

The councilman's face twisted with loathing at Duna's name.

"I saw a boy freely give his life because of his love for a total stranger." She nearly choked on the words as she thought of Ethan's willingness to die for his parents and for Damian. "That love doesn't exist in the world today because its source has been shut out."

Passion emboldened her words, edging them with a conviction she was only now able to comprehend. She didn't know the All-Powerful, but he had known her all along.

She could feel him pouring courage into her even now, filling her with a confidence she'd never had, and with a hope she hadn't thought possible.

"I'm confused." The councilman scratched his chin as two young kids gave him funny looks as they brushed past his robe. "Is your doma time travel or sophistry?"

"It isn't sophistry. And it doesn't take a doma to see what's happened. But it isn't your fault." She took a step toward him, the soft glow of the sunset adding much-needed warmth to his face. "You can see for yourself, and you can change it. You can make things right."

A shadow fell across the councilman's face as a low, roaring sound rumbled through the temple, muting the revelry as every instrument and voice fell silent. "You should have done more research."

"What are you talking about?" Chloe's eyes scanned the desecrated courtyard, certain that Iris and Tycho were nearby. If she could get the councilman to meet them, to listen to everything they knew...

"Run!"

The command echoed through the crowd, carried from person to person in a contagious surge of panic. The people who had been so carefree just moments ago, caught up in the bliss of the festival, began stampeding toward the portico like a herd of animals, dropping their banners, palm branches, and pieces of fruit as they went.

Black plumes of smoke rose beyond the inner courtyard, blocking out the sun, spearing the clouds with long bolts of lightning that reached the ground. A deafening crack, like a sonic boom, rang out from the mountain range encircling the city.

"You don't want to stick around for what's coming, Miss Zacharias," the councilman said. "That's a promise."

"What is it?" Chloe climbed onto a boulder to get a better view. But she could see nothing except the wall of smoke drawing nearer, growing taller, curling toward her like a tidal wave.

CHAPTER THIRTY-SIX
GENESIS

A small blond-haired boy stopped beside the rock on which Chloe stood and leaned forward onto his tiptoes, taking her finger. He spoke in Próta, but she didn't need an interpreter, or Carya's magic, to understand that he wanted her to go with him. His family shouted at him to move.

"Mania!" said the boy, pulling Chloe toward him. "Mania!" He pointed toward the blackening sky.

What an odd word for a child to use, Chloe thought.

Growing impatient, the boy's father scooped him up and carried him off, disappearing into the frenzied crowd. Chloe looked to the councilman, his expression cold and bizarrely calm despite the chaos around them.

The boulder began to tremble, and Chloe jumped off, only to land on quaking ground. The remaining upright columns swayed and quickly collapsed, and all the debris of a prior catastrophe shook in terror as gusts of wind gathered the dirt and created from it dozens of man-sized tornadoes that sped directly toward her.

"Mania is her name," said the councilman in a voice so low she could hardly hear him.

Chloe coughed as dust flew into her mouth. "Whose name?"

"The final Asher ever to have a place in history." The councilman turned to her, pulling up his sleeve to cover his face. "*Your* ancestor. You want to know why I've sworn to do away with you?" He stretched out his free arm as lightning struck the boulder on which Chloe had stood. "You, and all your kind, are dangerous, Miss Zacharias." He stabbed his finger into the air. "*This* is what Ashers become. *This* is what you do."

Chloe shook her head. "No. That's what you've been told to believe all your life." She shielded her face with her arm and stepped over to him, touching his hand. "But it's a lie, and if you won't make things right then I *will*."

She reached out and yanked the councilman's sleeve, pulling him toward her. "I could leave you here at her mercy," she said, clutching his cold, brittle arm and glancing up at the gray-green thunderheads churning above them.

He gave her a small, condescending smile and patted her hand. "But you won't."

"Why do you seem so sure of that?" she said, loosening her grip.

"Because you need answers. And I'm the only person on this planet who holds them."

((

One breath later, Chloe was in the sanctuary where she'd first seen the councilman all those years ago. He was beside her, standing on one of the square white mats reserved for the eight-year-olds who came here to learn about the last phase of life, about Coronations. He didn't seem to be afraid of her, even though he knew by now that all it took was a light touch and a single thought for her to send him to any place, and any time, in history.

"Are you through taking your doma for a spin, Miss Zacharias?"

"I haven't even started."

His eyebrows lifted as a snarl crept into his smirk. He tapped his ear and lowered his chin to his right shoulder. "Tell the aunt and uncle that their charges are wanted criminals. Make a public announcement of it. If anyone knows the whereabouts of Chloe and Damian Zacharias, they are to report it immediately."

He smiled at her, dark circles carving out purple crescents beneath his eyes. "You are hereby an exile, a heretic, a traitor, and a threat to the empire of Petros."

Chloe smiled back, feeling somehow that her parents knew what was happening, that they were watching her now...and waiting.

"I've been to hell," she said. "It isn't anything at all like the Coronations you taught us about. Did you know that?" She watched his eyes cloud over as the faintest wisp of fear floated across his countenance. "The worst monsters you ever read about in the myths are true, and they're even more evil than what the stories say. And the souls there are just shells of their former selves; they spend every waking hour picking flowers in a field covered with fake sky. And from what I hear, that's the *good* part of hell."

She stared up at the domed ceiling above them, picking out the familiar constellations within its lifelike painting of outer space. "They don't remember what they lived for, or who they loved. They don't know how they died. They don't know why or how they were ever born to begin with."

"You may stop talking now, girl." The councilman's cheeks were reddening with heightened rage.

"They don't know the one who created them because people like you made them forget."

"Shut up! You don't know what you're talking about."

"I would take you there myself if I could, but it doesn't exist anywhere in time. But that's the other thing about hell. It's eternal. That means you will be there *forever*."

The councilman's face contorted into a terrifying mask, as if it were made of wax and melting slowly off his skull. His eyes rolled back into his head, his white fingers spread, and his arms shot out to either side. He dropped his head, his black eyes peering up at her as though he were a panther crouched low in high grass.

"What I wouldn't give to kill you," he said. "As I killed your mother and father."

Chloe's heart pounded hard in her chest. Hot tears welled in her eyes. She'd known deep down that her parents' death was no accident, and yet hearing him confirm it sliced her heart in two all over again. She fell to her knees and wept as fresh waves of grief washed over her.

"Dry your tears." The voice that spoke through the councilman didn't belong to him. It was deeper, more sonorous, almost hypnotic, swinging like a pendulum through the air. "The All-Powerful hasn't allowed me to take your life, lucky for you."

The councilman's eyelids fluttered. His feet lifted off the floor, and he hovered in midair, looking like a scarecrow with its arms pulled straight and body sagging.

"But I have a feeling that in time," the voice continued, "you will step into death without having to be led. Hades will see you again. At your Coronation."

Whatever was speaking through the councilman released the old man and threw him to the ground. He lay curled up in the fetal position and groaned as he ripped out a syringe from his robe and stuck it into his arm.

For the first time, Chloe felt sorry for him. He wasn't to blame for her parents' deaths. He wasn't to blame for Orpheus luring her to Aeaea or to the River Styx. He was just a pawn, a dispensable puppet whose strings were being pulled by the true rulers of Petros. If she wanted to change the world, she knew it would take more than changing one man's mind. Even if he saw the truth, his peers would waste no time putting him to death and the tyranny would continue.

"Goodbye," Chloe said to the councilman. "I'll be praying for you." Then she closed her eyes, her thoughts focused on four people.

Four people she could save.

Four people who could change history.

"Chloe."

Chloe jumped and opened her eyes, but she wasn't in the sanctuary. In fact, she didn't know where she was. Walls that appeared to be made of clouds surrounded her, and her feet were wrapped in the hazy tendrils of a dying fog. Below her toes, faraway lights twinkled through the mist; a bright sphere, identical to the moon, hung between them.

And then a figure stepped in front of her. He wore a white tunic that shimmered as he moved, and golden sandals that hurt her eyes to look at. She stopped breathing when she saw his hair, the dark brown waves that grazed high, olive cheekbones.

A spark flickered in one of his sapphire eyes.

"Orpheus?" She gasped as if coming up for air after minutes under water. "What are you do—where are—" She moved closer to him to make sure her eyes weren't playing tricks on her. "It's really you."

He smiled, then stretched his hand into the cloud behind him and pulled it back like a curtain. Beyond were countless stars of every hue, all of them gleaming like brilliant gemstones set on fire. Surrounding them towered hundreds of nebulas, suspended like colossal cocoons of cosmic dust and plasma in which ancient giants slept.

"Beautiful, isn't it?" he said.

As Chloe nodded, Orpheus traced a circle in the cloud with his foot, forming a melon-sized hole below them.

Through it, Chloe could see Petros, a tiny blue-and-green marble floating perhaps a million miles away.

"Where am I?" The air in the cloud suddenly seemed very thin. How was she able to breathe? How was she able to stay warm?

"I can't say for sure, but I would call it a bridge. A bridge for the living to meet with the dead, at least this once."

"The last time you met with the living, the living ended up in Hades." Chloe's brain fought against itself. One half yearned to travel back to Petros, to get out of this celestial web before Orpheus tried his sly tactics again. But the other half, the stronger half, sensed something had changed since they'd last been together.

"I'm sorry for everything, Chloe. In his graciousness, Duna has allowed me to ask your forgiveness face to face."

"Duna? You know about Duna?"

"Yes. Ironically, it was when I returned to Hades that I placed my trust in him. And I died a second death."

"I...I forgive you. You did what you did because you love your wife." Tears welled in Chloe's eyes.

Orpheus's eyes were glistening, too. "No. I did what I did because I didn't have hope." He took a deep breath as if a great yoke had just been lifted off his shoulders. "All is well now. I am with my wife Eurydice again." He wiped his cheek and looked out into the universe, joy brightening his face like a sunrise. "We were sent to the Vale of Mourning and the Fields of Asphodel to proclaim the existence, and the grace, of the All-Powerful. The ones who believed are now free."

"That's wonderful news." It was all Chloe could get out.

Orpheus took a step forward and placed a hand on her shoulder. His face grew solemn. "Apollo and his followers will do everything in their power to stop you. You mustn't lose faith."

"I won't."

The cloudy nest that sheltered them began to break apart, fading into the ether like puffs of breath in winter air.

The glittering lights of the heavens dimmed, and soon Orpheus was gone, leaving not a trace save for his warmth still lingering on her shoulder.

All alone and enveloped in darkness, Chloe looked down at her feet. There was nothing supporting her, but at the same time everything was.

"Please, Duna, don't let me fall."

Then she set her gaze on her home below as unseen fingertips painted the Moonbow into the blackness around it, filling her heart with hope, and strength for the coming fight.

NOW AVAILABLE!

WAR OF THE ASHERS

Book 2 in the the The Petros Chronicles series.

www.amazon.com/dp/B078Z5D2RR

THE PETROS CHRONICLES
WAR OF THE ASHERS

CHAPTER ONE
HERMES

For the first time in thousands of years, Hermes felt tired. He'd been tracking the mortals' scent all night, his winged sandals fluttering through the trees, his golden wand lighting the way. He knew it was only a matter of time until the Ashers' invisibility wore off, and then they'd all be as good as dead.

The Moonbow had been waning for the last half hour as warm streaks of sunrise sprayed its arches with the rosy foam of dawn. It had been watching him since he emerged from Lake Thyra with his treacherous heart set against his brothers, the hell-bound lords of the Underworld, who would doubtless condemn him to a century of torture once they learned of his present errand.

But the Moonbow had bewitched the wandering messenger. Hermes could feel no fear nor contemplate remorse as long as its peaceful bands hovered over him. What he was doing was undeniably out of spite for his brothers, yet for some reason he couldn't help but feel that the Moonbow was smiling on him, nudging him onward even as his immortal limbs grew weak and heavy in the air.

Hermes' mind drifted as he stared through a net of leaves into the fading Moonbow that filled it. His thoughts traveled back to the last time he could recall ever feeling so weary. It had been immediately after The War against the All-Powerful, the night he and his brothers, the bold triumvirate, were expelled from heaven along with countless other rebels, all of whom had been hypnotized by Apollo's promise of unending power and a paradise of their own to rule as they pleased.

Hermes had been in on the lie from the start. Together with Poseidon, Apollo, Zeus, Hades, and the Titans, he had been plotting the coup for what seemed like eons within the timeless stretch of eternity. It was called The War, but no swords were wielded nor chariots mounted until the dreaded end, which each black-hearted devil knew full well was coming.

Before word of their treason reached the All-Powerful, the weapons had been innocuous words, whispers of rumors that infected heaven's streets like an insidious plague. The symptoms were mild at first, hardly noticeable. A few complaints, a few disputes, a furious brawl here and there when the devout grew defensive and could stand the heresies no longer.

In the beginning, the revolt comprised only a few small circles of murmuring adherents. But, little by little, even the most pious ears were tickled and the strongest minds corrupted. To Hermes' surprise, there was soon enough of them to form an entire army that could rise up, dethrone the All-Powerful, and make greedy gods of themselves. It was then that the faithful took up arms against the rebel forces and drove them outside the city walls, as ruthless and swift as when a ferocious squall besets a sailboat.

Spirits, every one of them, the rebels awoke in one piece, their wishes granted. Around them now was a kingdom all their own, far from the stifling sovereignty under which they'd served and worshiped for untold ages.

The world was a newly created planet called Petros, meaning stone, named for the rocky terrain and jagged mountains that defined it. To the rebels, the atmosphere was so dense that many swore that the fingers of Death, which did not yet exist, were wrapping around their throats. For millennia, they'd been accustomed to the pure, rarefied air of heaven; now, their lungs labored and burned with every breath.

The anemic color of the clouds hanging low over the sickly green hills was a sore to the rebels' eyes. They kicked the weeds and cursed the thorns as they hiked to the highest peak on which the three would erect their thrones and rest their flimsy shelters, all pigsties compared to their former abodes.

Hermes, one of the few with the gift of flight, had fallen from the sky, landed halfway to the summit and awoken half a day later, hoping it had all been a terrible dream, a hallucinatory warning from his subconscious. His conniving mind stopped scheming, slowing to assess the bruises and aches racking his body, this frightening pain he had never experienced. His ichor blood felt frozen as regret gripped his muscles and sorrow seeped into his bones.

He wanted to cry out to Duna, to confess that he'd made a grave mistake and that he'd do anything to escape this loathsome world and reenter heaven's gates. But the darkness within him would tolerate no remorse, nor would his brothers let him lie around idly for long, pitying his wounds and rethinking his choice. "Give it some time," they'd said, "for we have it here. And in time we shall all be kings."

They had been right. In time, the fatigue had worn off, the bruises had healed, and repentance had become as vulgar a notion as revolution had once been. Petros had become home, and Hermes had made himself one of its sovereigns.

For thousands of years he had been an indispensable part of the oligarchy, and then of the counterfeit trinity after Apollo imprisoned the Titans and his siblings within the bowels of Tartarus, and adopted Hermes and Hades as brothers. It was then that Hermes, true son of Zeus, began to prove himself more clever and cunning than his two "brothers" combined. It had been his duty, his greatest pleasure, to bend mortals to his will, to convince even himself that his gods-breathed, grandiose lies were true.

And then the Vessel had arisen, just as the Oracles had prophesied they would two thousand years before their birth. The whole Underworld knew the Vessel would be an Asher, one of the gifted mortals who received supernatural abilities when they reached eighteen. And because the All-Powerful had ordained long ago that there could only be one Asher per family, Hermes was sure the girl called Chloe was the one. He didn't consider her twin brother could be a threat as well.

That oversight was Hermes' undoing.

Apollo and Hades blamed him for the Ashers' escape. He was their eyes and ears, they'd said, but he might as well have been blind and deaf and unforgivably brainless. He wasn't needed anymore. They had their blessed Fantásmata, their brainwashed, power-crazed disciples with whom they communicated through drug-induced channeling and cataleptic trances.

He was nothing but an underling now, an impotent peon like the other rebels who stood guard around Hades' gates, as if they could ever fend off the All-Powerful for even a second were he to descend to their sulfuric depths. If he chose to, the All-Powerful could thresh them like wheat and grind them to grain with a single breath. The question of why he didn't had settled over Hermes' mind like a fog, filling the void where his ruses and plans once dominated. He'd rather be annihilated than continue living with countless gallons of mortal blood staining his conscience.

Perhaps this was his punishment, one much worse than being bound in Tartarus or cast into the Vale of Mourning.

Just hours ago, he'd been certain that the greatest torture was to possess a hubris matched only by two other spirits in the universe, and to have no purpose or outlet with which to gratify it. But something in the air this night, perhaps the Moonbow itself, had convinced him otherwise. The greatest torture was not to be deprived of satisfying his pride, but to recognize its repulsiveness, to feel the unbearable weight of blood caked onto his hands, to carry guilt like a yoke upon his shoulders, and to remember a peaceful existence before any of it.

Hermes' heartbeat quivered, one side fighting to beat fast with swelling offense and anger, the other side resisting, for it knew that blaming his brothers for his dismal fate was futile. Evil had been stagnant within him all along, and they'd known how to draw it out, capturing it like sap from a tree. But he wasn't dumb; the All-Powerful had created him to be one of the shrewdest of all. While others might have been manipulated and deceived, Hermes was fully aware of the choice he was making. There was no one to blame but himself.

Unable to fly any longer, Hermes grabbed onto the nearest tree branch and sat down. He leaned his head against the trunk and breathed in the Petrodian air, air that had once tasted so vile but was now nectar compared to the choking swelter of hell.

The amber glow surrounding the Moonbow dissolved into the clear blue canvas of sky. He pointed his wand at it, commanding it to stay, but of course it was impervious to his magic. It came and went as it wished, offering solace, delivering warnings, chasing down destinies, answering only to the All-Powerful.

Who would Hermes answer to now? He'd betrayed the All-Powerful. He'd been ostracized by his brothers. But the Moonbow—that silent messenger overlooking the deeds of mortals and spirits both—he had not antagonized. Perhaps by helping the Ashers it loved, he could win its favor. He could do something noble; something that might reach the All-Powerful's ear and lighten the load of guilt bearing down on him.

Hermes jumped as his reverie was shattered like glass by the sound of a man's voice a short stone's throw away.

"Damian, look!" the man shouted.

Hermes looked down through the density of looming Folói oaks, but saw nothing but a red fox scampering past.

And then he saw it, a faint glimmer spanning four feet of air on which transparent waves rippled and shook as if pebbles were skipping across it.

"It's fading again," came the same disembodied voice, much lower this time.

Slowly, the see-through apparition became obscured as flesh tones and flashes of clothing suffused them. Hermes could make out four human forms, all still hazy as they regained their corporeality. Only one was familiar to him: the one named Ethan, whose voice he'd heard.

Ethan and an older man and woman had their hands planted firmly on the fourth's shoulders and wrists, clinging to him like children to their mother. Reluctantly, as they regarded the sunshine and shadows on their skin and crunched the leaves beneath their feet, they removed their hands and stepped away.

So this was Damian, the Asher who had escaped Hermes' notice. The one responsible for his demise.

"No one to blame but yourself, old man," Hermes muttered to himself. Then he rose from the branch and flew down to the ground, smiling softly at the thought of both vengeance and redemption irresistibly within reach.

AFTERWORD

I hope you enjoyed the first installment of The Petros Chronicles. If you don't mind, I would appreciate it if you could head over to Amazon, Goodreads or your preferred website of choice and leave a brief review of this book. Your help in spreading the word is gratefully received and encourages me to keep reaching others through my writing.

Also, I invite you to join my Greek-mythology-related mailing list at www.dianaandersontyler.com, where you'll receive The Petros Chronicles prequel for free as a thank-you for your support. Each month I'll send you an exclusive short story and also run a fun giveaway.

DISCOVER MORE FROM DIANA

www.dianaandersontyler.com
dianatylerbooks.com

Facebook:
facebook.com/dianafit4faith

Twitter:
@dandersontyler

Instagram:
@dianaandersontyler
and @authordianatyler.

ABOUT THE AUTHOR

Diana has been writing all her life, starting with her own versions of Teenage Mutant Ninja Turtle comics when she was four. She's always been fascinated by Greek mythology and comic-book superheroes, all of which inspire her fantasy novels. She's also a gym rat who loves to pretend she's Wonder Woman while lifting heavy weights, and swinging from rings and pull-up bars. She co-owns CrossFit 925 in San Antonio, Texas with her husband Ben.

Diana currently writes entertainment and media-related articles for movieguide.org, and contributes regularly to charismamag.com. When she isn't writing or working out, she can be found playing Scrabble with her husband, watching Marvel and Pixar movies, and pinning recipes on Pinterest that she never gets around to cooking.

ACKNOWLEDGEMENTS

Every morning, I wake up and realize how extremely blessed I am, not just because I get to do what I love every day, but because I have the support and assistance of amazing people who have enriched both my writing and my life. Age of the Ashers and the whole Petros Chronicles series has been a tremendous journey, one I surely wouldn't have completed without the motivation, encouragement, tips and advice offered by the following people:

My husband Ben: my #1 fan who puts up with my writerly quirks, moods, compulsions, and extemporaneous brainstorming sessions.

My mom Barbara: who has always nurtured my dream of becoming a published author and patiently listens to me vent and cry on the bad days.

My beta readers and proofreaders, Jaime, Kara, Mr. Travis, Rich, David, and Soulla: you have no idea how invaluable your encouragement and feedback have been to me. Thank you for shooting straight with me, catching my mistakes, and enjoying the story. I owe you the moon and so much more!

My editor, Penny, at Book Cover Cafe: Words fail to adequately convey just how grateful 1 am for an editor who not only polishes and corrects, but also affirms and educates. Thank you for shaping me into a better writer, page by page.

Book Cover Café: who always do a fabulous job with typesetting, design, and e-book conversion.

Made in United States
Orlando, FL
10 March 2023

30916015R00246